Some doors should neve

When Rose Black's upon Jake Crowley for help, but the two get more than they bargained for. The search takes them on a twisting journey, where danger lies at every turn. From ancient pyramids to lost cities, deadly cultists and conspirators lie in wait as Jake and Rose navigate depths few have dared on a pulse-pounding search for the ANUBIS KEY!

Praise for David Wood and Alan Baxter

"A genuine up all night got to see what happens next thriller that grabs you from the first page and doesn't let go until the last." Steven Savile, author of *Silver*

"Mixing history and lore with science and action, David Wood and Alan Baxter have penned a thriller that is hard to put down." Jeremy Robinson, author of *Island 731*

"Bone-cracking terror from the stygian depths. Explodes off the page!." Lee Murray, author, *Into the Mist*

"One of the best, the most thoroughly delightful and satisfying, books that I've read in quite some time. A serious out-of-the-park type of home run hit." Christine Morgan, *The Horror Fiction Review*

"A sinister tale of black magic and horror – not for the faint hearted." Greig Beck, bestselling author of *Beneath the Dark Ice*

"With mysterious rituals, macabre rites and superb supernatural action scenes, Wood and Baxter deliver a fast-paced horror thriller." J.F.Penn, author of the bestselling *ARKANE* thriller series

"A story that thrills and makes one think beyond the boundaries of mere fiction and enter the world of 'why not'?" David Lynn Golemon,

ANUBIS KEY

A Jake Crowley Adventure

DAVID WOOD
ALAN BAXTER

ADRENALINE PRESS

Anubis Key- A Jake Crowley Adventure
Copyright 2016 by David Wood
All rights reserved
Edited by Melissa Bowersock

Published by Adrenaline Press
www.adrenaline.press

Adrenaline Press is an imprint of Gryphonwood Press
www.gryphonwoodpress.com

ISBN-10: 1-940095-68-9
ISBN-13: 978-1-940095-68-4

Books by David Wood and Alan Baxter

The Jake Crowley Adventures
Blood Codex
Anubis Key

Primordial
Dark Rite

Books by David Wood

The Dane Maddock Adventures
Dourado
Cibola
Quest
Icefall
Buccaneer
Atlantis
Ark
Xibalba
Loch

Dane and Bones Origins
Freedom
Hell Ship
Splashdown
Dead Ice
Liberty
Electra
Amber
Justice
Treasure of the Dead

Jade Ihara Adventures
Oracle
Changeling

Bones Bonebrake Adventures
Primitive
The Book of Bones

BOOKS BY ALAN BAXTER

CHAPTER 1

Jake Crowley looked out over his class and saw the usual spread of expressions, from attention to disinterest. Some students would always be keen to learn, others simply eager to leave. It had always been that way. As the gathered young people settled and sorted out their notebooks, tablets, laptops, Crowley checked over his notes about the Black Dog. A rueful smile twisted one corner of his mouth.

He'd had his own black dog lately, the infamous hound of depression. He wasn't actually prone to melancholy, so it was probably unfair to categorize his feelings that way, but he was blue, as he hadn't seen Rose Black for several weeks. A beautiful and mysterious woman, Rose had cut off contact, ghosted him, after the two of them had shared in a dangerous adventure. He'd reached out to her, but she had rebuffed his advances and wouldn't tell him why. He'd thought maybe they really had something. In fact, she had even suggested as much at one time, but then nothing. Was he being needy? He liked her a lot and wanted to at least stay friends. And hell, he'd saved the woman's life. That ought to count for something.

"Uh, sir?"

Crowley realized, to his embarrassment, that dozens of pairs of expectant eyes were on him. He smiled. "Okay, folks. Following on from yesterday, I told you all that we would start today talking about the legends of the black dog."

"You sad, Sir?" a smart aleck piped up from the back of the class. Sniggers rippled around the classroom.

Crowley shook his head. High schoolers, always thinking they were so funny. But it stung a little given his previous train of thought. He chose to ignore the interruption. "Within British folklore, a black dog is predominantly a nocturnal apparition, usually associated with the Devil in some way. Often it's referred to as a hellhound. In most cases, its appearance was a portent of death."

"In that case, I'm surprised there isn't one outside this classroom, Sir." That same class clown.

"One more word from you and it's a quick trip to the headmaster's office." The student bristled slightly, then quickly settled. Crowley went on. "Larger than a normal dog, with glowing eyes, or fire where its eyes should be, the black dog is to be found at crossroads, sites of execution, and ancient pathways. It enjoys electrical storms, or perhaps its presence triggers them. Regardless, these dogs are always associated with death and are in some form or another associated with the underworld, usually as guardians. Perhaps one of the most famous is Cerberus, a legend we'll look at in more detail shortly. Black dogs are..." Movement at the door caught Crowley's eye and he glanced over.

Through the glass top half of the door he saw a woman glance nervously in. Black hair in a tidy bob, beautiful, soft Asian features. His heart skipped. Rose Black, as if summoned by his thoughts like the black dog itself. Her eyebrows rose as their eyes met, imploring him. She mouthed the word, *Sorry!* and gestured for him to come over.

"Excuse me one moment, class."

Heads craned and several students made "Oooh!" noises and wolf-whistles.

Crowley turned back. "Pipe down!" His voice was a whip-crack that silenced the room. "Read chapter eleven of the textbook and we'll talk more in a moment."

A chorus of groans rose from the class as students took out their books.

Crowley stepped out into the hall and closed the door behind him. "It's good to see you. You haven't returned my calls or messages."

Rose shuffled awkwardly and looked down at the floor. "I'm sorry, Jake. Really I am. But I need your help. My sister is missing."

Crowley frowned, unhappy with the turn of events. She only came because she needed his help, not because she wanted to see him? "Where have you been, Rose?"

"Jake, it's complicated. I..."

Annoyance rose in Crowley's chest. "Why have you been avoiding me?" He kept his voice calm and soft, but his frustration came through nonetheless.

Rose put one warm palm briefly against his cheek. "I can't explain right now."

Her touch put a little thrill through him despite the

discomfort that hung between them like fog. "But you show up wanting my help?"

Rose's expression twisted in pain. "There's no one else."

Her obvious internal agony put Crowley on the back foot. Something was clearly very wrong. And she'd said her sister was missing. It was harsh of him to have ignored that for his own feelings. He remembered all that time ago in her apartment where he'd seen photos of Rose, with her parents, and just one with another young girl who, by the similarity of her looks, had to be Rose's sister. That had been the only photo of the other girl on display, and in it they had been in their mid-teens at most. Crowley had wondered at the time why there weren't other photos and in all the time they had spent together, Rose hadn't mentioned a sister.

"Okay," he said. "I'm sorry." He took her hand, squeezed it gently. "Let's talk, but not now. I have a class on."

"Of course. When do you finish?"

"After lunch. I'm supposed to spend the afternoon marking and prepping for tomorrow, but I can come to see you instead. You know the Victorian Bath House bar in Bishopsgate, just by Liverpool Street?"

"Yes, I know it. Never been though. Isn't it a private hire place?"

Jake smiled. "I know a guy."

"Old Army buddy like before?"

"Yep. How about we meet there at two?"

Rose smiled, relief softening her features. "Thank you. I'll see you there."

He watched her turn and head back toward the front entrance of the school. Perhaps suggesting the Bath House bar was a bit ostentatious. A bit too try-hard, like he wanted to impress her all over again, but it was too late now. When she turned the corner out of sight he shook his head and went back into the classroom. "This is going to be nothing but trouble," he muttered.

CHAPTER 2

Jake walked up Bishopsgate to the entrance to the Victorian Bath House. Incongruous against tall buildings of glass and steel, the small access building with its tan, yellow and blue tiling and small onion-like turret seemed completely out of place. Intricate stonework around the roofline and narrow arched windows drew the eye as he went to the discreet doorway of the converted Victorian Turkish bathhouse. Just inside the door he smiled at his old friend who stood by, ready to vet guests. "How are you, Smiffy?"

Smiffy grinned, his smile wide and bright in his dark face. "Jake bloody Crowley, as I live and breathe! How long's it been?"

"About three weeks?"

They laughed and shook hands. Crowley patted his friend's shoulder. They had shared things as British Army soldiers in the Middle East, experienced situations that would forever make them closer than brothers. Smiffy's grin faded slightly, the old hurt still evident even after all these years, and returned Crowley's shoulder slap. They owed each other their lives many times over.

"I'm glad you're here today," Crowley said. "Slip me and pal in for a drink?"

"Of course, you know I'll never turn you away. But you might be losing your mind, mate." He gestured to indicate that Crowley was alone.

"She's meeting me here. Keep an eye out for her? Chinese, well, half-Chinese, she had on jeans and a green jacket earlier, but might have changed, I suppose. Name of Rose Black." He hoped she hadn't changed clothes for the occasion, but assumed it wouldn't matter too much either way. Then he wondered if perhaps he should have changed from his staid teacher uniform of slacks, collared shirt, and blazer. He realized he was acting like a teenager on a first date. He shook it off and smiled at his old mate.

"Oh ho? Got a new lady friend, eh?" Smiffy's eyes sparkled with mischief.

Crowley laughed. "Something like that. Direct her down when she gets here?"

"Sure thing, man. We still on for poker at Steve's on Thursday?"

Crowley had forgotten the once-a-month old Army buddy poker night had come around again. He had a feeling that maybe he wouldn't make it this time. "Hope so!" he said anyway. "See you then."

He entered the self-proclaimed jewel in the heart of Bishopsgate, smiling at the grandeur and lavish displays of old world charm. He went down the stairs into the bar area, past small stained glass windows and walls papered in textured designs of fleur-de-lis arches and fired tile. He entered the dimly lighted space, richly decorated, with cozy alcoves around the edges containing plush velvet seats in scarlet and blue. Brightly lit recessed arches displayed bottles of expensive spirits and lead crystal glasses and decanters.

A low murmur from the gathered clientele filled the air as waiters in crisp white shirts and dark waistcoats moved on silent feet with silver trays of cocktails and bar snacks. Crowley spotted a vacant alcove and took a seat, suddenly self-conscious at his choice of meeting place. Was he really trying to impress Rose all over again? He genuinely enjoyed this highly bespoken establishment in the heart of London—it played to his love of the bizarre and foolish—but perhaps it was a strange place to discuss serious matters. Maybe he should have suggested a regular pub somewhere nearby.

His thoughts were quickly stopped by Rose's arrival. She appeared at the bottom of the stairs, eyes wide at her surroundings. She paused, looking a little lost as a mystified smile played around her lips. Crowley was pleased to see she hadn't changed clothes after all. For some reason that made him feel better.

He waved and she spotted him, hurried over.

"What on earth is this place?"

Crowley grinned sheepishly. "Amazing, isn't it? I think it's pretty cool."

Rose shook her head, still smiling, and sat opposite Crowley. They faced each other over the small hexagonal wooden table and Rose opened her mouth to speak when one of the gliding waiters slid into view. He held out cocktail menus. "Water while you look over the options?" he asked.

"They do excellent cocktails here," Crowley told Rose. "You have a favorite?"

"I'm not really in the mood for fancy drinks."

Crowley nodded. She was genuinely out of sorts. He supposed a missing sister would do that and he again felt like a fool for suggesting this venue.

"But I do like a Bloody Mary," she said.

"Certainly, madam. And for sir?"

"I'll have an Old-Fashioned," Crowley said.

"Bourbon or rye, sir?"

"Bourbon, thanks."

The waiter gave a deep nod and slid away.

"I'm sorry," Crowley said to Rose. "Perhaps this was a dumb place to suggest."

"You don't need to impress me, you know. You've proven yourself already, after everything that happened before."

"I guess so."

"And I'm sorry I made myself scarce the last few weeks. Like I said, it's complicated. Can we leave it at that for now?"

"Sure." It was the last thing Crowley really wanted, but what could he do? Demand she tell him? He wasn't that much of an arse, and she clearly had bigger problems on her mind.

The waiter returned with their drinks, smiled, and left without a word.

"So tell me what's going on," Crowley said.

Rose sipped her drink, her lips blood red for a moment from the tomato juice before her tongue darted out to lick it away. Crowley averted his gaze, determined to stay on topic, and took a sip of his own drink to mask his thoughts.

But Rose was staring into the middle distance, looking back into the past, perhaps. "My sister is called Lily," she said. "And she's missing. This will all seem very strange, so please don't judge me."

"Of course not."

Rose breathed deeply, sipped again. "Lily is two years older than me. She's a stubborn, independent woman, rebellious since we were little kids, but especially once she hit her mid-teens."

"What kind of rebellion?"

Rose paused, caught Crowley's eye, then looked away again. "Just typical teenager stuff."

Crowley didn't believe that for a second; she was clearly keeping something close to her chest. But he chose not to question it. "Okay."

"She seemed to get herself together again pretty quickly anyway, but that's not really the point. I'm just pointing out how headstrong she could be. And, I suppose, that we weren't exactly close. But she's still my sister."

"Independent, you said."

"Exactly. Always preferred to take care of herself."

"What does she do for a living?"

Rose blushed slightly, evident even in the low light of the bar. "I don't know. We were… estranged. For a long time."

"Really? Why?"

Rose ignored the question. "She was a graduate student at University College London, from their Institute of Archeology. She'd gone back to do a PhD, though I'm not sure what her particular area of concentration was, or her subjects of study beyond that. Honestly, I don't know much about her life at all other than she had gone back to uni."

"You said estranged," Crowley prompted.

"Yes." Rose still chose not to elaborate, sipped her drink again.

"So how do you know she's missing?"

Rose smiled. "Good question. Well, after everything with Landvik, what I went through, I got to thinking about how fragile life is, how easily I could have died then."

"On several occasions, for both of us." Crowley saw no need to elaborate.

"Exactly. So I thought it was silly to still harbor our… differences. To not try to rebuild my relationship with Lily. So I reached out again. I had done a few times here and there in the past, sent her an email or a text. While we haven't seen each other in years, our estrangement isn't total. My parents and I have always had contact details for her and she's always replied in some form, eventually. Usually terse and dismissive, but something."

"Not this time though?"

Rose frowned, looked down into her half-empty glass. "Not this time. I called, texted, emailed. No answer at all. We have an address for her, in case we have to forward mail, as we know we're never welcome to actually visit. But I finally went to her apartment and no one was there. I asked a neighbor who said she hadn't seen Lily in at least a couple of weeks. The neighbor gave me a stack of mail that had been building up, said she assumed Lily had moved out, but she hung onto the mail just in case."

"You've got the mail?"

"Yes, but I haven't looked at it. This was only yesterday. After the conversation with her neighbor I got really spooked. I went to the university archaeology department but was told the same thing – she'd been gone for a couple of weeks. Missed an exam, dropped the ball on a class she was teaching. Something is clearly wrong, and I don't know what to do. I've hit a dead end and I'm worried."

"So you came to me." Crowley really wanted to ask if she would have come back to him without her sister's disappearance, but Rose was clearly on edge and he guessed she wouldn't respond well to his pushing that particular subject.

"Yes, so I came to you. You're good at this stuff, right? Any ideas?"

Crowley gave her a reassuring smile. "There is one obvious next step, if you don't mind a little breaking and entering."

CHAPTER 3

Lily Black's apartment, Harrow on the Hill, London

It was late in the afternoon by the time Crowley and Rose arrived at Lily's apartment building. Crowley liked Harrow on the Hill, a suburb in the northwest of London. Lots of narrow streets, green hedges and trees, tightly packed pale brown brick buildings with dark gray slate roofs. A number of shops they had passed on the high street had been whitewashed, classic old London suburbia. He could have afforded it, not on his teacher's salary, but with the other money. However, it didn't seem the sort of place one went to live a lonely bachelor's life.

"Nice spot," Crowley said.

Rose nodded, lips pursed. "Lily bought this place a few years ago. No idea how she afforded it, but like I said, I don't know much about her life. I wish I did, now more than ever."

They entered the building and took a double flight of stairs up to the second story. Rose pointed. "That's her place. You really going to break in?"

Crowley laughed softly. "Don't be so shocked, Miss Black. When we first met I told you about how I demobbed from the army, young and stupid, and ran with a few London hoodlums. Nearly ended up in prison."

"Oh yeah, you did tell me that."

"So let's just say I picked up some useful skills back in those days." He crouched by the door, used his body to mask his furtive activity with a highly illegal lock-pick kit. He enjoyed Rose's closeness as she stood behind, watching over his shoulder. She regularly glanced back to ensure they remained alone in the hallway.

A sharp click and Crowley stood. "And there it is." He flashed a grin back over his shoulder and pushed Lily's door open. Rose followed him in and shut the door behind them.

He paused in the spacious lounge room, scanning the décor. A number of Egyptian themed artworks adorned the walls, a few vases and other ornaments clearly resonant of the pyramids, mummies and sarcophagi. A mirror hung above the mantelpiece, framed in alternating blue and gold bands, the top a spreading pair of wings in three shades of blue. Above the wings a cobra emerging from each side of a large red ball.

"That's a little…" Crowley wasn't sure how to describe it.

"Ostentatious? Pretentious?" Rose suggested.

"Yeah. That. Both of those."

"I feel weird, breaking in here," Rose said. "We were never welcome, never invited."

"Sure, but if we're going to find your sister, this is the only lead we have, right?" Crowley pointed to a wall of bookshelves. "Lots of Egyptology titles here, and lots of books on the occult and secret societies."

Rose joined him. "No surprise for someone doing a doctorate in archeology, I suppose." She ran a finger along a shelf of hardback spines.

"Guess not."

Crowley gestured towards a glass-topped table against one wall, supported by two proud leopards coated in gold leaf. Beside it sat a large rosewood chest inlaid with gold and turquoise tiles. "These things look expensive. Like genuine artifacts. Or at least, very valuable modern recreations."

Rose frowned. "What are you implying?"

"Well, I'm just surprised a PhD student can afford this stuff, not to mention this apartment."

"Yes, but like I said, I have no idea what she did before she went back to do her doctorate," Rose said. "She could have made a fortune on the stock exchange for all I know."

Crowley walked towards a desk in one corner. "Or maybe they're gifts from someone. A man, perhaps?"

Rose made a non-committal sound. "No idea."

Crowley moved behind the desk and opened a laptop lying there. He hit the power button and waited while it booted up only to be faced with a password. "Well, that's irritating, but not unexpected. You got that mail the neighbor gave you?"

Rose reached into the inside pocket of her jacket and pulled out a wad of a dozen or so envelopes. "Not much use, I don't think."

Crowley shuffled through the white and brown windowed packets. "No personal correspondence."

Rose laughed. "Like letters? How old are you? Fifty? No one writes letters anymore."

Crowley couldn't help laughing along. "Yeah, I can't remember the last time I wrote one. Probably not since my Gran died. Just hopeful, I guess." He turned over the last one and saw it was a credit card bill. "But this might be useful."

He slit the envelope open, pulled the bill out, and scanned the transactions. "I think I know where your sister has gone."

"Just like that?" Rose hurried to his side, looked at where he pointed to a line from a travel agent.

"She bought a plane ticket to Cairo."

Rose looked up from the bill to Crowley. "That doesn't explain why she isn't responding to her messages, though. She often makes me wait a day or two when I try to start a conversation, but she always replies. Even if she's not using her phone overseas, she checks email regularly, and I've sent a dozen emails in the past week alone."

Crowley rubbed a hand back over his close-cropped dark hair. He wasn't sure about any of this. "Let's keep poking around."

In the immaculately tidy bedroom, he found a small safe tucked into one side of the wardrobe. "Check this out," he called out.

Rose came through from the kitchen, looked into the dim cupboard. "Hmm. Now that's more interesting."

"It needs a four-digit code, though. Locks I can pick, but this has millions of possible combinations. Beyond my skills."

"Nineteen thirty-five," Rose said, without hesitation. "Our grandfather's year of birth. No one in the world meant more to her than he did. She was devastated when he died."

"Huh." Crowley punched in the year and the safe door popped open. He shared a smile with Rose. "First bit of luck we've had!"

He took out the small pile of documents from the top shelf of the safe and moved back into the light of the bedroom. A frown creased his brow. "Well, this only raises more questions."

"What is it?"

Crowley held up Lily's passport for Rose to see. "Not only her passport, but her other ID, driver's license, credit cards."

"How could she have left the country without those?" Rose asked.

Crowley held up another envelope, clearly showing the logo and name of the HM Passport Office. "This might explain it. The address is this apartment, but it's not for Lily Black."

"Who then?"

"You ever heard of Iris Brown?"

CHAPTER 4

Crowley agreed with Rose when she suggested that Iris Brown was a pretty lame fake name.

"It's keeping the family theme, though," Rose said. "Our English names have always been flowers since my paternal grandmother, and she was Iris. So that's where she picked it from, I expect."

"That's why you guys are Rose and Lily."

"And my dad was called Rowan. It's been that way for generations on that side of the family. The boys are trees and the girls are flowers. My mother's English name was Jasmine; she adopted that when she met my dad."

"So you have a Chinese name as well?"

Rose smiled. "Of course. Most Chinese immigrants take on a western name, but we all have Chinese names too. Well, maybe not all, but most."

Crowley tilted his head, considering that. "I can't imagine you as anything but Rose."

"Not surprising." Rose wore a half-smile, clearly enjoying his discomfort at this cultural avenue he had never been down before.

"So, er… what's your Chinese name?"

"Maybe I'll tell you one day. Maybe not."

Crowley laughed, shook his head. "You're incorrigible." He turned back to the safe, frustrated despite the amusement. He wanted to know everything about Rose and wondered how much more there might be to surprise him like this. The second shelf of the safe had more documents and he began shuffling through them.

"Lots of photocopies here of official forms. Applications for a driver's license, stuff like that." With a grin of triumph he held up a collection of small envelopes and note paper, all handwritten. "Aha! People do still write letters."

Rose rolled her eyes. "If they're love letters or something, let's not pry any more than necessary."

"Yeah, that stuff should stay private. But it might give us a clue as to where she's gone if there's a lover involved."

"Let me see them."

Rose spent several moments reading through the opening paragraphs of the half-dozen or so letters, her brow furrowed in concentration. Crowley stayed on his knees in front of the safe, looking up at her. He'd missed the sight of her more than he cared to admit.

"Mostly talking about organizing the false documents," Rose said eventually. "It's all addressed to Iris and in a kind of code, but given we know she has another identity, it's pretty clear."

"I'm surprised she didn't burn those then," Crowley said.

"Unless she's keeping them in case of trouble. You know, perhaps to use against whoever this John Smith is who's signed off on them all."

"You think she's that devious?"

Rose handed the letters back. "Lily is really smart and cunning, Jake. She ran rings around me when we were kids, always getting me into trouble. I never saw through her clever schemes. Of course, we were kids, so they weren't that clever, in hindsight. But for a mind that young? Yes, she was devious. If she took the same kind of thinking into adulthood, I wouldn't put anything past her. And we know she's up to something, right? Why else would she have a fake ID?"

"Yeah, she must be doing something weird," Crowley agreed. He held up a few credit card statements from the bottom of the safe. "And these are all in the name of Iris Brown, going back several months. She's obviously had this other ID for a while."

"But what else does that tell us? Does it help us find her?"

Crowley used his phone to snap a photo of one of the bills, then put everything back in the safe and closed the door. He stood up, looked around the neat bedroom. "Not really, no."

"Unless we use the credit card account to track her movements?" Rose said.

"You think it's maybe time to call up old friend Cameron Cray, huh?"

"He's your army buddy, so you tell me," Rose said. "He really helped us with all that Landvik stuff, so it might be worth a call."

Crowley saw desperation in her eyes. He couldn't blame her. But still… "We don't have any hard evidence to show that Lily is in trouble, though. I agree the false identity is odd for an ordinary grad student, but perhaps she's perfectly happy and doing these things for a good reason."

"But she's still missing!"

"I know. But maybe that's what she wants. Missing doesn't necessarily mean she's in trouble."

Rose let out an explosive breath of frustration. "I get that, sure. And I hardly even know my sister, rarely even talk to her. But something is up. I can just feel it. Can you trust me on this?"

"Sure, okay. But let's look around more first."

They moved out into the main lounge of the apartment again. Lots of other artifacts besides those Crowley had originally noticed adorned the walls and shelves. Taken individually, several looked to hold significant value. Together, the collection seemed well beyond the means of any regular person, let alone a grad student. As Rose had said, they had no way to know how much wealth Lily might possess, but it was an incongruous décor nonetheless.

"Is it possible Lily was involved in black market antiquities?" he asked.

Anger flashed in Rose's eyes, but quickly faded. She sighed. "I don't want to think that of her, but I suppose anything is possible." She glanced around the room, lips pressed together. "I can understand why you ask. But don't you think Lily would live in a nicer flat if that were the case?"

Crowley shrugged. "I don't know. This isn't a cheap area, but it may not be her only property. If she has more than one identity…"

Rose's eyebrows lifted as she considered that. "A whole new set of possibilities opens up if we follow that line of thinking. But you know what, even if that's all this is, Lily involved with the black market, that's reason enough for me to want to find her. Who knows what kind of criminal she might have run afoul of in some shady deal."

Crowley nodded, realizing the immediate future was being laid out before him. His teaching semester was almost over and if he declared a personal emergency he could get a substitute to cover exams for him. He couldn't deny he felt protective of Rose after what they'd been through together. And he really wanted to be close to her again, to understand why she cut off contact if nothing else.

"You can get leave from the museum to look into this?" he asked her.

"I have to, don't I? Will you take time off to help me? Can you?"

"I can." Crowley smiled. "So maybe let's start by giving Cameron a call and see what we can learn."

CHAPTER 5

Museum of Egyptian Antiquities, Cairo, Egypt

Crowley and Rose stood outside the Museum of Egyptian Antiquities, looking up at the large white arched entrance surrounded by deep ochre walls. Matching arched windows, running down to ground level, marched off to the left and right. Flags fluttered far above in the hot breeze. The place was a little rundown, but a new museum was under construction, the activity loud and feverish. A hot, dry breeze pulled at Crowley's clothes, carrying with it the scent of traffic and metal, and the noise of the busy city.

A tour of this place was one of the last things on "Iris Brown's" credit card, as hacked by Crowley's old army buddy, Cameron Cray, who still worked the intel game, though for private enterprise as much as the Defense Force these days. Cameron's contacts and levels of access were high, though Crowley had no idea how the man managed his activities. But that was Cameron's business. He had given Crowley some grief about getting involved in new shenanigans so soon after the last adventures.

His work had led them to the Cairo Museum, on this hot, dry day.

"Let's see what we can learn," Crowley said, and approached the entrance.

Rose put a hand on his arm, stopping him. "Let me go first. My museum contacts can circumvent the usual issues." She approached the entrance, had a quiet conversation with someone behind the glass, then smiled and waved Crowley in.

Crowley gave the official-looking man behind the desk a smile as he passed, but the man simply glowered from beneath thick, black brows. "I don't think he approves of your access."

Rose shrugged. "I suspect he doesn't approve of my gender, but there's nothing he can do about etiquette between museum employees. Dr. Phelps, my boss at the Natural History Museum, remember him?"

"I do."

Rose winked. "He's been pulling strings for me again, so we get to wander uninhibited." She flashed a pass, laminated, and hung it from her neck by an attached lanyard.

They went into the large, cool interior of the main lobby and looked around. Pale stone floor stretched out before them, enormous arches along both sides of the giant space leading off to other exhibition spaces.

"There are two main floors," Rose said. "Ground and first. Down here there's a huge collection of papyrus and coins from the ancient world. Most of the papyrus is in broken fragments, sadly, decayed over the last two thousand years. But lots of different languages are in evidence: Greek, Latin, Arabic, ancient Egyptian." As with her lectures in the Natural History Museum where she worked, she was perfectly at home in this place, so similar but so different, thousands of miles from home. He grinned. What she called her museum brain, her incredible recall of facts and figures, her easy nature with sharing it all, had kicked in.

"I've always wanted to come here," she said, "though I wish the circumstances were different." They passed a large glass cabinet of coins and she was instantly distracted. "The coins here are mostly gold, silver, and bronze, but not only Egyptian. Look there, ancient Greek, Roman. Those are old Islamic currency." She glanced up at him. "This is your field, actually. Historians have done great research of the history of Ancient Egyptian trade methods from the study of these."

"I read recently about a new discovery relating to Islamic trade in the region. I'll have to look it up again, now it has greater significance. Maybe I'll run a unit on this stuff next term."

Rose made a soft sound of enchantment as they approached a display of large, intricately decorated sarcophagi. "These are artifacts from the New Kingdom period, between 1550 and 1069 BCE. Can you imagine? Three and a half thousand years old! Upstairs they have artifacts from the last two great dynasties of Egypt. They've got stuff from the tombs of Thutmosis III, Thutmosis IV, Amenophis II, Hatshepsut, artifacts from the Valley of the Kings. They have material from the tombs of Tutankhamun and Psusennes I, which were originally found intact, not looted or damaged at all. We have to go upstairs! They have two special rooms with New Kingdom mummies, kings and their royal family members."

Her excitement was palpable, but Crowley held up a hand. "Let's take our time. Remember, we're here to find Lily first and foremost, right?"

Rose's face fell. "Of course. But I can't help getting carried away in a place like this."

"Me too, but let's go slowly. Ask around a bit."

Crowley approached a security guard leaning laconically against the upright of one arched entrance halfway down the large main room. The man looked at Crowley disdainfully as he approached.

Crowley swallowed his annoyance at the guard's attitude and held up a picture of Lily they had taken from her apartment. "We're looking for a missing person," he said. "This woman. Have you seen her?"

The guard glanced briefly at the photo, then shook his head, looking off over Crowley's shoulder like he was not worth the time to even engage.

"Thanks, you've been very helpful," Crowley said, sarcasm dripping off the words.

As they moved along, Rose said, "Let me try next time."

"Maybe," Crowley admitted. "But don't be too flirtatious. This is a Muslim country, after all."

They passed a museum guide leading a group of four Americans along and Crowley interrupted her politely. "Excuse me, have you seen this woman lately?"

The guide looked at the picture for a few seconds, then shook her head. "Sorry, I don't think so."

They thanked her and moved on, frustration growing as they asked several other employees and always got a reply in the negative. There were moments of distraction as Rose enthused briefly about some exhibit or another and Crowley couldn't help but share her joy. He was a history teacher, she a museum researcher and sometimes guide. This was excellent common ground for them both, feeding their curious souls. But the search continued and after half an hour they had got no further.

As they made their way to the first floor, another guide came along the hall toward them, this one leading a group of six. The guide was tall and thin, with a long beard and eyes large behind thick spectacles. He paused and spoke about a papyrus housed in a large glass frame on the wall, then stepped back to let his charges in for a closer look.

Crowley took his opportunity and held up the photo of Lily again. "Sorry to interrupt, but have you seen this woman lately?"

The guide looked at the picture, then at Rose and his eyes

widened.

"She's my sister," Rose said.

"You look very alike. I remember her, she was here a lot, took my tour twice."

"Do you have any idea where she might be now?" Crowley asked. "She's been missing for some time."

"Missing? That's not good. It was a while ago that I saw her, but she spent a lot of time talking to one of the other staff members, Amisi. She works in the Royal Mummies room." The guard pointed along the hall. "That way; she's working today."

CHAPTER 6

Museum of Egyptian Antiquities, Cairo, Egypt

Rose's heart rate increased suddenly and she glanced at Crowley. He thanked the tall guard and headed off along the hall. For the first time there was something concrete, beyond speculation or a paper trail. These people had seen and talked to Lily directly. Rose tried to hold her nerves in check; they were still a long way from finding her sister, but for the first time she felt a spark of hope.

The Royal Mummies room was dimmer than the other parts of the museum, but constructed of the same cool white and tan stone. Rose paused in the entrance, mouth agape in surprise and excitement. Glass cases lined the walls and stood side by side in the middle of the large room, each containing an actual mummy. Not the bandage-wrapped monsters from the movies, but real people, dark skin tightened across stark bones. Most were dressed in light linen or had a linen sheet over them for modesty, but heads and feet were clearly on display, arms crossed on their chests, fingers thin and crooked.

Rose knew the collection had received mixed responses, some balking at such a blatant display of the dead, but she was enthralled by it. She saw by Crowley's expression as he stood beside her that he shared her wonder. It was good to have him by her side again, his strength, confidence, and yes, his attractiveness. She pushed the thoughts aside, determined to concentrate on finding Lily. But the displays in front of her grabbed her attention again.

She walked slowly among the glass cabinets, marveling at the actual bodies of ancient luminaries like Ramses I, Seti I, his son Ramses the Great, Merenpath, Ramses III, and so many others. Studying on the plane from England she had read that some biblical historians, and some Egyptologists, linked several of these individuals to the alleged exodus of the Jews from Egypt, as described in the Old Testament.

The almost physical presence of age, epic stretches of time, seemed to hang over her shoulders like a cape, weighing her down.

"This is remarkable," Crowley whispered.

Rose chuckled. "I was just thinking the same."

They paused, looking down at a woman reclined in death, in a dress of wrapped white linen, yellowed with age. Even with her gray-black skin tight to her skull, her past beauty was evident, lips blackened, but shining, slightly parted. Her hands rested one atop the other just above her stomach, her eyes closed as if she simply slept.

"Despite the obvious degradation, she looks like she might wake any moment," Rose said quietly.

"I often think the same." The woman's voice beside them made both Rose and Crowley jump.

"I'm sorry," the woman said. "I didn't mean to startle you." She wore the uniform of a museum employee and a name badge that said Amisi. She frowned briefly as she met Rose's eye.

Rose took the opportunity. "You recognize me? Perhaps you've met my sister Li... Iris. Iris Brown."

Amisi nodded slowly. "Of course. Your sister?"

"Yes. Please, can you tell us where she might be?"

Amisi frowned again, looked down. "Oh, I don't know anything..."

"Please, she's been missing for a while and I'm trying to find her."

Amisi met Rose's eye again and Rose saw the sympathy there. Was her desperation that evident? "I did talk to Iris and her friend on a couple of occasions, yes. But I'm sorry, I wouldn't have any idea where she is."

"When did you last see her?" Crowley asked.

"I'm not sure. Some weeks ago, I think."

"You said she was with a friend," Rose said. "Who was that?"

Amisi raised her hands slightly, shrugged. "I didn't get a name. Tall fellow, wispy beard, man bun. He was rather cocky. Honestly, I didn't much like him."

"I don't think I ever like any fellow with a man bun," Crowley said.

Rose and Amisi both smiled at that. Rose thought perhaps it was something they could all agree on. "How was my sister to this man," Rose asked. "Did they act like colleagues? Lovers?"

"I couldn't really say." Amisi paused, thinking. "Iris did the talking. The man was... standoffish."

This guy made Rose nervous, the description of someone maybe not entirely pleasant. Perhaps he was nicer to Lily, but perhaps not. "What did you guys talk about?"

Amisi thought again. "Well, she asked a few questions about King Tut, but then brought the conversation around to the *Book of the Dead*. Do you know what that is?"

"Let's assume we don't," Crowley said. "I'm sure my knowledge is rudimentary at best."

Amisi's voice took on the tone of practiced lecturing. "Well, The Egyptian *Book of the Dead* is a collection of spells, designed to enable the soul of the deceased to navigate the afterlife. But that title is misleading, coined by western scholars. The correct translation of the title would be *The Book of Coming Forth by Day*, or perhaps *Spells for Going Forth by Day*. Although *The Book of the Dead* is an ancient compilation of texts written at different times, and finally gathered together in a single volume, it was never codified. No two copies of the work are exactly the same. Each one was created specifically for the individual who could afford to purchase it, a kind of personal manual to help them after death.

"They were in use from the beginning of the New Kingdom, around 1550 BCE, until around the year 50 BCE. The surviving papyri discovered over the years contain various religious and magical texts and vary considerably in their illustrations. They also vary in size and complexity. At this point we're aware of one hundred and ninety-two spells, though no single volume we've seen includes them all. Again, it seems they were custom made to suit the client. Some spells are intended to give the deceased mystical knowledge in the afterlife, or to identify them with the gods. Spell seventeen, for example, is an obscure and lengthy description of the god Atum. Most everything we've seen has no more than one hundred and eighty-nine chapters at most."

Amisi paused, looked from Rose to Crowley and back again. "I could go on for hours on this subject."

Rose smiled. "And I would love to listen to you. It's truly fascinating. But how might this help me find my sister? Was there anything in particular she wanted to know?"

"One odd question did stick with me," Amisi said. "She was specifically interested in Books of the Dead that had more than one hundred and eighty-nine chapters. I told her there was no such thing to my knowledge. To anyone's knowledge as far as I know."

"Do you have any idea where she went next or what she

planned, after she spoke to you?" Rose asked.

Amisi made an apologetic face. "I'm sorry, no. She was focused, almost terse, but not unkind. I'm sorry I can't tell you more."

"Thank you." Hope had risen, but sunk away again. The fact that Lily had been here was good to know, but it provided them with no leads, nowhere else to turn. Unless Crowley had any bright ideas.

Amisi put one hand on Rose's shoulder and squeezed gently, then turned away. Rose fell into step beside Crowley as they headed out of the mummies room and down the stairs in silence. They walked through the main museum, heading for the front door and Rose finally gave vent to her frustrations.

"We've run into a brick wall, haven't we?"

Crowley glanced once behind them. "For now, perhaps we have."

"For now? So what's our next move?"

"This instant," Crowley said quietly, "we have a bigger concern. Someone is following us."

CHAPTER 7

The streets of Cairo, Egypt

Crowley took Rose's hand, enjoying the warmth of it, but pre-occupied by their sudden tail. The man was middle-aged, iron gray hair over a narrow face, sporting a wide mustache and a light tan suit. Crowley had spotted him twice as they toured the museum and something in Crowley's internal early warning system had shivered, but he'd written it off. It was all too easy to grow paranoid when you knew you were up to no good, or when circumstances made a person edgy. But training lived deep in Crowley's bones and his well-honed instincts had caused him to ignore his conscious thoughts and keep the stranger in sight. While they spoke to Amisi, Crowley had realized the stranger was loitering nearby, ostensibly looking at the various mummies in their glass cases, but clearly paying attention.

As they left the mummies room, Crowley used the dim light and glass cabinets to surreptitiously watch the stranger's reflection, and sure enough the man had tailed them at a discreet distance. Down through the main room he came. By the time Crowley took Rose's hand at the main entrance, he was buzzing with adrenaline.

"What do we do?" Rose whispered, her grip tight.

Crowley looked both ways. He pointed to the left. "The river is that way, the Nile. We'll potentially trap ourselves against it." He moved off to the right, heading for the busy main road, Meret Basha, picking up his pace as he went. "Let's get lost in the busy side streets across the way there and see how determined this guy is."

"He's still there?"

They reached the main road and Crowley checked the traffic, took the opportunity to cast a passing look back behind them. The man in the tan suit was taking long strides to catch up, one hand held in his suit jacket. "Yep, he's coming. Might be armed. Let's go."

"Armed?"

Crowley didn't bother to answer, but ran out across the busy four-lane road. Cars beeped and swerved, one man hanging out the driver's window to yell a stream of Egyptian invective.

Without pause, Crowley leaped the central footpath, yellow and black curb stones running along both sides, and hauled Rose directly across the two northbound lanes. More horns blared and he ran between tall buildings, past a small supermarket, narrowly missing an old woman pushing a rickety cart.

Rose shook off his hand, but kept pace alongside. "You don't need to lead me!"

"Sorry."

They reached another road running obliquely across their path, less busy than the last one and Crowley turned left, letting his natural hunter's nose lead them deeper into the city. Sweat trickled down his back, his lungs starting to burn despite his fitness. The hot, dry air of Cairo made any exercise hard work. Rose panted too, but showed no sign of slowing.

The footpaths were busy with people, causing Crowley and Rose to duck left and right, often going opposite sides of some person or crowd only to converge on each other again as their flight continued. They turned at the next street, heading right past a small café. Several tables littered the footpath, one surrounded by four old men with faces wrinkled as walnuts, passing the tube of a *nargileh* between them. One man, aromatic smoke streaming in twin jets from his nostrils, laughed and said something Crowley wouldn't have understood even if he'd heard it clearly.

As they made a turn, Crowley glanced back again and sure enough the tan-suited man still tailed them. His face was twisted in determination, doing nothing now to hide his pursuit, as he pushed people aside. He ignored their protestations and raised one hand towards Crowley. Not waiting to see if it maybe held a gun, Crowley pushed Rose sideways into a narrow alley.

"Hey!"

"He's still coming."

They burst out of the alley into a street with neat brickwork underfoot and a garish blast of color everywhere else. Yellowing buildings rose on either side and the shopfronts and footpaths were covered with awnings and market stalls. Men and women called out, selling clothing and vegetables, *nargileh* in a hundred shades of colored glass, rugs and baskets, trinkets and ornaments. The aroma of spice and fruity hookah smoke mingled with the petrol and exhaust fumes drifting in from nearby.

"He's still coming," Crowley said. "We need to change

tack."

"And do what?"

Crowley pointed. "You keep going that way, don't look back."

"Where are you going?"

"I'll be ahead. You lead him, and as he passes, I'll jump him."

Rose's eyes widened. "I'm the bait?"

Crowley grinned. "No time. Go!" And he sprinted ahead, praying she would follow him at a more leisurely pace.

Gasping and sweating, his lungs burning, he spotted a wide doorway leading into some kind of shady courtyard. But the archway containing the doors was deep in shadow. Crowley ducked in and crouched, taking long deep breaths to control his breathing. Peeking out, he saw Rose jogging along, less than a hundred meters away, and the stranger turned into the busy market street only another fifty meters behind her.

Rose squinted forward, her mouth twisted in annoyance. Crowley smiled. If she hadn't spotted where he went, the stranger certainly wouldn't. The man in the tan suit had closed the gap to twenty meters by the time Rose ran past Crowley's hiding place. She still stared ahead, scanning the crowds shopping, no doubt looking for Crowley's pale blue, short-sleeved shirt.

The stranger hurried past and Crowley shot out of the shadows right behind him. He reached an arm around the man's neck, the other around his chest, pinning the left arm tight to the man's body, and trapping that hand in the jacket pocket.

The stranger let out a yelp and tried to bat Crowley's hands away.

"Don't struggle!" Crowley snapped. He raised his voice. "Rose!"

She turned, face splitting into a smile, and jogged back to them.

Ignoring the sudden interest of several stallholders and shoppers, Crowley dragged the man back into the shadows he had hidden in moments before.

"I mean you no harm!" the man said, voice heavily accented, thick with fear.

Crowley could feel the trembling throughout the man's body and the heat of his exertions. Feeling down the man's arm, Crowley found only a withered bony hand in the jacket pocket.

The man lifted it, the skin a much darker shade than the deep tan of the rest of his skin. The fingers were crooked like talons, the flesh all but gone, thin bones poking up like rails. "The result of an unfortunate incident in my youth. It has been useless for decades."

Crowley frowned, sympathetic and mildly disgusted at the same time. "What does that to a person?"

"A long story that we don't have time for. Nor do I have the inclination to tell you."

"What do you want?" Rose demanded. "Why are you following us?"

"As I said, I mean you no harm. I simply wanted to warn you. I couldn't understand why you ran from me."

"You following us is pretty suspicious, don't you think?" Crowley said.

The man made a face to show that was a fair point. "Perhaps, but your reaction makes you also seem suspicious. Like you're up to no good."

"We're not the ones following people," Crowley said.

"True. I just didn't want to talk inside the museum."

"Why not?"

"There are ears everywhere, and not all of them friendly."

"So what did you want to warn us about?" Rose asked.

The man drew a deep breath, then sighed. "The path you follow leads to the Anubis Key... and certain death."

CHAPTER 8

The man they had caught in the markets refused to give them any more information. Rose didn't like him anyway, and was glad to be out of his company, but she had tried along with Crowley to press the fellow for more details. As soon as he had delivered the melodramatic statement about the Anubis Key, whatever that was, he had clammed up and tried to leave.

They both cajoled him, offered him money even, to tell them more. To tell them what he knew. But he simply shook his head, lips together.

Eventually he said, "I have made a promise to myself many years ago, that I would do what I could to prevent others making the mistakes I made as a young man. I've done that now by warning you. I will not be drawn back into that which nearly killed me. That which did kill all those close to me and left me... lesser." He raised his withered hand again and pushed Crowley aside with his good arm.

They watched him stalk off back down the street towards the museum and the river.

"Well, that was proper creepy," Crowley said.

They returned to their hotel to try to piece together what little they had learned. The tall gold and green building pushed a dozen stories or so up into the impossibly blue sky. Stepping into the cream marble interior, Crowley and Rose both sighed with relief as they were enveloped in air-conditioned cool. They had adjoining rooms, both identical in earthy shades of brown, tan and cream, with a generous queen bed and a wide window that gave a beautiful view over the broad expanse of the Nile. The skyline on the other side was blocky and lit gold as the afternoon began to wear toward evening.

They went into Crowley's room and Rose fell onto the bed, staring up at the ceiling, as Crowley sank heavily into a large armchair and put his feet up on the matching footstool.

"What now?" she asked.

Crowley pulled a tablet from his messenger bag and said, "Let's do some research. I'll look more into the *Book of the Dead* that your sister was so interested in. You see what you can learn, if anything, about the Anubis Key that crazy guy was talking about."

Rose sighed and sat up. Grief tugged at her chest, along with a myriad of other conflicting emotions. She needed to know where her sister was, but she was angry with Lily, too. Angry with her for going missing, but also for their estrangement over all these years. What Lily had done, that Rose could never forgive. Lily made life so difficult for everyone, always so combative, so vindictive. Then, just as Rose or her parents, or both, were about to declare the woman a lost cause and give up on her, Lily would do something loving or kind, something redemptive. Or show up for one of her rare in-person appearances, and make the family think perhaps there was something worth holding onto after all. This time, Rose would find Lily and she would demand to know not only what was happening now, but what the story was for all these past years. What Lily expected of her family. An ultimatum, perhaps, to try to stem this tide of heartache.

With another sigh, Rose pulled out her laptop and logged onto the hotel wifi. She thought back to the strange man in the market. *The path you follow leads to the Anubis Key... and certain death.* She would have simply written him off as a crank if it weren't for the disturbing state of his left hand and arm. It looked like the mummies they had been so enthralled by only minutes before. He may well be a crank, after all, but perhaps not one they could ignore.

She began a search for the Anubis Key. Not surprisingly, there were hundreds of results for Anubis himself, the Egyptian dog-headed god of mummification and the afterlife. Anubis had varying roles in different contexts, sometimes depicted as a protector of graves, an embalmer, lord of the underworld until Osiris took over that role. Among the most prominent of his roles was the god who ushered souls into the afterlife, attending the "Weighing of the Heart" to determine whether a soul would be allowed to enter the realm of the dead or not. For all his frequent mentions in the Egyptian pantheon, Anubis played almost no role in Egyptian myths. Rose went back to her original search. All this about Anubis himself was no news to her, common knowledge to anyone with even a rudimentary understanding of Egyptian mythology. The Anubis Key was the important thing and that garnered few mentions.

She skimmed over a few wild notions on a variety of

conspiracy theory websites. They all seemed to speculate of the existence of the Anubis Key, but none had any concrete ideas about what it might be. Rose frowned. Was it a physical object, an idea, a place? All the stories she looked at agreed it had something to do with summoning the dead.

Then Rose found a few suggestions that it might be a spell or incantation, and that played into the idea of raising the dead.

She sat back, stretched her arms high over her head. Crowley watched her, glanced quickly away when she saw him looking. Poor Jake, forced to share her life again but not a bed. They had more important concerns right now, but she would have to talk to him at some point about why she had distanced herself. She owed him at least that much. Maybe more. She derailed that train of thought and brought herself back to the present predicament.

"Anything?" she asked.

Crowley shook his head, put his tablet face down on his lap. "Nothing we didn't already know. You?"

"Not really. Except one possibility. There's some conjecture here that the Anubis Key might be some kind of spell relating to the summoning of the dead."

"Interesting."

"And Lily was really focused on the *Book of the Dead*, right? Which consists of various spells related to the afterlife."

Crowley nodded slowly, eyes narrow. "Right. But what's your point?"

Rose wasn't sure herself where she was going with this, but she let her mouth run away with it to see where it led. "Well, Lily was looking for a *Book of the Dead* with more than the one hundred and eighty-nine known spells. So what if that guy with the weird arm overheard us asking about that and suspects that the Anubis Key might be a previously unknown spell. Or a spell thought to be lost, but that might be found in a book containing more than the standard set? Or maybe he knows the spell and it did that horrible thing to his hand."

Crowley tapped his fingertips together, thinking silently for a moment. Eventually he said, "You could be right, although the hand thing is maybe a bit of a leap. It would connect *the Book of the Dead* with whatever that guy feared. Regardless, it's the only thing close to a lead we've got, so it's worth following up. And according to what I've been reading here about the *Book of the Dead* and its various incarnations, there's only one scholar who seems halfway reliable."

Rose smiled, daring to hope they might have found a way forward. "Okay, then. Let's go and talk to him."

CHAPTER 9

Siwa Oasis, Egypt

The Siwa Oasis lay between the Qattara Depression and the Egyptian Sand Sea in the Western Desert, some thirty miles east of the Libyan border. The trip of nearly three hundred fifty miles from Cairo into the desert had reminded Crowley unpleasantly of tours in Iraq and Afghanistan, but had afforded them time to study up on the oasis. According to the research Crowley had done the previous evening, Siwa Oasis was about fifty miles long and twelve wide, and one of Egypt's most isolated settlements. Around twenty-three thousand people lived there, mostly Berbers, who had apparently developed a unique culture and a distinct language called Siwi. The place gained its reputation mainly from its historical role as home to an oracle of Ammon, which gave it its ancient name, Ammonium. The associated ruins had become a popular tourist attraction.

After the dry landscape they'd driven through, the greenery surprised Crowley. Lush trees surrounded the large town, the blocky pale tan sandstone buildings standing out against a range of conical hills in the distance behind. The late afternoon sun painted one side of every building a deep gold as Crowley guided the Land Rover up the main street, between buildings with darkened windows. People in white or pale pastel *thawb,* the flowing ankle length clothing common throughout the region, watched as Crowley cruised by. Their eyes in deep tan faces under checkered headscarves were narrowed in interest, but perhaps not unfriendly.

"So this Professor," Rose said.

"Dado Hamza," Crowley reminded her.

"Right, Professor Hamza. He's not in the town itself, you said."

"Well, he's probably living here, but working at the Amun Oracle dig, which is at the mostly abandoned village of Aghurmi, about two kilometers east."

"Can we drive there?"

"Yeah." Crowley looked at the map he held open on the steering wheel, then squinted out the windshield again. "This way, I think."

It wasn't long before the road led them out between the trees again and soon to a broken down sandstone village, the tumbled buildings casting long afternoon shadows across the ground. The place was largely deserted and Crowley parked the Land Rover in one of those deep shadows. When they stepped out, the dry heat hit them like a wall. Crowley sniffed, picking up the aromas of plant life and water, incongruent in the desiccated environs all around.

Crowley pointed. "That's the Temple of the Oracle of Amun. The dig is apparently on the other side of the mount."

As they walked, Rose said, "I was reading about this last night. Some people think it's an ancient solar calendar thing, you know, like Stonehenge, only a temple."

Crowley laughed. "Yeah, I got lost in a lot of conspiracy theory and whackjob websites last night, too. It's a pretty interesting place."

They gained the top of the flat rock on which the Temple stood and walked in across the sandy floors among the fallen stones. From one point they saw across the tops of dark green trees to a series of rugged mountains, striped in alternating layers of light and dark rock. No one else seemed to be around.

"I guess all the tourists have left for the day," Crowley said. "Maybe we're too late as well."

"Over here," Rose said.

Crowley moved to see where she pointed and saw the archeological dig on the far side of the temple. From their elevated position it was clearly laid out below them, a grid of trenches, surrounded by tents and vehicles. Several people milled around, seemingly packing up tools and equipment.

"Or perhaps we're just in time," Crowley said.

They made their way down and approached the first people they met, a man and a woman loading up a battered old pickup truck with plastic crates.

"Professor Dado Hamza?" Crowley asked.

The woman frowned, but turned and pointed to a tarpaulin supported on four long poles, rippling slightly in the hot breeze. An old man stood in the shade beneath it, talking to a small group of people.

Crowley and Rose waited respectfully outside the covered area until the man stopped talking and the group moved away. As they approached, Professor Hamza looked up and seemed momentarily startled. Crowley realized he'd spotted Rose and thought he recognized her. The Professor's face hardened.

"Yes?"

"We'd really like to talk to you about something important," Crowley said.

Hamza shook his head, his shock of iron-gray hair waggling comically. "Sorry, I can't help you." His voice was deep, heavily accented. "You've wasted your time coming all the way out here."

Crowley bristled, annoyed at the summary dismissal, but Rose put a hand on his arm before he could speak up.

"You recognized me at first," she said. "You thought I was Lily."

Hamza frowned. "Lily?"

"Sorry, you thought I was Iris. Iris Brown. Her real name is Lily and she's my sister. She's missing and I really need your help, sir."

Hamza looked around nervously, his face twisted in indecision. After a moment, he sighed. "We can't talk here. Go back to town, find the Kenooz Siwa Restaurant. I'll see you on the roof terrace there at eight." Without another word he turned and strode away.

CHAPTER 10

The restaurant Professor Hamza had suggested turned out to be on the roof terrace of the Shali Lodge in the middle of Siwa Oasis. Crowley and Rose had found themselves a place to stay nearby, then wondered the streets of Siwa as the day gently cooled into evening. Heat still clogged the air, but not oppressively like it did during the day. By around seven pm, they headed up to the Kenooz Siwa Restaurant and got a table beside a sandstone arch where they could look out over the town. Stars began appearing in the indigo sky as evening fell slowly into night, an aromatic breeze drifted past, bearing scents of spices and night blossoms.

Their table was low to the ground and they sat on thick white cushions. Palm trees grew along one part of the wall to their left, their deep green leaves shifting and whispering in the soft breeze. They ordered mint tea and some of the restaurant's Siwan specialties, baked lentils, eggplant with pomegranate sauce, and a goat curry with a rich, spicy sauce.

They didn't talk much, enjoying the moment's peace and calm as they ate. Eventually, Crowley said, "Are you okay?"

She raised an eyebrow. "Within the context of what's happening, sure. Why do you ask?"

Crowley swallowed down nerves and said, "It's just that you've been avoiding me a bit. I'm not trying to seem possessive or stalkery or anything, I'm just concerned that everything's all right with you." He felt a little creepy, wished he could have kept his promise to himself and let her address the subject in her own time, but he genuinely worried about her. And his ego was slightly bruised; that was undeniable.

Rose finished her mouthful, looking down at the table. Then she raised her gaze to meet his and opened her mouth to speak, but something behind him distracted her. Crowley glanced around and saw Professor Hamza approaching. Great timing, old man! Crowley thought, but shook his head slightly. It would have to wait.

He stood and shook Hamza's hand. Rose did the same.

"Thank you for your time," Rose said.

They sat down again and Crowley gestured to their food. "We have plenty here, please help yourself."

"Thank you, but I've eaten." Hamza caught a waiter's eye and ordered an iced tea.

"Earlier, you did mistake me for my sister, didn't you?" Rose said after the waiter had left.

Hamza nodded, looking at Rose with narrowed eyes. "You say her name is Lily?"

"Yes, though she seems to be traveling under another identity, Iris Brown. Her real name is Lily Black. I'm Rose Black. And this is my friend, Jake Crowley."

Crowley smiled but kept quiet to let the two of them talk.

Hamza looked over the low wall, his attention drifting out across Siwa Oasis, and maybe across time as well. "She did come to me, yes. You look a lot alike, but she's older, yes?"

"That's right."

His gaze returned to Rose. "I see the differences now I'm paying more attention."

Rose smiled. "People so often thought we were twins when we were kids. What did she ask you about, Professor?"

"She initially expressed interest in the *Siwan Manuscript*. You've heard of it?"

"I read a little last night, but I know very little about this area or its history."

Hamza accepted his iced tea from the waiter with a smile. "The Siwan Manuscript was written during the middle ages. It's the best example we have of a local history book. It tells of a benevolent man who arrived here and planted an orchard. Afterward, he went to Mecca and brought back thirsty Arabs and Berbers, and subsequently established himself, along with his followers, in the western part of Shali. But Iris's interests…I mean Lily's interest, didn't really lie with our history. She guided our conversation around to the Anubis Key."

Crowley's heart gave a quick extra thump of excitement at the connection, the long journey seemingly not wasted after all. If Rose shared his enthusiasm, she hid it well.

"We've heard about that, but only in passing. What is it?"

Hamza frowned, looked around himself as though checking no one else was in earshot. Then he shook his head. "It's a myth, nothing more. And that's what I told your sister."

"Humor us," Crowley said. "Suppose it's real, just pretend, you know? What can you tell us about it?"

Hamza sighed, sipped his iced tea and thought for a moment. Then, "Okay, let's start with Anubis. He is the god of mummification and the afterlife in ancient Egyptian religion. A man with a canine head, yes?" Hamza smiled. "Did you know, archeologists had originally identified the sacred animal of Anubis as an Egyptian canid. At the time it was called the golden jackal, but recent genetic testing has meant the Egyptian animal needed to be reclassified as the African golden wolf."

"A wolf, really? I'd always heard the jackal association." Rose's interest was genuine. Crowley smiled inwardly, enjoying the sight of museum brain engaging again.

Hamza nodded. "But I digress. So Anubis had many roles depending where in history you read about him, but probably most famously he ushered souls into the afterlife, weighing their hearts to determine if they would be permitted to enter the realm of the dead."

Crowley knew all this, and he was certain Rose would know it too, but she was smart enough to let the professor talk at his own pace. The more they claimed to know, the more he would clam up, Crowley was sure. As an academic himself, he knew that to let a professor speak on his area of expertise was the best way to put that professor at ease.

"Anyway," Hamza went on, "assuming that the Anubis Key is a real thing, which it isn't…" He paused and looked from Rose to Crowley. Crowley motioned for him to go on. Hamza shook his head. "Well, assuming it is real, there are a few theories. One is that, since Anubis was the protector of tombs, that perhaps the Anubis Key is a spell to protect tombs, or even to open tombs. Another theory, related to Anubis's association with mummification, is that the Anubis Key explains the Egyptians' secrets of mummification. This, incidentally, is the theory I would consider most likely. The most pragmatic answer is usually the right one. It's easy to get caught up in ideas of spells and magic and mysticism, but we are intelligent, educated adults, are we not?"

"We are, of course," Rose said quietly. "But are there any other theories? Perhaps things that educated adults might scoff at but that remain theories nonetheless?"

Hamza smiled crookedly. "We would be delving into the most far-fetched."

"Let's do that," Crowley said. "Just for fun."

"All right. Given that Anubis is the spirit guide and the

weigher of hearts, some believe the Anubis Key unlocks the door to the world of the dead." He shook his head, his expression clearly betraying what he thought of that idea.

"What would that mean, exactly?" Rose asked sharply.

Crowley frowned, her reaction a bit strong to his mind, but Hamza didn't seem to notice.

The old professor shrugged. "It means some think the Anubis Key is a spell or a device to allow a person to visit the underworld. Or to communicate with the dead, perhaps even bring the dead back."

Rose blanched, lips pressed tightly together.

"Is there anything more you can tell us?" Crowley asked.

Hamza shook his head, more decisively this time. "No. I'm sorry, but we need to wrap this up. It's no good for my reputation to be overheard talking about this stuff."

"We really need to find Lily," Crowley said. "Where might she go if she was on the trail of the Anubis Key, be it real or otherwise?"

"I don't know. Look, I only ever mentioned the damn thing once during an interview about Egyptian legends. Ever since then my name has been scattered across message boards, and conspiracy theorists won't leave me alone. It's why Lily sought me out in the first place and I told her I couldn't help. I realize you're not crazies like some out there, I understand you're simply trying to find your sister, but I can't tell you any more. I wish you the best of luck, really, but I must go."

He stood and Crowley quickly joined him, held out one hand to shake. "Thank you, Professor. We really appreciate your time."

Rose stood and shook his hand too, though she was clearly crestfallen. "Thank you, Professor," she said quietly. "Lily didn't tell you anything about her plans? Nothing at all?"

"No, I'm sorry." Hamza gave each of them a polite nod, then walked away.

"You okay?" Crowley asked Rose as they sat on their cushions again.

She smiled sadly. "You keep asking me that lately. But I'm fine. Just upset that we've hit a dead end."

"I don't think so."

She looked up, mirrored the grin she saw on his face. "Really? What do you mean?"

"I was watching the old man closely. I'm a pretty good

judge of people and he's hiding something."

"Like what?"

"I don't know," Crowley said. "But we're going to find out tonight."

CHAPTER 11

The night was cool and dim, lit only by the stars and a quarter moon. It meant that Crowley and Rose were able to see once their eyes had adjusted, but the shadows were deep, pitch dark and mysterious. The breeze caused tarpaulins and tent flaps around the dig site to flap gently, occasionally slapping like restless sails. There were no guards, no people at all, as the two made their way silently through the site, looking nervously left and right.

After a tentative pass through, getting the lay of the land and ensuring they were, in fact, entirely alone, Crowley pointed to the large covered area where they had first spotted Professor Dado Hamza. "Let's start there," he whispered.

"What do you expect to find?" Rose was equally sotto voce even though they had established they were alone. Something about the darkness and their uninvited snooping about made them both cautious.

"No idea, really. But Hamza was hiding something, I know it. If we can't turn up anything here, I'll find out where he's staying and pay the man a visit. Extract the answers from him."

He felt Rose's disapproval as she asked, "What do you mean by that?"

"Use your imagination."

The covered area didn't give up much, only tools and sketches of the different areas being investigated. As they made their way to other tents nearby, they began to relax. A tapping, like someone knocking rapidly on stone, rang out and they froze. Heart racing, Crowley scanned the darkness, Rose beside him doing the same.

"What was that?" she whispered eventually.

"No idea. Animal?"

"Maybe not!"

"Come on."

They crept forward again, on high alert now. Crowley tried to pierce every shadow with his vision, but the darkest areas were inky and impenetrable. He thought his ears must be standing out from the sides of his head he was listening so hard.

The soft crunch of sand and gravel under their careful steps, the breeze gently stropping the tent sides, the rustle of palm leaves and occasional chatter of a night bird. Though the night was cool, sweat trickled along Crowley's spine under his shirt.

Each of the dig trenches was like a grave, filled with darkness. In some they could vaguely make out silhouettes of disturbed earth at the bottom, others seemingly abysses falling away forever. Crowley briefly entertained they idea of tripping and tumbling into one, spinning through darkness for eternity.

He sniffed, took a deep breath. The place was giving him the creeps. *It's just an empty desert settlement!* he chided himself, but the thought felt hollow even in his own mind.

Something on the air tickled his nose and he couldn't place it. But it felt wrong, out of place somehow. Fragrant, vaguely floral. Perhaps another of the night blossoms they had smelled in the town. Though it wasn't quite the same.

A row of small tents marked one side of the dig and they approached slowly, trying to look everywhere at once. Then that rapid tapping again, or perhaps a clicking. They froze.

"What is that?" Rose's voice was tight in her throat.

Crowley shook his head. "Maybe a lizard? I know there are geckos in Asia and Australia that make that kind of sound."

It didn't repeat and, after another minute or so, Crowley moved on. He lifted one tent flap, held his breath while he flicked on the flashlight app on his phone and shone it around inside. Tools, crates, a table with some interesting small items on it, earthenware that seemed ancient. The next couple of tents were the same.

What did he expect to find here? Crowley became frustrated, the sensation of failure settling over him. Hamza had definitely been withholding something, some information about Lily or about this mysterious Anubis Key. He didn't know what, but the man had every sign of the nervous interviewee. And he had quickly concluded their meeting once Rose and he had pressed for more about things the Professor seemed to write off as complete superstition. There was certainly some valuable detail to be found somewhere, but perhaps it wasn't here. Maybe Crowley would have to have another, more private, conversation with Hamza. The thought made him squirm. He had used all kinds of less than civilized techniques over his army career, and more recently during his and Rose's last adventure, but he would never like those methods.

Crowley spotted a larger tent, out away from the others. He pointed and Rose nodded. When they reached it, Crowley lifted one side of the entrance, tried to pierce the darkness, but couldn't. He flicked on his phone flashlight again and played it around inside. The tent was completely empty but for a large hole in the center of the covered ground.

He crept nearer, shone his light in and saw ancient stone steps leading down some three or four meters to an excavated passageway. The passage disappeared into impenetrable shadow. And that aroma again, stronger now, drifting up from below. Incense, Crowley realized, being burned somewhere far along in the darkness.

He cautiously took the first few steps down, then crouched to listen. Voices, muffled and distant, singsong. He glanced up to Rose to see if she heard it too and she gave a single nod, her eyes wide in concern.

He turned out his light and descended the last few steps into blackness. He heard a soft scuff as Rose followed, then she put a hand on his shoulder. She leaned close, her breath hot against his ear. "Are you sure?"

"We'll just go a little closer, see what we find."

The passage sloped slowly downwards, curving subtly to the left. After a while, a weak golden glow began to light the pale sandstone blocks that made up the walls, floor and ceiling.

The voices they heard resolved into a strange chanting, the language not anything Crowley had ever heard before. The golden glow began to flicker and the passage opened out into a large circular room, dome-ceilinged. The flickering light came from a circle of thick candles, pushing back the shadows to writhe around the walls like silhouettes of dancers. In the circle, four men in full length deep crimson robes, hoods pulled over to hide their faces in shadow, were gathered around another figure, worshipping as they chanted.

Crowley gasped at the sight of the tall, dog-headed figure in the center, candlelight reflecting off the gold and precious stones of its long skirt and intricately-patterned broad necklace.

Anubis looked up, black head swiveling to stare directly at Crowley as he tried to duck back into the shadows of the passage. Crowley quickly realized Anubis was simply a man in elaborate costume, but he been seen.

A voice yelled out. "Intruders! Grab them!"

CHAPTER 12

Aghurmi Mound, Siwa Oasis, Egypt

Crowley cursed as Rose gasped in surprise and they backed up quickly into the shadows. But the worshippers were already charging forward in a ragged line.

"Game on!" Crowley said, and dropped into a ready crouch. He sensed Rose beside him, equally prepared. He'd seen her fight before; her kickboxing and other training made her fit, strong, formidable. But five against two odds were tough, even for trained professionals. However, facing the fight was infinitely preferable to turning his tail to them.

Anubis hung back while the four worshippers ran on. Crowley slipped to the left as Rose dodged right, the two of them operating on an unspoken natural sense, working as a team. Crowley shot out a fast lead hand punch as the first cultist, or whatever they were, closed the distance and his knuckles cracked into the man's surprisingly hard jaw. But hard or not, that one crumpled like a dropped sack of rocks and lay still.

Rose engaged another worshipper, trading blows and blocks while the remaining two both turned to face Crowley. Rose delivered a devastating forearm smash to her attacker and he howled and fell to the floor, writhing but mostly unconscious as blood poured from his crushed nose.

These fools have no idea how to fight! Crowley thought as he feinted with a looping left and then kicked one man directly in the stomach. Air rushed out of the man along with a pained grunt and the man clutched his midriff and collapsed to his knees gasping.

The last of the four ducked, arms over his head, and bolted off up the corridor, heading for the outside world. The man Rose had flattened sat up, face twisted in pain and fear, and raised his hands pleadingly. Rose whipped a kick to his temple and he dropped bonelessly, out cold.

Crowley grinned. Rose was a woman who took crap from no one. He respected the hell out of that.

"You need to stand very still!"

Crowley turned to see Anubis, keeping his distance but holding a long bronze knife in front of himself threateningly.

"He's gone to get help, you know!" Anubis said. "Best you stand still and keep your hands down!"

"Get help? You'd better hope at least a few of them know how to fight," Rose said, one side of her mouth hitched up in amusement.

Crowley saw the adrenaline sparkling in her eyes, knew she felt the same rush he did from the action and the combat. It was especially addictive when it was this easy. He also saw the hand holding the knife trembling. "I don't think anyone else is coming," he said. "What's going on down here is obviously a secret, else you wouldn't be doing it in the middle of the night."

He stalked toward Anubis, who hesitated briefly, then raised the knife. With a cry of fear as much as aggression, the tall man in the faintly ridiculous headdress launched forward and tried to plunge the long blade down at Crowley. But Crowley's training, and his confidence, meant there was never any threat. He raised his forearm, blocked the clumsy downward stroke, and cranked the man's arm over, putting painful pressure against the elbow joint. Anubis howled again.

"One more centimeter and your elbow pops and will never work properly again," Crowley growled between clenched teeth.

The man dropped the knife and it rang like a bell off the stone floor, echoing along the narrow, dim passageway. Crowley turned the arm over, moved behind Anubis and pinned his arm tight against his back. Rose stepped forward and yanked the mask off his head.

"Professor Hamza?" she said, aghast.

"Please," Dado Hamza said. "Let me go. This is none of your concern."

"Oh, we'll let you go, of course," Crowley said. "But not until we get some real answers."

CHAPTER 13

Dado Hamza quaked at the fury in Crowley's voice. He tried to pull away, but his efforts were futile. "What do you mean by real answers?" he asked.

Crowley ground his teeth, quickly losing patience with the frustrating old man. He cranked the arm he held, made the man yelp. "You know what we asked you about only a few hours ago."

Rose dropped the headdress to one side and stepped in front of Hamza. Her face and voice were soft. "Why don't you start by telling us what you're doing here. What is all this?"

"I'm a priest of the Cult of Anubis," Hamza said, defiantly proud. "I lead this chapter."

"And what is the Cult of Anubis?" Crowley asked.

Hamza tried to glance back and see Crowley, but his arm was held too tightly. "We worship Anubis."

Crowley wanted to smack the fool for wasting his time stating the obvious. He cranked the arm again, about to speak, but Rose held up a calming hand. "To what end do you worship Anubis? What do you hope to achieve?"

"We commune with the dead."

Crowley snorted. "That's ridiculous."

But he looked over Hamza's shoulder to Rose, remembering her strange experiences not so long ago, being hypnotically regressed through past lives, into the minds and actions of Vikings hundreds of years dead. He still wasn't sure how much to believe of any of that, but couldn't deny a lot of it remained well outside the realms of anything most people might consider normal. But was it really supernatural? He simply couldn't say. He saw his thought process reflected in Rose's eyes, felt sure she was remembering too. And her memories would be so much more detailed, first hand as they had been. Here we go again, he thought. "Is it like performing a séance?" he asked Hamza.

The man shrugged. "I suppose it could be seen that way. But we seek to bridge the gap in a more concrete way."

"Actually talking to and seeing dead people?" Crowley said.

"That's mental."

"Look, we harm no one," Hamza insisted. "Everyone has suffered terrible loss, yes? Everyone is touched by death sooner or later. The Anubis Cult reaches out to close the gap between those who have died and we who remain living."

"And have you succeeded?" Rose's voice hardened, skepticism touching its edges.

"I'm not sure how to answer that."

"How about just yes or no?" Crowley said, beginning to lose patience again. The man talked in circles and riddles like all carnival barkers and snake oil salesmen.

Hamza shook his head, swallowed. "We all feel a greater connection with those we've lost since we began these rituals. Some claim their lost loved ones have actually spoken to them."

Crowley let the man's arm go and pushed him back against the wall. Hamza, he decided, was not a dangerous man, only a stupid one. He moved next to Rose and Hamza looked nervously from one to the other and back again. He seemed older than ever in the low light, afraid, his scrawny bare chest rising and falling rapidly. Ribs and gray hair stood out in the candle glow.

"You really believe all this?" Crowley asked. "Do you truly think the Egyptian gods existed?"

"Yes." Hamza's tone was strong, dead serious. "They not only existed, I think they still exist."

Rose frowned. "Explain."

Hamza drew a long, trembling breath. "It started on my first ever dig in Egypt. I won't bore you with names and places. But it was old tomb, the sandstone weak, crumbling in many places. The sensation of presence was strong, I could feel something beyond the normal there. One night I worked late, alone in the depths of the tomb, and as I uncovered some bones I heard a sigh. Almost a soft wail. I looked up, 'Who's there?' I demanded. But no one answered. I continued my work, and as I excavated more bones, I heard it again. I turned, looked everywhere. Nothing. I moved away from the bones and looked out the door of the small space, saw and felt nothing but the cool dry air of the tomb. When I turned back, movement made me freeze. Something like mist was drifting up from the bones I had uncovered. I was terrified, but mesmerized, as the mist slowly coalesced into the shape of a man, gossamer-like, a pale reflection, but a man nonetheless. He looked at me, raised one hand imploringly, then another shape formed from the shadows in the corner. Equally insubstantial, the shape of Anubis approached the man. In one hand, the god held a set of scales and on one side lay a heart, still beating. With his free hand, Anubis reached out and took the spirit's palm and together they took two or three steps and faded into the darkness.

"Of course, this all happened in just a few seconds, in semi-darkness, before my very tired eyes. But I do not doubt what I saw. I could go on, I could tell you other experiences. But suffice it to say, the spiritual plane is real, and the gods exist on it." Hamza raised his bony hands, palms up. "Maybe other gods besides the Egyptians."

He fell silent. Crowley could not simply dismiss the man's story as lunatic ravings, for he didn't seem genuinely mad. Then again, what did real madness look like? Not all lunatics were raving. Hamza clearly believed in every word he said. That, or he was a hell of an actor.

"Do you know a man in Cairo?" Crowley asked. "Late middle-age, his left hand is all withered and blackened."

Hamza winced, recognition clear. "Yes. I know who you mean."

"What's his story?"

Hamza pursed his lips, then shook his head. "His story is his to tell. He was part of our cult, but he left. Call it a clash of personalities."

"Before or after the thing with his hand?"

"Oh, long after. He's had that… injury since he was a young man. Long before I knew him. That was part of our falling out. He insisted it was connected to the Anubis Key."

Rose sucked in a quick breath. "So you do know more about that! What is it?"

Hamza sighed. "I told you, it's nonsense. It's a large part of why he and I fell out. He claimed the Anubis Key did that to him, but I wouldn't hear any of that nonsense."

"But you'll happily try to commune with the dead?" Crowley said with a smirk.

Hamza saw the look in Crowley's eyes and his face creased in desperation. "Please, just let me go. I'm harming no one and I'm no use to you."

"You can go," Rose said, "after you tell us where we can find my sister."

Hamza sighed heavily. "I honestly don't know. All I can tell you is what I told her. Where I suggested she look next."

CHAPTER 14

Dahshur Complex, south of Cairo

The Black Pyramid at Darshur lay some twenty-five miles south of Cairo. To Crowley's disappointment, it was mostly a pile of rubble. Named for its dark appearance as it devolved, it stood blocky against the lightly overcast sky, one side fallen into two large squares of ragged stone, the other a sloping scree of tumbled rocks. The pale sand and stone leading up to its base were warm under the occluded sun.

"Compared to the magnificent order of the pyramids at Giza right by Cairo, this is something of a disappointment," Crowley said with a laugh.

Rose smiled. "Yeah, to say the least." She had studied on the journey back, after their conversation had waned, and found the site fascinating despite its decrepitude.

The journey back from Siwa Oasis had been long and uneventful. They'd used some of the time to talk about Hamza and the stories he told. Neither could decide how much they believed, but they both agreed that it was clear Hamza himself believed every word of it.

"You know, The Black Pyramid was the first to house both the deceased pharaoh and his queens," she said.

"That right?" Crowley flashed her a grin.

She frowned. "Well, if you're not interested…"

He quickly raised his hands, eyes wide in apology. "No, no! I love your museum brain. Your smarts and your fighting skills are probably the most attract… amazing things about you."

She gave him the benefit of looking away as the color rose in his cheeks. He had nearly said attractive and she couldn't help being a bit pleased about that. He was attractive, too. She pushed the thoughts aside, again refusing to address the inconveniently, constantly present concerns of their friendship. Her sister came first, and whatever was happening with her.

She looked up at the imposing edifice instead and recited other facts she had recently learned. "It was built by King Amenemhat III during the Middle Kingdom of Egypt. Five remain of the original eleven pyramids here at Dahshur. The excavations were begun by Jacques de Morgan, on a French mission, in 1892. The German Archaeological Institute of Cairo completed excavation nearly a hundred years later, in 1983. Two nearby are among the oldest, largest and best-preserved pyramids in Egypt, built between 2613 and 2589 BCE. Can you even imagine that age?"

Crowley whistled between his teeth. "When it comes to ancient history, nothing comes close to Egypt."

Rose paused, looking up at the imposing edifice of the Black Pyramid. "It's a family affair," she said, almost wistfully. "For all its age and size, these things come down to individuals."

"No one person built these!" Crowley said.

"That's not what I mean. Of course, hundreds or thousands of people were involved in actually building them, but the impetus came from individuals. The pyramids here were a learning experience for the Egyptians, because they were transitioning from step-sided to smooth-sided pyramids. During the reign of Pharaoh Sneferu, more than four and a half thousand years ago, the Bent Pyramid nearby was the first attempt to make one smooth-sided. Ultimately unsuccessful though. The design flaw was an unstable base made of desert gravel and clay that had a tendency to subside when a large amount of weight was put on top. And the blocks were cut in such a way that caused the weight of the pyramid to push down towards the center. That's thought to be the reason the pyramid is 'bent'. It changes angles about halfway up the sides."

"I'm guessing old Sneferu wasn't best pleased about that," Crowley said drily.

Rose laughed. "Indeed not. So he built another, called the Red Pyramid because of the color it goes after it rains. *That* one was the first true smooth-sided pyramid. And that's what I meant by a family affair. The Red Pyramid is huge, thought to be where Sneferu is buried, and the biggest of its kind until Sneferu's son, Khufu, built a bigger one. And Khufu's is the Great Pyramid of Giza, the really famous one, which is 490 feet tall! But Khufu could only build that because of the knowledge gained by his father." She smiled at Crowley. "Individuals, you see?"

Crowley pointed up at the crumbling mass of the Black Pyramid. "But this one was built much later, wasn't it?"

"Yes, by five hundred or even a thousand years at best guess."

"So why is it so crappy?"

Rose laughed. "Where's your respect? This one was originally about seventy-five meters tall, much smaller than the Red or Giza, but typical for the Middle Kingdom. It was encased in limestone like the others, but made of mud brick and clay instead of stone."

"Why?"

Rose shrugged. "Possibly to reduce weight as it's so close to the Nile. But it began to sink, like the Bent Pyramid of Sneferu did. That's about a kilometer and a half that way." She pointed. "This one was abandoned after it started to crush the underground chambers. The builders tried to save it with supporting beams and mud brick walls to stop the sinking, but it was too little, too late."

Crowley scanned the enormous ruin. "Amazing to consider, isn't it. The panic, the process, all the hours of labor. Such mammoth undertakings."

"And all so long ago. But we're not really here for history, are we." Rose looked about them. Small groups of tourists wandered nearby, but the area was not busy. She had hoped there would be people whom they could ask about Lily, archaeologists perhaps, but the lack of activity dented her optimism.

Crowley appeared to have read her mind. He pointed to a bus parked nearby and said, "What about that guy?"

The bus had a tour company logo emblazoned on its sides and the man Crowley pointed out stood on the step of the front door addressing a crowd gathered around. They moved closer to listen, smiled as the guide repeated a lot of what Rose had recently shared.

"So you weren't making all that up," Crowley whispered.

She swatted his shoulder, shook her head. "Hush!"

Crowley bowed his head slightly by way of apology. "But given that he clearly knows his stuff, perhaps he comes here regularly."

"Would Lily join a tour?" Rose said.

"Maybe. But even if not, that doesn't mean that fellow didn't see her."

The guide sent his tour group off with a wave. "You have one hour, then we move on to the Bent Pyramid," he said, his voice accented, but with an American twang underneath.

Rose approached as his charges drifted away. "Excuse me?"

"Yes, madam?" The man was young, maybe early thirties at

most, lean but fit-looking, with short black hair and deep brown eyes. He let his gaze roam quickly down and back up as Rose closed the distance between them.

She sighed internally; men were always so predictable. She noticed he wore a name badge that read, *Kenny*. "Do you tour here regularly?"

"Yes, but I'm afraid you can't join halfway through. You need to book in Cairo…"

She held up a hand to interrupt. "No, no, that's okay. I was wondering if you'd seen my sister." She pulled the photo both she and Crowley carried, showed it to the guide.

Kenny stepped down, taking the photo for a closer look. He smiled. "I have seen her. And it's no surprise you're her sister, you're very alike. Normally I wouldn't remember, I see so many people day to day, tourists, you understand? But I like the Asian look." He flashed an embarrassed glance at Rose. "No offense intended!"

She ignored the comment, glad he had recognized her sister. "Did you speak with her? Or see anything?"

"See anything?"

"She's missing. I'm trying to find her."

Kenny pursed his lips, made a sound of sympathy. "That's no good. I didn't talk to her, but I noticed her here two days running. That's why I remember her, I think. She and another man were talking with Kasim, a tour guide from a different company. Kasim is short and fat, a greasy man with a thick mustache."

"Sounds like you don't like him," Crowley observed.

The guide smiled crookedly. "He's not so bad. But he works for the opposition. One of many competitors. You can ask for him at the Sacred Tours Company in Cairo. You'll find him there."

Rose felt a thrill of excitement ripple up, a new hope sparking into life. Another person who had dealt directly with Lily, more recently. Perhaps they were getting closer. And Lily had been with another man, apparently. Could that be the guy with the man-bun they had learned about before? They would need to find out who he was. "Thank you so much," she said, shaking the guide's hand.

Crowley moved forward slightly. "Incidentally, are you aware of any connections to Anubis in Dahshur."

Kenny seemed to flinch slightly at the mention of the god's

name. "Anubis? Connections?"

"Statues, images, locations associated with him in this region?" Rose said.

"No. I hope you find your sister. I'm sorry, I have to…" He gestured over his shoulder at the bus and climbed back aboard without another word.

"That was a bit weird," Rose said.

"Wasn't it."

"But did you notice something?"

Crowley smiled, nodding. "If you mean the way his eyes flitted to the Black Pyramid just now, then yes."

She smiled back, pleased to be picking up tricks from Crowley when it came to reading people. "Shall we?"

CHAPTER 15

The Black Pyramid, Dahshur, Egypt

As Crowley and Rose made their way towards the Black Pyramid, Crowley reflected on how well they worked together. Rose had definitely found her stride with this situation and was probably using the focus to distract her from the bigger issue, that her sister was missing. She developed new skills every day and Crowley had to admit that he had learned from her as well. They made a formidable pairing when it came to this stuff. The previous adventure with Landvik and all that had entailed seemed like it might have been a one-off, some random lucky sequence of events. But these last few days were proving that Crowley and Rose were well-suited to investigations of this kind, and together they were far stronger than either would have been alone.

"We should keep an eye out for this Kasim character," Rose said, interrupting his thoughts.

"Short and fat, greasy man with a thick mustache." Crowley parroted Kenny's description in his best impression of the man's faux-American accent.

Rose laughed. "That's him. I imagine that could match any number of people, but Kenny said he worked for Sacred Tours, right?"

"That's it. Well remembered. And yeah, let's keep an eye out, but I didn't see any buses marked with that company."

As they rounded a corner of the tumbled down old pyramid, another tour guide, obvious from his logo-emblazoned t-shirt, addressed a group of a dozen or so tourists. They were too far away to hear what he said, but whatever it was seemed to be a conclusion and he disappeared inside, his group trailing behind.

"Let's catch up," Crowley said, jogging forward. "We'll slip away inside if we need to, but we might learn something."

The pyramid entrance led immediately to a steep downward slope, the hot day left behind in an instant. The cool, dim interior was a relief and the guide's voice echoed back in the confined space.

"...explained before that so close to the Nile, the

groundwater leaked into various areas, causing the pyramid to sink and become unstable. Lots of areas are compromised, but there are still numerous passages and chambers accessible. This network of passages contains the king's section, which remains mostly intact and has a sarcophagus and canopic jar, but the king was not buried there. The queen's section was long ago broken into and looted, and there are four other burial chambers but it is unknown to whom they belong. Some scholars postulate that two of them were for King Amenemhet IV and Queen Sobekneferu."

The steep passageway leveled out and the guide led them through various chambers and corridors, the pale stone lit with low wattage electric lights that caused their shadows to flit and dance.

"After the sinking caused underground chambers to be crushed," the guide went on, "the pyramid was abandoned."

"We know all this stuff," Crowley said. "It's interesting, but not really relevant. No mention of Anubis, nothing to indicate he had any particular influence here."

Rose put a hand on his arm to slow him and he looked at her expectantly. She smiled, put a finger to her lips as the group moved away from them, then rounded a corner into a small side chamber.

"I saved this image to my phone." She pulled it out, the screen bright in the dim space. It showed a three-dimensional diagram of the underground network they were in.

"Where did you get that?" Crowley asked.

She grinned. "Wikipedia. It's amazing what fantastic info is just lying around on the Internet these days."

He wasn't sure if she was mocking him or not, but he chose not to pursue that. "So where are we?"

She pointed, using her pinky so as not to cover the small display. "Right here. But we've missed this side passage. That guide didn't even mention it."

"Maybe it's buried and inaccessible. He said several were."

"Yeah, but I saw it. There's at least some open passageway we can get into. And I'm bored of his lecture, aren't you?"

Crowley smiled. "We work better alone anyway."

They headed back and slipped into the side passage just as the sound of the guide's droning voice became louder. They pressed themselves to one wall around a corner of blocked stone and held their breath as the tour group passed by.

"That's better," Rose whispered after they had gone. "Now maybe we've got the place to ourselves for a little while. This way."

Disappointment was quick when the passage ended in a solid wall and no further chambers. Rose frowned. "Damn it."

"There was another passage alongside this one, wasn't there?" Crowley said, recalling the diagram she'd saved.

"There was. Let's try it."

A few minutes later they found themselves at another dead end, this time in a large square chamber.

"Well, this is a boring maze." Rose pocketed her phone, put her hands on her hips. "Maybe we've run into a dead end in our hunt too. Should we go and find this Kasim?"

Crowley paused, something niggling at him. What had he seen? "Just a second." He took out his phone and turned on the flashlight. By its small but bright white glow, he checked the walls and floor again.

"What are you looking for?"

Crowley drew a deep breath. "Something caught my eye. I can't see it now... Ah!" He grinned, moved aside and waved Rose forward.

"What is it?"

Shining his light to get the best angle of light and shadow across the floor by the far wall, he said, "What do you see?"

"A wall. Stone floor. Dust. Footprints."

"Yep. Keep looking."

Rose frowned, annoyance playing over her face, then her eyebrows shot up when she spotted some of the footprints in the dust heading straight into the wall and not coming back. One was neatly bisected by the wall itself, like the huge stones had come down right on top of it.

"There must be a way through there," she said.

Crowley crouched low, shining his light close to the ground. A dark line between the floor and wall showed the two weren't quite connected. "This section of wall must be a doorway. But how to open it?"

He stood back, looked left and right. The floor and wall, in fact the entire chamber, was empty and featureless.

"There must be a hidden control somewhere." He began looking closely at the floor stones, pressing them with his feet, feeling along the wall. His frustration grew as nothing yielded. Then he jumped at a sudden scraping of rock, and hopped back as a section of the wall about a meter wide and two high swung slowly open.

He turned to see Rose on the far side of the chamber. She grinned at him from beside a stone that she had moved aside to expose a small lever set back out of sight.

"You were looking too near the door," she said. "I guess it makes sense to have a secret control further away. Helps to stop people stumbling across it."

"I suppose so." Crowley looked into the dark space she had revealed. Even with his phone flashlight, the shadows obscured everything beyond a few meters. "Shall we explore?"

Rose slid the stone back into place to conceal the lever and joined him. She gestured politely, grinning. "After you!"

CHAPTER 16

The Black Pyramid, Dahshur, Egypt

As they entered the dim passageway, something still tickled at the back of Crowley's mind. He paused and Rose bumped into him from behind. She laughed and began to speak, but Crowley whipped up a hand to quiet her.

"What is it?" she whispered, voice tight with tension.

Crowley pointed to the ground, finally realizing what his subconscious had been digging him about. "I think there's someone up ahead."

"How do you know?"

"There's a single set of new footprints going in." He pointed, keeping his voice barely audible. "See how the dust is all disturbed and several sets of prints go back and forth."

"Yes."

He moved his flashlight. "Now, look here."

Another set of prints, pressed into the dust recently and not yet disturbed or scuffed over. They went forward, but no similar prints came back. "I think whoever made these is still in there."

He doused his light and ran his fingertips along the rough wall to sense the way forward. Behind him, Rose put one hand on Crowley's shoulder. He enjoyed the closeness and the warmth of her touch, but nerves rippled through his skin nonetheless.

After creeping forward several meters, the passage turned sharply to the right and a weak light illuminated the walls. The stones were covered in hieroglyphs, every inch crawling with tightly carved ancient writing, deep black in the shadows of the thin orange light. Ahead the passage opened out into a chamber, lit by flickering candles.

The massed hieroglyphics continued into the room and covered every wall but one. That wall was dominated by a massive image of Anubis. His face was twisted in a snarl, black ears standing tall out of his complicated striped headdress. He held his hands out to either side, his left holding a two long white feathers, his right a bleeding, dripping heart. Behind him a set of scales was etched in simple geometric lines.

Crowley and Rose stopped dead at a soft scuffing noise.

They couldn't see the entire chamber yet, but something had moved inside. Crowley slowly released a held breath and took another step forward to see properly around the corner. More candles flickered around a stone altar in the center of the large space, atop which stood a set of golden scales, glittering in the dancing candlelight. Kneeling before the altar was a man in a khaki shirt, tan jodhpurs and brown boots. Crowley smirked. All the man needed was a pith helmet to complete the ensemble. Thankfully there was no one else in the room and Crowley could tell from his position that he was bigger than whoever knelt in worship. Never assume any potential enemy is easy prey, the Army had taught him that only too well, but this fellow appeared largely harmless.

Crowley cleared his throat and the man nearly jumped out of his skin. He leaped up, spun around in a half-crouch, eyes wide. His dark skin glistened in the low light with a subtle sheen of sweat. "Good God, you startled me!" He had a deep voice, a distinct upper-class British accent. He took a deep breath, quickly recovering himself. "What are you doing?"

Rose stepped up beside Crowley. "We got separated from our tour group."

The man took a few menacing steps forward, his face set in a grim expression. He opened his mouth to speak, then paused, looked more intensely at Rose, then shook his head as if to clear his thoughts. "I suggest you rejoin your group immediately," he said, injecting authority into his voice. "You shouldn't be here." But the authority he tried to convey was empty, shaking with nerves the man was finding it harder and harder to contain.

Crowley stepped up to him. "We need help with something first."

"I have no idea how I can help. You need to…"

"Got a name?" Crowley interrupted. He'd dealt with this type before and it wouldn't take much to deflate the man's artificially inflated bravado.

"Leonard," the man said, clearly intimidated already.

Crowley almost felt sorry for him. He jabbed a thumb back towards Rose. "We're looking for my friend's sister." Leonard grimaced, opened his mouth to speak, but before he could deny knowing anything again, Crowley said, "I saw the way you looked at her. For a moment, you thought you'd seen her before."

Leonard slumped. "A woman called Iris was here a week or

so ago. Sisters, eh? Makes sense. The resemblance is remarkable."

Crowley nodded, though he disagreed. He supposed if you'd only seen each woman briefly the resemblance was stark, but he knew Rose well enough to see that her similarity to her sister was superficial. They were clearly family, but really didn't look that much alike. Regardless, the family look seemed to be assisting them in their search so he was glad of it. "And what did Iris want?"

"She said she was a doctoral student doing her thesis on Anubis. That she'd heard about this chamber."

"What, exactly, is this chamber?" Rose asked.

Leonard looked around, proud as though the space were his own property. "It's only recently been discovered. The translation of the hieroglyphs is incomplete, as there are some that are previously unknown, but it seems to have been a place of worship for a cult of Anubis."

Rose pulled out her phone and began photographing the walls.

"You can't do that!" Leonard said, his voice high in outrage. He strode forward, reached for her phone, but Crowley quickly closed the gap between them and grabbed his wrist.

Leonard gasped, looked at Crowley's strong fingers wrapped around his flesh as though it were an absolute atrocity. "Unhand me!"

Crowley kept his hold as Rose took detailed photos of the entire chamber.

"What did you and Lily… Iris talk about?" Crowley asked as Leonard began to shake with an impotent rage.

Leonard looked from Crowley's grip to his face and back again. He shook his arm ineffectually.

Crowley tightened his grip, grinding the man's wrist bones slightly. Leonard yelped.

"What did you talk about?"

Leonard let out a sharp breath of annoyance. "She asked about this chamber. When it was discovered, what we had learned, stuff like that."

"And?"

"And if there were any new insights about Anubis based on the discovery. She wanted to take photos too, but she respected my wishes when I asked her not to."

Crowley smiled crookedly. "Yeah, well I'm sort of an ass, I

guess. Anything else you can tell us about her visit?"

Leonard shook his head, upset at his treatment.

"Was she with a man?" Crowley asked.

"She was, actually. Quiet chap, hair tied up on top in some ridiculous style. Didn't say a word except to thank me when they left."

"Did they say where they were going next?"

"No, and I didn't ask. I just wanted them to leave me to my work." He drilled Crowley with a piercing gaze, making the point that he required the same of him and Rose.

Rose finished taking her photos and came to stand beside Crowley. "The hieroglyphs that have been translated. Do they say anything about the Anubis Key?"

Crowley shot her a look, couldn't believe she had blurted it out like that, but there was nothing to be done about it now.

"No," Leonard said, much too quickly in Crowley's opinion. "I've never heard of it."

Crowley decided he had had enough of the man's obfuscation. The fellow could be forgiven for not being particularly receptive to the treatment he had received, but things were more important than this guy's pride or whatever he felt had been compromised. Crowley twisted the man's wrist over, used his other hand to lift and turn over the elbow, quickly putting the unfortunate bloke into a painful arm lock.

Leonard howled, struggled briefly but quickly stopped when that only made the pain worse.

"A woman is missing," Crowley growled. "Her life is at stake. You're going to tell us all you know. You can do it voluntarily or I can... persuade you."

Leonard let out a frustrated half-sob. "All right, all right. They did ask about the Anubis Key, but I honestly don't know what it is. I heard the name years ago, but when I dug into it, I concluded it was nothing but rank foolishness. The sort of thing nutters believe in. I told the woman so."

Crowley nodded, considering. But he wasn't fooled. In a flash, he released the arm lock, drew his knife and pressed its keen edge against Leonard's throat as he backed the man up against the wall. Rose gasped as Leonard staggered into the hard stone and froze there, eyes wide.

"You're holding something back," Crowley said, his voice brooking no further misdirection. Anger surged through him and he knew it was reflected on his face. "What aren't you telling us?"

Leonard sagged. "They found the bone room."

CHAPTER 17

Rose couldn't help grimacing at Crowley's treatment of poor Leonard. The man had every reason to be annoyed at their questioning, at their invasion of his space and his work. But she had to admit that Crowley's methods worked. She was pleased Crowley always seemed judicious with use of force, always intimidation first rather than outright violence.

"What's the bone room?" she asked.

Leonard swallowed against the knife edge. "I believe there were sacrifices performed here and the victims' remains were left in a room just over there." He rolled his eyes toward the huge mural of Anubis.

During her photographing, Rose had realized it was a carving rather than a painting as she had first suspected. Intricately, expertly crafted, beautiful with detail. Every barb of every vane on each feather, the blood vessels of the dripping heart, the fur of Anubis's face and the individual precious stones of his headdress, all rendered in exquisite detail. But she saw no room. Obviously it was another secret chamber.

"And my sister found this room? What did she find inside?"

"I don't know, but they left quite excited. I've been trying to figure out what it was that caught their interest so thoroughly." Leonard paused. "I wanted to keep the room to myself until I understood it. I can't keep this place a secret much longer."

Crowley looked in the direction of the carving. "Show us." He lowered the knife but kept it in plain sight, held casually but ready in front of his chest.

Leonard retrieved a small set of steps from beside the altar and carried them to the Anubis carving. He set them down, climbed up so he could reach the top crossbar of the carved scales. A small hole, hidden from the casual eye in the darkness of the carving, disappeared into the rock at the point where the crossbar ended, the left scale hanging from it. Leonard slipped his finger into the hole and pulled down.

A grating sound echoed in the chamber and a rectangular block of stone, encompassing Anubis's lower half, slid down into the floor. It revealed another chamber beyond.

Leonard climbed down and led the way inside. The floor was strewn with skeletons, bones piled high against the walls. Rose gasped, put one hand over her mouth. There were a lot of bodies crammed in here, clearly eons ago. A narrow path had been cleared down the middle of the room, the pale stone of the floor dark against the yellowing bones.

"Your sister and her friend spent a lot of time down at that end," Leonard said, pointing to the far side of the cleared area. "I've looked it over a dozen times. All I see are some squiggly lines, but they aren't any writing I've ever seen and they certainly aren't hieroglyphs."

Rose hurried to the other end of the chamber, followed by Leonard and then Crowley. Leg bones - femurs, tibias, and fibulas - were stacked like cord wood to either side, dozens of skulls lying atop them as if on display.

Leonard directed the beam of his flashlight on a section of wall. "This is where your sister and her companion found the markings."

Rose crouched, twisting sideways to not block the light Leonard held. There were strange lines carved into the sandy stone, sinuous, snakelike, with no obvious pattern. She pulled out her phone once more and snapped a few pictures.

She looked back over her shoulder. "What do you think, Jake?"

Crowley came to crouch beside her, brow creased in consternation. "I'm not an expert in this stuff, but I've never seen anything like it. And I assume Leonard is an expert and he says he has no idea what it is. Unless he's holding out on us again."

"She did say something about an airport," Leonard said, his voice low and musing.

"An airport?"

"Yes. She said, 'It's the same design as at the airport!' Then she said to her friend, 'I bet this is proof they moved it from here to America.'"

"Moved what?" Rose asked.

"I don't know. When I asked her what she was talking about, she clammed up. It was like she'd forgotten I was there for a moment and become careless."

Rose ground her teeth. "Clearly Lily thought it was important. What else did she know that made this discovery so exciting?"

Rose leaned forward, looking more closely. "I wish I had paper so I could make a rubbing of it, to get a life size representation. Do you have any theories at all on what this is?" she asked, turning to address Leonard.

But a flash of movement interrupted her and Crowley slumped to the floor, clutching his head. Leonard loomed over her, wielding a heavy leg bone, and swung it down. Pain burst out and everything went dark.

CHAPTER 18

Crowley heard Rose's cry and the sound of running feet even as he struggled to maintain consciousness. Damn that idiot Leonard; people watched too many movies. A genuine knockout could cause a person extreme brain injury. And even with the glancing blow he'd received, almost dodging Leonard's wild swing, the pain was blinding. He put a hand to his head, felt wetness and heat. His vision swam, nausea briefly surging as he rolled onto his knees. He prayed Rose hadn't been hit harder, her skull cracked like an egg.

He turned and slumped back against the wall, one palm pressed hard to the throbbing, bleeding cut on the side of his head. He blinked, vision beginning to clear, and saw the chamber door closing and then everything was blackness.

He scrambled in his pocket with his free hand and managed to find his phone and get the light on. Rose groaned and shifted next to him, pulled herself up to a sitting position.

"You okay?" He was pleased to hear his speech wasn't slurred.

"That son of a bitch!" Rose sounded more angry than hurt and that was a good thing.

"Were you unconscious?"

Rose drew a deep breath in through her nose, rubbed her head just above her left eyebrow. "No, I saw it coming and ducked. But he clipped me and knocked me down."

Relief flowed through Crowley. "Sounds like we were both lucky." He didn't feel lucky; his head throbbed with pain and a deep headache pulsed up from the back of his neck, but his bones were intact and his brain remained undamaged. Rose's too, thankfully. "He even mocked us, suggesting Lily had got careless in his presence."

She moved her hand and he winced at the egg forming there.

"He got you good, though. You sure you weren't unconscious?"

She smiled weakly. "Yes, I'm sure. Why are you so concerned?"

He returned her smile, blinking against the pain that didn't seem to be subsiding. "Life isn't like the movies, that's all."

They took a few minutes to gather themselves and Crowley relaxed when the hammering pain began to reduce to a dull ache. The blood dried and he thought maybe he would get away without stitches. The headache he expected to persist for a while though.

He turned to Rose. "I'm sorry."

"What for?"

He gestured around. "This! I took my eye off Leonard, stopped paying enough attention."

"You were distracted by this discovery. We both were."

"Sure, but it's my job to stay alert. To protect you."

Rose laughed and that stung a little. "Thank you, Sir Crowley, but I prefer to see it like we're in this together. Looking out for each other. We both messed up this time. We both underestimated Leonard."

Crowley paused, but had to agree. It was a better way to look at things. "Okay. So let's both agree that we don't take our eyes off people in situations like this again."

Rose squeezed his shoulder. "Let's hope there aren't situations like this again." She looked around, suddenly concerned. "And let's hope that's not because we're stuck in here forever to become more bones for the pile!"

"Yeah. There must be a way out."

Rose stood tentatively, found her phone and switched on its light. "Must there? Maybe the only access is via that mechanism outside. After all, these poor sacrificed souls wouldn't need a way out."

Crowley chose not to think too hard about that rather too likely possibility. "Let's look for a way out."

They moved carefully, ensuring they didn't upset the neatly ordered ossuary. Crowley thought it stood to reason that any exit mechanism would be free of skeletal remains, but the small chamber afforded little in the way of unoccupied space.

"How long do you think these bones have been here?" Rose said.

"Thousands of years, I would imagine." Something caught Crowley's eye and his heart did a double beat of shock. "Or not."

Rose looked back towards him. "What?"

Crowley moved to one side, played his light over one stack

of old bones to see better the next pile. A flash of color among the dark stones and pale remains. "There's a body here," he said tightly.

Rose laughed. "No wonder they call you Jake Sherlock."

He smiled despite himself. "No, I mean a recent one. Concealed under this pile." He pulled the bones aside, as carefully as he could, to reveal the corpse of an older man. He had the appearance of a local as best as Crowley could see, though his skin was dried tight to the bone, eyes wide open, teeth bared. His clothes were shabby, threadbare, but the body was weeks old at best. "Not all of the dead are ancient, it seems."

Rose hurried over. She muttered a low curse, pointed at the man's chest. His shirt lay torn open, stained dark brown with copious amounts of dried blood, a gaping hole in his chest.

"His heart has been cut out."

Anger washed through Crowley. "The Anubis Cult. Alive and well, unlike this poor bugger."

"You think they're performing occult rituals?" Rose asked.

"Looks like it. And I don't intend on us being their next victims."

Rose looked at him sharply. "You think Leonard..?"

He shrugged. "I don't know. But we can only assume he's gone for help and I don't imagine that help will be of any benefit to us. Or if he's not in the Anubis Cult, then whoever is will come back eventually and find us here. Or we'll never know because we've starved to death in the meantime."

"Jake!"

He smiled, put a hand on her shoulder. "So let's get out of here, yeah?"

They resumed their search and Crowley tried not to let despair get the better of him. This chamber was a box, made of stone, with one entrance built into that Anubis carving. And the only release for it was the one Leonard had used on the other side. After a good ten minutes of searching, even moving piles of bones to check the floor underneath, he sat back against one wall and put his chin in his hands. Never one to quit, never one to give in. But he was out of ideas.

Rose looked over, his concerns echoed on her features. "What do we do?"

He shook his head. "I don't know. Maybe someone will come for us and we'll have to fight our way out."

"I don't think Leonard will make the mistake of

underestimating you."

Crowley winced. She was only being honest, but that cut deeply. He had made a grave error letting his attention waver from Leonard and it might have cost them everything. He tipped his head back against the wall, staring up at nothing.

No, not nothing. The ceiling of the chamber didn't look quite right. He tipped his head left, then right. "Rose," he said quietly. "Can you move aside, please?"

She looked at him quizzically, but did as he asked. He pointed his light at the ceiling, then the floor, and a slight smile pushed up his lips.

"What have you seen?" Rose asked.

He pointed up to where the ceiling met the wall on the opposite side of the room. "Look how the ceiling sags there."

She turned to look, eyebrows creased together. "Yeah, I see it. This place is thousands of years old, after all."

"Yes, but remember what all the guides keep talking about? It's built too close to the Nile, there's ground water, the weight of the pyramid caused it to sink, to crush the underground chambers."

Rose's eyes went wide. "You think we can, what, collapse this place? How will that help?"

Crowley laughed. "Well, collapsing it might just help to kill us extra quick. But if this area is subject to some subsidence, then it means the general structure is compromised. We can use that. Look along the side of that block near the middle at the top. See the crack in the mortar? If the walls have shifted, if they've sunk, they'll be loosened, right?"

"I don't know…"

Crowley picked up a heavy tibia and whacked it hard against the ground, breaking the ball joint of the hip off the end. With the resulting ragged point of bone he reached up high and began digging at the thin line of mortar around a large stone just below ceiling level. He ignored Rose's concerned scrutiny, working hard at the job, building up a sweat as he went. After a few minutes he'd cleared a fair amount of mortar from the sides and underneath the block. Unable to reach properly to get leverage, he muttered an apology to the long dead and pushed a heap of bones up against the wall to use as a makeshift step. They crunched and cracked as he stepped up on them, but gave him the boost he needed. He scraped more, cleared more mortar. Deciding that might be enough, he leaned back and then slammed both palms hard against block. There was a deep creak and dust rained down all around him.

"Jake!" Rose's voice was high.

He dug in again, cleared more, then double-palmed the block again. This time it shifted a good half its width out into the chamber beyond. The next block down shifted an inch or two as well and the ceiling rained more debris.

"What if you bring this whole place down?" Rose asked, panic making her speak quickly.

Crowley paused. "I don't think it'll collapse entirely. Or we can wait to see who comes." He watched her, serious about the choices. He would abide by whatever she chose.

She pursed her lips for a moment, then resignation softened her face. "Don't crush us, please."

He grinned. "I'll try."

He worked more carefully now he'd made a start in the block's removal. If the structure had been compromised by the slowly sinking edifice, but was still standing, he felt sure removing one block wouldn't be enough to cause a catastrophic collapse. "We only need one of these out for you to squeeze through," he said as he cleared more mortar.

"Me?"

"I'm too big."

After a moment he pushed against the first block, more cautiously this time, and it slid forward then dropped with a dull crack to the floor outside. The ceiling creaked and moaned, dust danced through their flashlight beams as it sifted down. With a sharp crack the large block of ceiling above Crowley shifted and dropped. With a cry he leaped backward, staggering off his bone pile as adrenaline flooded him. The ceiling stone fell at an angle, maybe ten inches below its original level at one end, but still held up by the greater part of the wall at the other. Everything settled.

"Holy crap," he said quietly. Then he smiled. "But it's holding. You can get through there, right?"

A deep groan rumbled through the pyramid, seeming to be both far above them and far below them at the same time.

Rose blew out an exasperated breath and stepped forward. Crowley cupped his hands together to give her a boost and she went up the wall, arms first through the small hole. It pressed and scraped at her hips and Crowley had a moment of fright thinking she might get stuck there, but another shove against the soles of her feet sent her through. He heard her drop and roll on the other side, grunting with the effort.

Crowley stepped back. "Quickly, pull that mechanism!"

A dull grinding sound filled their ears and the small door at the base of the wall slid up. Crowley shot through and into the main chamber. The carving of Anubis had been marred, his left shoulder fallen to the floor and broken where Crowley had pushed the block out. But he didn't stop to consider the damage. Maybe some enterprising archaeologist would oversee repairs. For now, he was only concerned with leaving.

"Come on!" Rose said, pulling at his sleeve.

He grinned. "Right behind you."

CHAPTER 19

Outside the Black Pyramid, Dahshur, Egypt

Leonard hurried out of the underground chamber, through the dim passage and up the steep incline into the sun. Panic made his heart beat faster along with the physical exercise as he ran for his car, trying not to look suspicious. He kept glancing over his shoulder, fearing the two intruders would escape and come after him. He was no fighter, as their easy humiliation of him had already proven. But he was no fool, and no pushover. They had paid dearly for underestimating him. But it wasn't over yet.

He glanced back again, certain he'd see that angry face bearing down on him. That woman alongside, beautiful but fearsome, determined to make him suffer for striking her. He didn't even know their names. She claimed to be the sister of that Iris Brown woman, and certainly looked so alike she couldn't be lying, but he knew no more than that. And he got the impression that Iris Brown was a fake name. Hadn't that rough fellow said another name before correcting himself? Lily! That was it. Ah, nothing made any sense, and none of it mattered. He had trapped them in the bone room and there was no way out of there, he knew that for a fact. Enough paranoia, just make the call.

He reached his jeep parked on the far side of the lot and unlocked it, took his phone from the glove box. He hit the quick dial and waited, chewing his lip as it rang, then a gruff voice answered.

"Yes?"

"There's a problem," Leonard said.

"What kind of problem?"

"The girl who came last week? Remember her? She has a sister. She just showed up asking questions."

"She came alone?"

Leonard sighed, remembering his impotence to stand against her friend. "No. She came with a big guy. Bigger than me anyway, six foot tall probably, muscular. He had the bearing of a military guy, you know?"

"Military? You know that for sure?"

"No, just the impression I got. He incapacitated me easily,

had all the hallmarks of some special forces type."

A soft chuckle on the other end made Leonard wince. "Okay, if you say so. How much do they know?"

"I can't say for certain," Leonard admitted. "They claimed they were looking for the sister, said she was missing, but…" He hesitated, scared. Then he said, "They did ask about the Anubis Cult."

The person on the other end let out a slow exhale.

"They didn't seem to know anything about it," Leonard added quickly. "I had the impression it was just something they'd heard about while searching for the sister. But they're the kind to cause trouble, I'm sure of that."

"Anything else?"

Leonard hesitated again, cold sweat prickling his brow, his heart racing. "They asked…" His throat was suddenly dry and he swallowed hard. "They asked about the Anubis Key."

Silence from the other end of the line. Leonard kept his own peace for several seconds until he began to fear that he'd been cut off. He took the phone away from his ear, glanced at the screen, but the signal was strong, the call connected. "Hello?"

There was a slow sigh from the other end. "Do you know where they went?"

Leonard brightened, finally having something positive to report. "I shut them up in the bone room."

"Really? I thought you said he incapacitated you."

Leonard rolled his eyes. "He did, but I turned things around."

"I'm not sure you know what 'incapacitate' means, but all right. Where are you now?"

"In my car," Leonard said, ignoring the jibe. "I needed a signal."

"Have you left yet?"

"Not yet."

The voice on the other end sounded calm now. "Good. Hold tight and keep an eye on the pyramid in case they get out. If they reappear, do not let them out of your sight, understand?"

"They can't get out, I'm sure of it. You know how that mechanism works."

"Just in case."

Leonard's shoulders sagged. "Okay."

"And keep me posted on where they are. I'm sending

someone right away."

Leonard began to nod, then thought about the man he had locked in that room. "If you really think there's a chance they might get out, you might want to send several someones."

CHAPTER 20

As they made their way back out into the daylight, Rose kept looking back at the pyramid, expecting it to sigh and slump down, collapsing into rubble and clouds of dust, like in the movies. But it didn't. She didn't think she'd get the image of that drooping ceiling slab out of her mind for years, if ever. She anticipated it would be front and center of several future nightmares. Had Crowley really been confident his gambit would pay off or was he genuinely gambling with their lives back there? Then again, he had a point about waiting for someone else to come. If Leonard was so concerned by their investigation that he was prepared to brain them and lock them in a sealed chamber, it made sense he wouldn't have their best interests at heart on his return. Not to mention that poor soul with his heart removed, hidden under the bones. No way could Leonard have missed that, so if he knew about it, surely he had something to do with it.

Regardless, Rose simply wanted to get away. What had Lily got herself into? This whole situation was far more dangerous and complicated than Rose had ever considered. She expected maybe some crooked antiquities dealers, not heart-removing cultists of ancient gods.

"I want to find Leonard," Crowley said, scanning the area around the pyramid with angry eyes.

Tourists milled around, cars and buses moved nearby, but she couldn't see the dark-skinned fellow in his pale cliché of a costume.

"Surely he's long gone," Rose said.

Crowley scowled, but reluctantly agreed. "Keep an eye out for him, anywhere. Back in Cairo, even. Seriously, if I ever set eyes on that guy again, I want to settle the score."

He winced as he talked, kept pressing a hand to the dried blood on the side of his head. He had obviously been more seriously hurt than she had. For her, it had been little more than a glancing blow that knocked her down. Crowley had copped a far greater blow. She would have to watch him for signs of concussion.

"So I guess we head to Cairo and try to track down this Kasim," Crowley said.

Rose began to nod in agreement, then paused, smiling. "Or maybe not." She pointed.

Across the way a tour bus was parked; bright blue and yellow lettering along the side read *Sacred Tours Cairo*. A man stood by the door, chatting casually with people as they disembarked.

Crowley laughed. "Short. Fat. Thick mustache. Can't tell if he's greasy from this far away, but I'll bet he is."

"I'll let you know," Rose said. "I think maybe I should talk to him alone."

"You think because he's greasy he'll be sleazy?" Crowley asked with a grin.

"Well, I hadn't thought of that, actually." She gestured at his head. "But you know, the blood and all. Might put him off answering any questions."

"That's a good point. You've quite an impressive lump above your eyebrow too, you know. We should find something to ice it with."

She smiled. Always trying to look after her, trying to be the provider of care and intel and plans. She knew he didn't mean it that way, but he could be such an infuriating man at times. "I'll worry about that later. You go and find somewhere to wash yourself off and I'll talk to Kasim."

"Okay. But I'll be nearby."

She rolled her eyes, but smiled to show she was only poking fun. Infuriating though he could be, it came from a place of genuine care and she couldn't hold that against him. "All right. I'll come and find you soon."

Rose headed across to Kasim's bus. From the description she realized she had been expecting someone old and unpleasant, but it was obviously Kenny's prejudice shining through. Kasim, his identity confirmed by an embroidered patch on the pocket of his shirt, was a young guy. He was overweight, but not morbidly, and had a wide friendly face, set off well by his neatly groomed mustache. He had green eyes that glittered in the sun as he turned to face her. "Hello, can I help you?"

"I hope so. I'm searching for my sister, who's been missing for a while now. I'm very worried." She took the photo of Lily from her bag and held it out.

Kasim took the photo and nodded immediately. "Yes, I

remember her. Iris Brown. I met her…" He paused, looking up at nothing as he mentally calculated. "Five days ago," he decided. "At the end of my tour as I was giving the group a last chance for photographs before we boarded the bus again. She had just come from inside the pyramid. Friendly lady, I was enjoying her company. I thought we were hitting it off fairly well, you know? Until her boyfriend showed up."

"Her boyfriend?"

Kasim shrugged. "Well, I assume it was her boyfriend. Tall, thin, hair tied up on top. The guy was courteous, but he seemed…" Kasim made a circular gesture with his hand as he searched for the word in English. "Possessive? I think that's the best description."

"I know the type," Rose said, a rueful smile on her face.

"Your sister, you say? I can see that." Kasim looked her up and down, not impolitely. "I don't know if I can help you find her, though. She asked a lot of intelligent questions about the pyramid at first. I was enjoying the conversation. You can imagine, I have the same superficial conversations a dozen times a day usually."

"At first?" Rose asked.

"Yes. After a few minutes the questions got strange."

"Strange how?"

"She was asking about things I'd never heard of… far-fetched legends about Anubis worship and sacrifice. I mean, this is my job, yes? I've heard about most of the weird things people think about our culture. But her questions were really out there. Then she asked about ancient Egyptian seafaring."

Rose nearly did a double-take. She hadn't expected that.

Kasim saw her reaction, smiled. "Exactly! You see what I mean? She got really strange. She specifically wanted to know if they could have crossed the Atlantic."

"Ancient Egyptians?"

"Yes. When I told her that I had no idea about any of that, she abruptly ended the conversation."

Rose understood the man's confusion. What had Lily expected to hear? How had she got from Anubis cults to ancient people crossing such a vast expanse of ocean? And why?

"I'm really worried about my sister," she said. "I'm desperate to track her down. Do you have any idea where she might have gone?"

"No, not really. I'm sorry." Kasim paused, then looked up,

his expression hopeful. "Although I do remember hearing one thing. As she and her guy friend were walking away, I heard him say, 'It's a long flight to Colorado.' I remember thinking at the time that going from here to Colorado seemed strange given Iris was so obviously British. Her accent English like yours, you know?"

Rose smiled. "That is unusual. I have no idea why she would go to Colorado."

"Neither do I," Kasim said. "But then, I know as much about Colorado as I know about the surface of the moon, so perhaps there is a connection."

Unless that's the airport Lily mentioned to Leonard, Rose wondered.

"Thank you," she said. "I appreciate your time."

"You're welcome. I hope you find your sister. And maybe you'll come and take my tour some day? I'm the best there is!"

"Maybe I will."

She walked away from the nice young man, lost in thought. Colorado? It wasn't much of a lead, but perhaps it was better than nothing. Crowley was good at thinking about this stuff, maybe he would spot a connection.

She saw Crowley in the shadow of the pyramid. He had a bottle of water he'd bought somewhere and was washing the dried blood off his head, gingerly testing the wound with his fingertips. She told him about all she had learned, little though it was.

"Don't write it off," Crowley said. "It's a good lead."

"Is it, though?"

"Sure. Anything is good if it's a genuine lead. When a trail goes cold, that's it. Dead. But all the time there's something to follow up, we're in business. An avalanche can be triggered by the tiniest stone moving."

Rose smiled, encouraged by his enthusiasm even if she wasn't entirely convinced by it.

"I called Cameron while I waited too," Crowley said. "He still hasn't had any success hacking Lily's fake identity, but says he's getting somewhere slowly. It's laborious work. Maybe the Colorado lead will help." He tapped out a message to his army intel buddy as he spoke, then looked up with a smile.

"So it sounds like our next move is to Colorado," Rose said. "Shall we head back to Cairo and book flights? Where to exactly?"

Crowley shrugged. "Denver, maybe. Let's see what Cameron suggests."

"I wish I could see the connection."

They climbed into their car and Crowley started the engine. "It's just another puzzle to solve."

They drove in silence for a long while, Rose lost in thought about the events in the pyramid, the possibilities ahead of them. She assumed Crowley was thinking similar things until she noticed an odd look on his face. They had made most of the journey back to Cairo, one long and uninteresting road, but now Crowley watched the rear view mirror with a frown, glanced regularly to the side mirrors.

Rose sensed his tension. "Jake, what's wrong?"

"We're being followed."

Chapter 21

Cairo, Egypt

Rose was thrown back in her seat as Crowley suddenly floored the accelerator and yanked the wheel over into a hard right turn. She cried out in surprise, sat forward and put her hands out to grip the dashboard, but bit down on her fear. She had to trust his skills now.

"They followed us from the Black Pyramid?" she asked.

"Yep. Think so. Spotted them about twenty kilometers back, realized they were tailing us. Badly." He grunted, braked hard and turned left. They rocked forward in their seats, the belts pulling hard across their chests. "Once we got into the Cairo suburbs I made some random turns and even went entirely around one block. And they're still there."

Rose had been so lost in thought she hadn't even noticed Crowley had been driving in circles. She was thankful he was on the ball. They barreled into the suburb of Giza, west of the Nile. The old Land Rover roared in protest at the rough treatment, black smoke roiling back from the exhaust pipe. Tires screeched as Crowley drove hard into a tight bend, then braked almost to a standstill to turn hard left.

"I hope this thing doesn't fall to pieces!" Rose said.

"Me too," Crowley said through gritted teeth. "Because they're still there."

He floored it again, hammering through a junction to a symphony of angry car horns. Rose braced her feet against the floor pan and held the grip above the door until her knuckles turned white. A series of small shops, neon signs and varied stock hanging on racks outside, whipped past her window in a riot of color.

"Hang on!" Crowley said.

She didn't bother to state the obvious, that she'd been hanging on for some time already, as Crowley mounted a curb, blaring his own horn to make pedestrians leap, faces wide in shock, out of his path.

"What are you doing?" Rose cried, but he ignored her.

Then she saw it. A narrow alley that he needed room to turn into. Some poor trader's cart exploded into splinters off the corner of the Land Rover, plastic drink bottles thumping and rattling over the roof, as Crowley made the turn into the alley. Rose caught a glimpse of the drink seller's furious expression, then a *crang* made her sit back sharply.

The Land Rover barely fit between the high brick buildings, the wing mirrors dragging across the stones with showers of sparks.

"There goes our deposit!" Crowley said, but he sounded strangely elated.

"Let's just stay alive, Jake!"

He squinted up into the rear view mirror and cursed eloquently.

"Still there?" Rose asked.

"Their car is much smaller than ours. It's easier for them in these narrow streets. But it's faster too, so no point trying to outrun them on bigger roads." He hauled the wheel to the left and the big Land Rover slewed out across the road at the end of the alley, tires screaming. More horns voiced brash displeasure.

"So what do we do?" Rose asked.

"Outdrive them."

"I don't know why I'm bothering, but please be careful!"

He grinned. "It's okay. Defensive driving courses in the Army use scenarios like this all the time. I've done before."

"For real?"

"Well, no. In training."

"Jake!"

He glanced over and winked. "British Army training is the best in the world. Here we go."

Rose swallowed and held on, determined not to distract him with any more talk. He was surely pushing his limits, but obviously enjoying himself too. She decided it was time to shut up and let him get on with it.

The traffic thickened and Crowley began blasting his horn, pushing through tiny gaps between cars that didn't look big enough for a wheelbarrow let alone a Land Rover. But he made it work. A swarm of people on bicycles appeared suddenly, dozens of them, their eyes widening at the huge car bearing down on them. Crowley cursed again and swerved, bounced the car violently across a curbed median and then they were screeching left and right to avoid oncoming cars.

Rose began praying to any gods who might listen, though she really didn't believe in any of them. Perhaps if they got through this she might start. Crowley turned sharply again, slamming Rose across her seat and back again, then they were rattling along a narrow cobbled street. Much quieter for traffic, but with carts and pedestrians everywhere. The people quickly dove aside and Crowley braked hard, turned right.

A green wagon piled high with bright yellow bananas suddenly rolled out in front of them. Crowley braked, but there was no time and the cart spun away from the front bumper with a loud crack. Fruit sailed up and around, bounced off the hood and the windshield. The fruit seller, an old woman with a gnarled cane, hammered against the side of the car and Crowley yelled, "Sorry!" and drove on.

"It's not worth killing someone over," Rose said.

"I know. But I think we've lost them."

Relief flooded through Rose. "Have we?"

"Pale metallic blue Peugeot," Crowley said.

A small car turned into the road directly ahead of them. "Like that one?" Rose asked.

"Bollocks!" Crowley yelled, and slammed the Land rover into reverse. The car whined as he roared backward and the old woman began battering the side door with her cane again, glad of another chance to berate them.

"Hold tight," Crowley said, then braked and hauled the wheel, spinning the car one hundred and eighty degrees in a reverse bootlegger turn.

Rose yelled out, unable to endure the screeching slide without giving voice to her panic, but Crowley pulled it off and accelerated away again, the Peugeot hot on their tail.

"Don't go back out onto that road with all the traffic!" Rose said. "It's too dangerous."

Crowley turned again. More cobbled streets rumbled under the car's large tires, then another side street packed with market stalls and milling crowds. Crowley cursed, braked and turned the other way. The Peugeot was right on their tail. Rose saw it in her side mirror, even though the glass was cracked from its previous encounter with the alley wall. An arm appeared from the passenger window holding a pistol.

"They're going to shoot!" she shouted.

Crowley roared wordlessly and slammed the pedal down. A junction came up on them fast, traffic busy left and right. Crowley let out a yell of defiance and yanked the wheel left and right, dodging between two cars and a bus that screeched and blared their horns. Traffic was suddenly mayhem behind them as Crowley shot the Land Rover out the other side, into a street strangely quiet. More screeches echoed to them and Rose saw the Peugeot skid sideways, then slam into the broad side of the bus Crowley had narrowly missed.

"They crashed!" she said excitedly. "You can slow down! They're gone."

Crowley let out a long breath and eased up on the accelerator. "Thank goodness for that."

"How much did you just risk our lives?"

He grinned at her. "I was in total control the whole time."

She shook her head, laughing despite her fear at the relief of it all. Crowley drove them on to the airport and the company they had rented the Land Rover from. When they arrived, the owner stepped out and his mouth fell open. He pressed one palm to each cheek, staring dumbfounded.

Rose and Crowley climbed out and saw why he was so upset. Not a single panel was free from dents or scratches. Most of both front wings were bent out of shape, one almost torn completely off. All the lights and indicators on the front were smashed. One side was pebbled with a field of small dents, all about the size of that old lady's cane.

"We ran into a little trouble," Crowley said. "Really sorry about that." He turned to Rose. "I'm glad we paid extra on the insurance waiver though, to get the excess down to a sensible amount."

"My car!" the dealer managed, finally finding his voice.

Crowley threw the keys to the man, who scrabbled in the air and managed to catch them. "The paperwork's all in order," Crowley said. "Really sorry about the car, but the insurance will cover it, right?"

He turned and walked away, pulling Rose along with him.

"We should fill out forms or something, surely?" she said.

"No doubt. But do you want to? Let's make the most of his shock."

They hurried away and ducked into the crowds heading for the airport as the man began shouting streams of invective.

"Let's just get on the first plane to America," Crowley said. "We need to leave this country behind, especially before whoever was chasing us catches up again."

Rose nodded. She couldn't agree more.

CHAPTER 22

On the plane to New York, the first destination out of Egypt they had found, Crowley and Rose found themselves exhausted and slept as much as was possible in the cramped economy seats. Crowley's body ached from the exertions of the last few days and his mind ached at all they'd had to learn and figure out. Not to mention the throbbing headache from the blow that git Leonard had given him. He was pleased to note that he showed no signs of concussion and the wound had dried well. He was less pleased to know that he would probably never get a shot at evening the score with the guy.

Of greater concern was the threat of whomever Leonard must have called, who had subsequently chased them through Cairo. That had been too close for comfort and Crowley didn't know how much information about himself and Rose those people might have garnered. Was it enough to track them down further? They had escaped this time, but he had to assume they had a permanent tail now and he would need to keep his wits about him. Getting a head start out of the country was the best thing they could have done, but it wouldn't stop him fretting over it. Regardless, for now, dozing in the airline chair, however fitful, was a decent reprieve.

He woke with a couple of hours flying time left as the flight crew pushed trolleys up the narrow aisles offering food. He realized he was ravenous and woke Rose so they could both eat. Over plastic trays of dried out chicken and soggy vegetables, they tried to go over all they had learned thus far.

"Who do you think Lily is traveling with?" Crowley asked.

Rose shook her head, swallowed with a grimace. "This possessive guy? No idea. Like I said originally, we've been largely estranged for years. She could have any number of friends or associates I know nothing about. Or she could have only recently met him."

Crowley considered that. "Maybe he's connected with the Anubis Cult?"

"Or maybe he's equally interested in learning more about it."

Crowley knew he was on thin ice with some questions that rattled in the back of his mind, but he needed to consider all the angles. It seemed that although Rose and Lily were largely estranged, as she put it, Rose still acted fiercely protective of her sister. Family dynamics had always mystified him. He was an only child, after all, his father having died in the Falklands War before Crowley was born. Raised by his mother and maternal grandmother, he'd had few other family members around, never liked school, and quit at sixteen and joined the army, in order to be like his dad. He did eight years and the army became the closest thing to a real family, besides his mother and grandmother, he had ever known. He still had several friends he considered as close, or closer, than siblings. But for all that, he had no idea how things might be between two actual sisters, who had grown up together, shared everything, even if things drifted or broke apart later on. He still needed to ask hard questions to understand Lily's motivations now, and perhaps predict what she might do next.

He finished his meal, pushed the empty container aside. Then he took a deep breath. "Why would Lily get involved in this hunt for the Anubis Key, do you think? I mean, whatever it really is, why is she so driven?"

Rose glanced over at him, her expression wooden. "Lily's an archeologist. An Egyptologist. She probably wants to find something no one else has. Make a name for herself."

"You think that's all?"

Rose frowned. "What are you trying to say?"

"Back in her apartment you mentioned that she was devastated when your grandfather died. You said he was the most important person in your lives."

"Sure. My parents worked hard. Dad comes from generations of working class Londoners, always driven his cab day and night. Still does. Mum's Chinese, so her work ethic is maybe more ingrained than Dad's. She worked eighteen-hour days in hospitality and hotels for years when I was little, then finally managed to retrain as a bookkeeper. And she still works hard. They'd love to retire, but claim they can't afford to. I think they can, but they won't listen to me." Rose laughed softly. "You can't tell a bookkeeper about budgeting for retirement. Not one like my mum anyway."

"So your grandfather was around a lot to take care of you?"

"Yeah. My dad's dad. He was so kind. He'd collect us from

school, play with us at home, often put us to bed and sometimes still be there in the morning for breakfast and to take us back to school."

Crowley nodded, understanding why the connection was so strong. "No grandmother?"

"We never knew her. She died when Lily was a baby, before I was born. And my mum's parents are still out in Guangzhou. It's time I visited them again, to be honest. They're getting really old."

"And your grandfather died recently?"

Rose smiled sadly, eyes a little wet. "Last year. We both loved him dearly, but Lily was especially broken up. His death was sudden, unexpected. I mean, he was old, you know, in his late seventies. But a stroke took him in an instant with no warning. Lily grieved hard. She and he were always closer than he and I. It's like they, I don't know, like they shared a secret or something. Some bond that never quite took with me. He loved us both equally, of course, but Lily loved him far more deeply, I think, than I can quite understand."

Crowley took the plunge to raise the concern he harbored. "You don't think she's trying to, I don't know, bring him back or something?"

Rose flared up suddenly, her cheeks reddening. "What?"

Crowley raised a hand to placate her. For all her talk of Lily grieving hard, this was clearly a strongly emotive subject for Rose as well. "I just mean that perhaps she thinks this Anubis Key, if it's real, might mean she can talk to your grandfather again."

"Bring him back, you said!"

"Well, maybe she thinks that's possible."

Rose shook her head, looked away. "No!" They lapsed into stony silence.

Crowley decided to let it go and pulled out his laptop to check his email.

"Hey," he said, keeping his voice light to try to break the tension he'd inadvertently triggered between them. "I've got a message from Cam."

Rose quirked an eyebrow. "What's he say?"

Crowley was pleased to see that she didn't appear to harbor any anger toward him. He had to trust they were good enough friends to disagree without taking personal offense. He read through the email, then paraphrased for Rose. "Says he's still trying to hack Lily's credit card account, and he thinks he's getting close. But this is more interesting. With the help of a buddy in Russia, he's accessed security footage at Denver International Airport and he found Lily and her companion."

Rose turned in her seat, excitement brightening her expression. "Found her?"

"Well, found evidence of her, not where she is now. I told him about the Colorado comment, so he obviously started trawling through their CCTV. Cameron says he has no clue where she went afterward, but she did spend a lot of time examining something unusual. He's attached a video clip."

"So let's watch it!"

"I'm downloading it now. The airplane WiFi is slower than old dial-up modems! And you pay a fortune for it."

Rose laughed. "You act outraged, but you are sitting at thirty thousand feet on the way to New York, downloading video footage from a contact in England."

Crowley grinned. "True. But the future is never fast enough. Look at this though." He pointed to the screen. "Listen to this. I'll read from Cameron's email. 'By the way, this Denver airport, it's weird. I mean really weird. Look it up so you know what you're headed into. Or at least what this girl is into.'" He looked up at Rose. "Sounds ominous."

Rose frowned. "How weird can an airport be?"

"Who knows? Ah, the clip is ready."

He double-clicked in the icon and the video started. It was slightly grainy and stuttered occasionally, but the clarity was still impressive. The vision showed a young woman who looked a lot like Rose, along with a tall, dark-haired man, that hair gathered on top of his head, standing in front of a truly disturbing mural.

"That's her!" Rose said. "It's really Lily."

"And that tall fellow must be the companion we've been hearing about."

"What are they looking at?"

The CCTV angle was slightly oblique, but the mural was partially visible. It showed a man in a Nazi uniform, wearing a gas mask, armed with a rifle and scimitar, standing over dead children.

"That's one of the most disturbing images I've seen in a while," Crowley said.

"Why is that in an airport?" Rose asked.

Crowley shook his head. "I guess this is what Cameron was

talking about when he said it was weird."

As they watched, Lily moved to the right and knelt to inspect something in the bottom corner of the mural. Crowley couldn't make out what it was in the small video window, but Lily took great interest, snapping photos with her phone and then taking out a notepad and scribbling furiously. Her companion glanced around, then leaned down and tapped Lily on the shoulder. The two stood and hurried away. The clip ended.

Crowley backed it up, paused it with Lily crouched down and pointed at the corner of the mural. "We need to find out what's there that's so interesting."

"Look it up online," Rose said. "There must be photos others have taken that are better resolution. Or pictures on the airport website."

The airplane PA crackled and the pilot came on to announce they were beginning their descent into New York. Tray tables up, seats up and seat belts on and in-flight wifi was being turned off.

"I guess," Crowley said, closing his laptop, "that when we land in New York we need to find a connection directly to Denver and check that out in person."

CHAPTER 23

When they arrived in Denver International Airport, fatigue had set in again. They traveled with carry-on bags only, a few changes of clothes and other essentials in order to stay light. They grabbed them from the overhead locker and buffeted along with the line of people deplaning.

"All this running around and then sitting on planes is exhausting," Rose said with a laugh.

Crowley pointed to a refreshments cart in the gate area as they emerged from the tunnel off the plane. "Coffee?"

"Good idea!"

They ordered coffees and snacks and then sat with them at a small plastic table. Crowley pulled out his laptop and fired it up.

"Let's follow up on what Cameron said about this place. Check out what we can learn before we look around aimlessly." He started an online search and soon his eyebrows rose and he was shaking his head.

Rose shifted her chair next to his to see the screen. "What is it?"

"This place is nuts. The murals we saw in the clip are in the baggage claim area, so we can go and look for those in a while. But this is bizarre."

He pointed to a statue of a huge horse, a giant blue mustang with fiery red eyes, rearing up on its hide legs, kicking at the air.

"That's here?" Rose asked.

"Right out front. Meet Blucifer."

Rose laughed. "Blucifer?"

Crowley laughed with her, scanning the text. "That's what the locals call it. It's actually called Blue Mustang, but it has a bloody history. It's thirty-two feet high and weighs nine thousand pounds. Those red eyes light up at night like some kind of demon horse."

"Denver Broncos though, right?" Rose said. "That's a local team."

"Sure, but blue with glowing red eyes?"

"Good point. What do you mean by a bloody history?"

Crowley grinned. "Old Blucifer here killed his creator."

"What?"

"The commissioned artist was a guy called Luis Jimenez. But before the thing was even unveiled, a section of it fell and severed an artery in Luis's leg and he died!"

Rose grimaced. "That's awful."

Crowley read on then said, "A lot of people seem to think the sculpture is a representation of one of the horses of the apocalypse."

Rose gave him a skeptical look. "That's a bit far-fetched."

"I don't know. Maybe not when you hear what else is going on here. There's a lot here that doesn't make much sense. There was already a perfectly good airport only six miles from Denver, then this one was commissioned and it's twenty-five miles from the city. It's the biggest airport in the US, the second biggest in the world. This place is big. It's fifty-three square miles!"

Rose whistled softly. "That's..." She shrugged. "Why?"

"Exactly. As of 2010, it's the fifth busiest in the world, so I guess it needs to be big. But this big? It cost a fortune, came in two billion dollars over budget."

"Sounds like typical politicians wasting the public's money," Rose said with a sneer.

"You don't know the half of it. Apparently there were five original buildings that were completely constructed but then those in charge decided they were incorrectly positioned. So they buried them."

"Buried them? They didn't knock them down to start again?"

Crowley raised his hands, genuinely nonplussed by what he was reading. "Yep. They were buried and the airport built on top, leading many people to think they're deliberately constructed bunkers in case of some catastrophic event."

"Bunkers for whom?"

Crowley grinned again. "The elite!" At Rose's frown, he went on. "There's a massive network of tunnels left underneath that airport which officials maintain are used to ferry baggage around. Much safer than driving it around on the runways above, apparently."

"Well, that makes sense."

"I guess. But it still doesn't explain why there are these huge, multiple story buildings under there. The airport says they're four stories deep, but some theorists maintain there are blueprints showing them to be six stories."

"Maybe some enterprising billionaires are preparing for the apocalypse," Rose said.

"They might be."

"But who might those enterprising billionaires be?"

"Just a sec." Crowley did a couple of extra searches, double-checking what he had read. "Well, there are several sources here looking at the Illuminati."

Rose made a disdainful sound and sat back in her seat. "Seriously?"

Crowley pointed to the screen and she leaned back in to see. He showed her a photo of a square block, carved with the Masonic symbol of the set square and compass. At the top of the block, five lines radiated downward like the sun's rays. Beneath that was written Denver International Airport Dedication Capstone. Two names were recorded lower down, both listed as Grand Master Masons, then the date of March 19, 1994.

Rose laughed. "Masons aren't automatically Illuminati."

Crowley pointed to a small line of text carved into the stone below the date. "Look there."

Rose read aloud. "New World Airport Commission. Like New World Order? What the hell? Why would you call yourself that? No one's that stupid, surely."

"And there's no record anywhere else in the world, except for the capstone, of that name."

Rose was shaking her head, still looking at the photo. "So why be so blatant?"

"Maybe it's a misdirection."

Rose looked from the photo to Crowley then back again. "A misdirection from what?"

Crowley flicked over his browser windows to show an aerial photograph of the entire airport. "Look at the layout of the runways."

Rose gaped. "A swastika." She shook her head again, as if trying to clear it. "This place can't be real. Maybe we're still on the plane and I'm having a vivid dream."

Crowley chuckled. "And all this is only the tip of the iceberg." He drained his coffee and put the laptop back into his bag. "Come on. Let's check this crazy place out."

CHAPTER 24

Crowley and Rose shouldered their messenger bags and towed their carry-on cases behind them as they strolled at random through the huge airport. Rose was eager to see the mural that had so captured Lily's attention and Crowley understood her enthusiasm for that, but he needed to see more. Everything he had learned about the place gave him the creeps and unsettled him in ways he couldn't articulate. There were any number of reasons for the strangeness of the Denver International Airport, lots of them completely benign. But the conspiracy theorists had a lot of meat on the bones they were chewing and after everything that had happened last time he and Rose had found themselves working together, Crowley was reluctant to write anything off. Something was hugely awry here and he didn't want to miss any small detail that might be important later on.

"Look at that!" Rose pointed up to the wall to their left.

Atop a pillar against the marble wall, just below the high ceiling, stood a grotesque sculpture. It depicted a suitcase, sat on its base and opened, with a gargoyle of some kind sitting in it. The creature had large wings and a horned head, its knees drawn up to its chest and its head resting disconsolately in its hands.

"Why the hell would they have something like that just randomly sitting up the wall?" Rose asked.

Crowley shook his head, looking up at the thing. "It looks kinda sad, don't you think?"

Rose smiled. "Lost luggage? Maybe he expected to go somewhere else, and doesn't want to be in Denver."

"He'd be more at home on the roof of a church in England."

Rose sighed, looked away. "It's bizarre. I can't imagine why anyone would put that in an airport."

They walked on and Crowley pointed to the marble surface beneath their feet. "Look at all these symbols embossed in gold in the floor."

Some of the designs were obvious, the kind of thing a person might expect to see, like the outline of an airplane. But others were patterns less readily understood, the meaning obscure. Rose used her phone to snap pictures of each of them. A security guard leaning against one wall noticed and smiled, ruefully shook his head.

"Apparently we aren't the first to take an interest in the oddities of this place," Crowley said. "And I'm not surprised. Honestly, it's a conspiracy theorist's nirvana."

Rose pointed out one pattern on the ground ahead of them. "Is it me or does that look familiar?"

Crowley paused, staring down at the strange design. It was familiar, but he couldn't place why. He walked around the uneven square, lines branching out all around. As he got to the other side, he had a moment of revelation.

"Hey, look up on your phone. That diagram you found of the passageways underneath the Black Pyramid."

"Oh yeah." Rose flicked up her camera app and started swiping through her saved photos. She moved around to stand next to Crowley and they compared the two images.

Crowley looked from the design to Rose's phone, then up to catch her eye. "I'm not mad, am I?"

"Nope. That's it, almost exactly. Just represented two-dimensionally."

They continued on, Rose taking pictures of all the odd-looking shapes in the floor. They came to one area with a huge design of overlapping circles, different colored stone making a kind of interlocking geometric design.

"That part looks like a black disc eclipsing the sun," Crowley said. "The Nazis revered a black sun."

"And this area is called the Great Hall," Rose said. "Which is what Masons call their meeting halls."

Crowley shook his head, paused walking to turn in a slow circle on the spot. "Masons and Nazis. Swastika runways. Massive underground bunkers."

"Gargoyles and maps of pyramid catacombs," Rose said, taking up the litany of the bizarre. "What the hell is going on here?"

"I don't know." And he genuinely didn't, but he also realized they were being distracted. It was too much information to process. "Besides, you were right before. We need to focus on the main problem, which is finding your sister. Let's look at that mural."

When they had seen the painting in part from Cameron's clip, Crowley had found it discomforting. Standing before it, in all its full-color glory and size, it was truly disturbing. The soldier wore a Nazi-style uniform with an eagle on the hat. It was hard to tell if he was wearing a gas mask or if his face was, in fact, a gas mask. He held a rifle in his left hand, its bayonet pointing at the sky. In his left, pointing down, he held a huge, curved scimitar. He stood among ruined buildings, the point of the scimitar stabbing a white dove. The sharp edge of the blade hovered above supine children, their eyes closed, either in terror or death. To the left, a sweeping design of a terrified woman clutching her dead infant repeated ad infinitum into the distance. Bizarrely, sweeping out from under the large skirts of the Nazi's greatcoat, a brightly colored rainbow arced off to the top left of the mural.

"This is just about the creepiest thing I've ever seen," Rose said.

Crowley could only mutely agree, nodding as he looked the terrible image over again and again.

"That scimitar reminds me of another Masonic symbol," Rose said quietly. She tapped on her phone for a moment, then turned the screen for Crowley to see. It showed an image of a curved blade, beneath which was suspended a star, a crescent moon, and the head of a pharaoh.

"More Masonic and Egyptian connections," Crowley said. The small symbol disturbed him almost as much as the huge mural, though he couldn't say why. He noticed an image in the bottom right of the mural, a page with writing on it. He moved closer and read it aloud for Rose. "I was once a little child who longed for other worlds. But I am no more a child for I have known fear. I have learned to hate… How tragic, then, is youth which lives with enemies, with gallows ropes. Yet, I still believe I only sleep today, that I'll wake up, a child again, and start to laugh and play." He looked up at Rose, knew his expression was haunted.

"That's terrible," Rose said quietly.

Crowley frowned, looked down at the floor while he racked his brains. "It's familiar," he muttered. He took out his phone, dialed up a browser and typed in the first line. Numerous results came back. "Of course. I knew I'd read that before."

"What is it?"

"No less terrible, I'm afraid. That's word for word from an actual letter written by a fourteen-year-old child named Hama Herchenberg, who died December 18, 1943, in the Auschwitz

Concentration Camp."

Rose blanched, looked away from the mural with one hand over her mouth. After a moment she looked back at Crowley. "Humanity sucks," she said, voice constricted with referred grief.

He nodded, lost for words.

Rose pointed to the rainbow-colored ribbon, stretching across the background and wrapping around behind the dark figure. "You think that's maybe a symbol of hope?"

Crowley wanted to reassure her, but he didn't think it was. "Look at how the colors fade, turning to a silvery gray, and come to a point like a sword under the soldier. I guess maybe it depends which way you look at it. I can't help thinking the rainbow is fading out if we read the image left to right."

Rose frowned, shook her head. "Look at those children under the Nazi. There are no marks of violence on them. No bullet wounds or sword cuts. They're just… dead."

Crowley nodded slowly. "And the Nazi is stabbing a dove of peace. The rainbow fades to gray, the children die, peace dies. Good grief, this is horrible."

"Some people say the rainbow represents a chemical agent."

Crowley and Rose both jumped, and turned around quickly.

An old Latino man, clad in an airport janitor's uniform, stood right behind them. His nametag read, 'Mike'. "Sorry, I didn't mean to startle you."

Crowley smiled, taking a breath to calm his racing heart. Everything about this place was putting him on edge. "That's okay. You know a bit about this?"

Mike shouldered a mop, and moved his bucket nearer to the wall to avoid blocking passersby. "I've worked here a long time, heard a lot of stuff. You two were paying some serious attention to the mural."

"Most people don't stop to look?" Rose asked.

"Oh, just about everybody stops to look. But not for long. It was interesting to hear you try to figure out the meaning, though."

"What do you think they mean?" Crowley asked.

Mike smiled, shook his head. He avoided the question. "You know, there are four murals, all painted by a guy named Leo Tanguma. They're supposed to represent peace, harmony and nature. But it doesn't look that way, does it? Everybody says that Tanguma was given guidelines for all four paintings and they paid him big." Mike rubbed his thumb and forefingers together for emphasis. "But when they asked him about it later, he was all, 'No way.' He said there aren't any hidden meanings in his work. But if you look up his other stuff? Very different, like it's not even by the same guy."

"You said the rainbow represents a chemical agent?" Rose prompted.

Mike shrugged. "That's what they say. Like you said, the dead children aren't hurt or nothing, just dead. Like they're sleeping, you know? And the dude's wearing a gas mask." He pointed up at the soldier.

"So the children were gassed and the rainbow represents that?" Crowley asked.

Mike pointed to a nearby image on the floor. It depicted a mine cart with the letters *Au Ag* inscribed on it.

"I thought those were the chemical symbols for gold and silver," Rose said. "Not some kind of gas."

Mike cocked his head, and then smiled. "They are, yes. But there's a double meaning, which is why this particular symbol is located in front of this particular mural."

"And what's that?" Crowley asked.

Mike lowered his voice. "They say the Au Ag stands for, um…" He paused, took off his cap, and scratched his head. His brow furrowed for a moment, and then his face brightened. "Yeah, the Australian Antigen Virus."

CHAPTER 25

Crowley frowned, unsure if the man's interpretation could be right. He'd never heard of the virus Mike referred to.

"What's the Australian Antigen virus?" Rose asked, echoing his thoughts.

"I don't know the science," Mike said. "Just that it's a biological agent for mass deployment. The conspiracy theorists say it'll bring the earth's population down to a manageable level. I hope they start with the Raiders fans." He grinned, but neither Crowley nor Rose had any idea what a Raider was.

"A human mass extinction virus?" Crowley asked. He had trouble believing so blunt an instrument would ever be deployed.

Mike nodded. "The virus is… I don't know, programmed for people with certain gene types."

"Targeted for what? Race?" Crowley asked, horrified.

Mike shrugged. "Plenty of people would like to see a whole lot less of me and mine, if you know what I mean."

"That's a bit far-fetched," Rose said, shaking her head slightly. Crowley saw her eyes and a fear was reflected there, a paranoia that such a thing was maybe possible. He shared her concern, though he was loathe to admit it.

Mike didn't argue. He pointed to the next mural. "Like I said, these murals are all by the same artist. They seem to be telling the story of the world suffering a big disaster, and a remnant little bit of humanity surviving. Look here." He led them to another painting, this one depicting children, along with extinct and endangered animals, gathered around three open caskets. In the background, a forest burned furiously, and in the far distance loomed a city lost in a poisonous-looking haze, as if the entire place were being gassed. The three coffins each held a different body. On the left, an African woman in native garb, interred with drums and flowers. On the right, a blonde girl child holding a bible. On her dress was a yellow star.

Crowley pointed to the design. "That's a 'Juden' star. Used by the Nazi to identify Jews."

In the center coffin lay a Native American woman, also garbed in traditional dress.

"What's that doll she's holding?" Rose asked.

Mike tapped his nose, smiling like she was a particularly astute student in his class. "That's a *Kachina*. It's a totem that represents a Hopi spirit and a connection to the Fifth World."

Crowley felt discomforting connections to their current predicament beginning to drop into place. "Fifth World?"

Mike nodded. "The world that's to come after this one."

Rose glanced at Crowley and raised an eyebrow. She was thinking the same things as him. "Does this Kachina represent a particular spirit?" Rose asked.

"That one is Masuwa, also known as 'Skeleton Man'."

"What's his significance?"

Mike paused for dramatic effect. "He's the Lord of the Dead."

A shiver ran through Crowley at the mention of the Lord of the Dead. He couldn't be sure if it was simply the general weirdness of these murals, in an airport of all places, but he was becoming ever more disturbed. Considering their own search so far had been leading toward another lord of the dead, these similarities seemed too unlikely to ignore.

"Would you believe," Mike said, "this mural is called 'In Peace and Harmony with Nature'?"

Crowley huffed a humorless laugh. "Nothing like a bit of irony."

Mike chuckled. "It's technically only half of the mural. Check this out."

He led them to another section, pointed to the next huge painting along. This one depicted happy children gathered around a brightly colored plant. All the endangered or extinct animals from before were alive and well again. A white dove seemed to be appearing from within the plant itself.

"Well, this is more positive," Rose said, smiling nervously.

"Is it?" Mike asked. "Even if you ignore the fact that the plant is totally alien, look beneath the surface, literally."

Crowley let his gaze drift down the glowing plant, shining in all the colors of the rainbow, to the roots. They were inky black with sinister-looking tendrils spreading in every direction.

Mike pointed to some tigers in the painting. "Look there. See they have human faces? The other animals are happy. Everything about this seems modified. Synthesized."

"Genetically modified?" Crowley mused.

"Maybe. This is like an artificial world. A new, created world perhaps."

"Well, that certainly puts a damper on things," Rose said, brow creased.

"What about the other two murals?" Crowley asked. "Are all of these a single work of art?"

Mike nodded. "They're called 'Children of the World Dream of Peace.' It begins with the one you already looked at."

Crowley couldn't help glancing again at the disturbing soldier standing amidst death and destruction. Mike beckoned and they moved along again.

"When you first look at this," Mike said, as they reached the next painting, "it seems like everything worked out okay."

The painting they stood before this time depicted the children of the world carrying bundled swords, all wrapped up in their national flags. A boy was joyfully pounding those swords into plowshares. The sweeping rainbow design was in evidence again, framing the entire mural. Beneath the boy's anvil, the Nazi soldier in the gas mask lay dead.

Rose sighed, clearly expecting the initial impression to hide something deeper and less pleasant. "So, what's the problem with this one?"

"I think I get it," Crowley said. "They're not just bringing him weapons. See how they're wrapped? They're all surrendering the flags of their countries."

Mike smiled. "Bingo. They're giving up weapons, giving up fighting for their country and culture. One world. A New World Order, maybe?"

"Seems a stretch," Rose said, frowning. She clearly didn't like what she saw.

"I think there's more," Crowley said. "They're bringing everything to that one boy. See what he's wearing?"

Rose leaned forward to look. "Lederhosen. He's German. Is that relevant?"

Crowley laughed. "I tell you, I'm way beyond even guessing now. I'm seeing relevance in every detail and I have no idea if that's what it means or if I'm just making stuff up."

Rose smiled. "Yeah. And is a one world order really that bad? I mean, think about *Star Trek*? They went to the stars after the Earth put aside its differences and worked together, right? Humanity, as a whole, not individual nations at war."

"Well, sure," Crowley said. "But it depends who's in control of that new world order, right?"

"Remember what the dead looked like in the other murals?" Mike said. "Eyes either closed or rolled back in their heads, yes? Look at the supposedly dead Nazi under the anvil here."

Crowley did as Mike suggested. The gas mask worn by the soldier was empty, black, hollow sockets peered back at him. "He's not there. That isn't a dead body, just an empty uniform."

"So, the painting depicts what? A ruse perpetrated on the earth?" Rose asked.

"That's it," Mike said. "The people of all the nations don't even know they're surrendering to the enemy they thought they beat long ago. And to top it all off, check out the rainbow."

Crowley looked up at the multi-colored band that framed the picture. At its beginning, it was comprised of several colors, but it grew darker as it wrapped around and under the image. And then, one by one, colors were torn from it as the nations surrendered their flags, until only one color remained. Blood red.

"I just noticed something else," Rose said. "Almost everyone is focused on the German boy, but look over there." She pointed to the far right, where a young man faced in the opposite direction, eyes wide, crying out. "He sees something. And so does that dove." She pointed to two white doves of peace perched on the hollow shell of the Nazi uniform. One looked up at the young German boy working the anvil, but the other's attention was diverted. It stared off to the right in the same direction as the young man on the far right of the painting.

"Something is coming," Crowley said quietly. "And no one else sees it."

"Maybe," Mike said. "But notice that this is the left half of the mural."

Rose stepped back, looked left and right at the spread of huge paintings. "What do you mean?"

"Take a few steps further back and try to see them as one."

Crowley and Rose did as the man suggested. They stared for a moment, trying to read the artwork as a single statement. Then shock rippled through Crowley's core. "Oh my God."

CHAPTER 26

Denver International Airport

Looking at the two main halves of the mural as one, Crowley saw immediately how the they worked, connected by the rainbow, into a single narrative.

"The illusion of peace is the beginning," he said.

Rose had seen it too. She nodded subtly as she spoke. "The swords into plowshares, empty Nazi uniform... The world believes the threat is ended. But from the blood of the Second World War comes something that appears beautiful, but is actually deadly."

Crowley's eyes followed the rainbow as it wrapped around the happy, distracted children, to the scene of horror, where it faded into a huge blade, honed for slaughter. "The boy and the dove are seeing the future no one else yet sees," Crowley said.

"A future where the dove of peace is dead and the Nazis rise again," Mike said in a low voice.

Crowley couldn't tear his gaze away from the Nazi's sword stabbing the white dove mid-flight. That single portion, among all the other weirdness of the paintings, made his gut tighten. Eventually he looked at Mike. "I have to say, you are the world's darkest art critic."

Mike laughed. "I'm just telling you what smarter people than me have said. Or at least, people who are a whole lot more paranoid than me."

Rose narrowed her eyes, swept her hair back with one hand. "So what part was Lily interested in? Remember in the CCTV clip she was focused on one particular area. If we read the mural this way, the *final* image contains the bit that Lily..." She cut off in mid-sentence and hurried over to the corner of the mural.

Crowley had reached the same conclusion, remembered the letter painted into the lower corner. Lost in their contemplations, they hadn't considered which part had so fascinated Lily. But he remembered, the letter from the child who died at Auschwitz. Sorrow tugged at him once more as he recalled reading it earlier.

Rose crouched before the metal railing that prevented people getting close enough to touch the artwork. She read aloud. "I was once a little child who longed for other worlds. But

I am no more a child for I have known fear. I have learned to hate…" Her voice caught, grew husky with emotion, but she pressed on. "How tragic, then, is youth which lives with enemies, with gallows ropes. Yet, I still believe I only sleep today, that I'll wake up, a child again, and start to laugh and play."

"You know the history of that letter?" Mike asked.

"We do," Crowley said.

"So, yes, if you interpret the painting from left to right, that's what we're left with. Tragedy, hate, and death." He sighed. "Word is, the airport is planning on painting over the darker halves of these murals, but who knows?"

"What the hell are things like this even doing in an international airport?" Rose asked, her face twisted in a kind of grief. "I mean, this stuff, the demon in a suitcase, the giant hell horse out front? What's going on here?"

Neither Crowley or Mike had any real answer for her, but the question seemed largely rhetorical anyway. She didn't wait for an answer, but turned back to the mural and snapped a photo of the letter. She stood, drew a hand back over her hair again, visibly shaken.

Crowley wanted to comfort her, longed to gather her in a hug and try to reassure her, but he wasn't sure she would welcome it.

"Are you okay?" Mike asked. He looked to Crowley then back to Rose, made a face of chagrin like it was his fault. Perhaps he thought his stories had frightened Rose, but it ran deeper than that.

Rose shook her head. "It's fine. It's not you. I'm sorry. My sister is missing, and we have reason to believe she came here and took a particular interest in this painting. This letter in fact."

Mike smiled gently. "Sister. Last week, I had pretty much the same conversation with her that I had with you. Nice girl. I almost said something, but I didn't want to sound like one of those 'all Asians look the same' kind of people."

Rose managed a smile in return. "Did my sister say anything about where she might be going?"

Mike pursed his lips, shook his head. "The only thing I can tell you is she was really interested in the Great Hall."

"Like the Freemasons call the room where they perform their rituals," Crowley said. "We already looked around there."

Mike shrugged. "This way." He led them away from the

paintings. "Around here it's what we call the Main Concourse. I'll show you something."

As they walked, Rose looked at Mike. "So, we've got a painting depicting the rise of the Nazis and the slaughter of much of the world's population, at an airport with swastika-shaped runways and a horse statue that symbolizes the apocalypse." She let out a laugh, shook her head, still obviously having trouble believing what she was saying. But she went on. "Is it possible that there really is an underground city here that's designed to protect, I don't know, the Illuminati or whoever from what's to come?"

Mike drew in a long breath, looked suddenly serious. "I don't know what's down there. Some of it really is used for running the airport. Tunnels for baggage transport and the like. There's room for vehicles and it's much easier and safer than driving around above, on the runways. But that's the only part I've seen. It's all that any outsiders have been allowed to see. But I know there's more. Much more." A shudder ran through his body. "They say…" He paused, looked at the ground.

Rose put a hand on his shoulder. "They say what?"

Mike swallowed, looked Rose directly in the eyes. "They say sometimes workers go in and they don't come out."

Rose recoiled slightly, eyes widening. "Seriously?"

Mike frowned. "I stay as far away from the underground as I can. No one's going to miss a janitor."

They reached the concourse and he pointed out a painting. It was a Native American-style work showing an alien-looking figure hovering in front of a mountain range. The figure was stylized, a horned headdress above a long neck, arms out to either side. On its diamond-shaped body was a design of a kind of plant with radial lines either side and a descending root like a constellation. On the right of the figure a bird sat on a stalk of corn. On the left, a baby floated on its back.

"This is what my sister was interested in?" Rose asked.

Mike nodded. "She took pictures, stared at it forever, did stuff on her phone. She kept looking between it and her phone, like she was trying to match something up."

"You were watching her?" Crowley asked.

Mike looked a little sheepish. "Keeping an eye out, you know? I don't meet many people who are that into the artwork. We had a good talk, like I've had with you two."

Rose nodded. "You like to discuss this stuff, huh?"

"It's pretty cool, I think."

Rose laughed. "Bizarre is what it is. Thank you for looking out for Lily while she was here."

"She was a nice girl, traveling all alone. Just seemed like something wasn't right, I guess."

"She wasn't with a man?" Crowley asked.

Mike shook his head. "Not that I saw."

"Can you tell us anything else that might help us find her?" Rose asked.

Mike pursed his lips in thought. "Actually, maybe. I said she ought to visit the Denver Museum of Nature and Science. They have a new Egyptian mummy exhibit there and some visiting experts. So maybe she went there and talked to someone? They might be able to tell you more." He glanced at his watch. "I got to get back to work. I'll be in trouble."

They thanked him, and then Crowley thought of one more question. "Is there anything in the airport connected to Anubis, by any chance?"

Mike laughed. "Other than the big-ass statue of him?"

"You're joking." Crowley couldn't help laughing himself. This was all too strange. "That would qualify, yeah."

Chapter 27

Cruise smoothed the lapels of his gray suit, leaned back, crossed his ankles, and peered over the top of the novel he was pretending to read. He watched the airport maintenance worker talking to the two tourists. Considering the length of the conversation, and the urgency they displayed, he suspected they weren't tourists at all. Finally, the janitor shook hands with them both, smiled, and pushed his cleaning trolley away.

Cruise watched the remaining pair as they stared up at the large mural before them. The man was Caucasian, around six feet tall, his dark hair cut short. He was lean but muscular under his jeans and jacket. The woman looked to be around five-eight or so, Asian in appearance, her black hair in a tidy bob. She had a trim, athletic figure. Cruise let his mind wander for a moment, imagining her without the jeans and sweater she wore. Then he pulled a cell phone from his inside jacket pocket.

Trying to appear nonchalant, he tapped a saved number and waited for an answer.

The reply was curt when it came. "Yep."

"It's probably nothing," Cruise said, "but we've got a couple of people showing a lot more interest in the airport than usual."

"Too much interest?" the voice asked.

"Yeah, maybe. They're asking a lot of questions."

"What do they look like?"

Cruise gave a cursory description, mentioned the voices he had overheard.

"A young Asian woman with a British accent, you say?" asked the voice at the other end.

"That's right."

"Interesting. Any idea what they're up to?"

"Not really, but they're definitely not asking the usual tourist questions. They spent a long time talking to a janitor, asked a ton of questions. Could be more conspiracy theorist idiots, of course, but it might be something worse. I could follow them."

"I've got them on camera now. See what this busybody janitor has to say and then check back in. I'll let you know if they leave."

Cruise scanned the large main concourse. His gaze finally fell on the maintenance worker, pushing his trolley toward a side exit. "Will do," he said, and hung up.

He walked fast, his stride long and confident, and quickly caught up the worker, whose name badge read 'Mike'.

Mike looked up and his eyes widened. He went to push his trolley back out into the crowded concourse, but Cruise guided his arm, pushed him into the quiet corridor. "We need to talk."

Mike forced a smile, shook his head. "Sorry, señor. I very busy!" His accent was comical, overplayed given the conversation on which Cruise had just eavesdropped.

Cruise slipped a pistol from inside his jacket, keeping it close to his body but making sure Mike saw it. "You can make time, amigo."

"Before we go to where Mike said the statue was, I want to check on something," Crowley said.

Rose frowned. "Check on what? This place gives me the creeps, I want to get moving."

"Yeah, but there's more here, right? Mike said about the underground places he won't go?"

"And you want to go there?"

Crowley inclined his head towards an open door to the side, beyond it a shallow ramp led downwards, then switched back on itself and went down further. The door was slowly closing on a hydraulic arm as someone walked quickly down the ramp. "Come on!"

Rose started to protest, but Crowley dragged her along and they slipped through the gap just in time. "Jake, this will get us arrested."

Crowley grinned. "Just a quick look. Act like you're supposed to be here. Confidence is key."

They waited to give whoever had passed through the door time to move away, then walked down the ramp, followed it as it turned, then came to another double door. Crowley pushed through, a corridor ahead of them with several doors along either side. At the end of the corridor, stairs led down. They took the stairs, moving from clean white corridors to industrial gray cement and exposed metal conduits. The space opened out into a vast thoroughfare, wider than a highway. A baggage train, one cart pulling half a dozen flatbed trailers loaded with cases, cruised by them, the driver frowning. Crowley nodded to one side and they hurried around an outcropping of pipework covered in a variety of warning labels.

"Here," Crowley said, looking through the reinforced glass window of another door. "More stairs going down."

"How far down does it go?" Rose wondered.

Crowley gestured back over his shoulder. "If this level is where they move the luggage around, then anything below this has to be for other purposes."

"Like what?"

"That's exactly what I'd like to know." He tried the door and it opened. He grinned back at her and headed down.

The stairs seemed to go more than a single level, four flights switching back and forth. They emerged into a cement corridor lit by bright neon tubes. At the end of the corridor was a heavy door, like something from a bank's vault, steel with a large wheel in the center. Set into the metal were two electronic keypads of some sort. More importantly, at the side of the corridor in front of the door was a desk. A man stood quickly from behind the desk, his face angry.

"The hell are you doing here?"

He wore an airport uniform, but had an automatic rifle slung across his chest. Crowley swallowed hard at the sight of a small badge stitched onto the shoulder of the man's shirt. It showed a pyramid, an eye suspended above, and several lines radiating out from the eye.

Crowley forced a laugh. "You won't believe how lost we are!" He pointed at Rose. "I told her the restaurant wasn't this way!"

"Don't blame me!" Rose spluttered and Crowley wasn't sure if she was playing along or genuinely outraged.

"Just stand right where you are!" The armed guard pulled a radio from his hip and keyed it. "Command, this is Gaston at sub-three-zero-one."

As Crowley drew a breath to turn and run, hoping Rose would not hesitate to run with him, footsteps rattled down the stairs behind him.

"I got it, Gaston," another man said. He was dressed the same, equally armed. "I saw them on the CCTV. I'll take 'em out."

Crowley flinched internally at 'take 'em out', wondering if the man meant to escort them from the premises or disappear them permanently. He decided to act up the dumb tourist. He turned the English accent up to eleven. "I'm bally well sorry, chaps, I'm sure we're causing you no end of bother. We're really quite exhausted and jetlagged, and we're just trying to find a bite to eat."

"He won't listen to me," Rose said, turning her own English accent on. "He always thinks he knows where he's going. You know, he once tried to drive us from London to Leeds without a map. Without a map! Honestly, you men need to learn to ask for directions once in a while and then actually listen when someone tries to help."

Crowley turned to her, suppressing a smile. "My dear, you do me a disservice telling the story like that. The journey to Leeds is really quite simple. It was the address at the far end that caused the consternation."

Rose drew breath to speak again when the first guard, Gaston, cut across them. "Enough, already, for God's sake. Bill, just get these two back up to the concourse."

Bill blew out air. "Gladly. This way, please."

Crowley and Rose walked ahead of him as Bill directed them back up to the concourse and then pointed out a sign.

"There's your directions to the restaurant, okay?"

Crowley smiled. "Got it. Thank you so much, and terribly sorry to have been any trouble."

Bill shook his head and disappeared back through the doors that closed heavily behind him.

"Too damned close, Jake!" Rose said with a scowl.

"Yeah. But there's definitely something going on down there right? That door, the guns? What the hell is happening in this place?"

"I just want to keep moving," Rose said.

Crowley gave her shoulder a quick squeeze of reassurance. "You're right. Let's go and see the place Mike said that Anubis statue used to be."

CHAPTER 28

Denver International Airport

From outside, Denver International Airport looked like it had grown there rather than been built. The roofing was reminiscent of a collection of circus big tops, crammed together like mushrooms. Beneath the bizarre, spiky top, the airport buildings were layers of sandy stone and reflective glass.

A cool breeze ruffled Crowley's jacket, but he was glad of the freshness following the air-conditioned interior under fluorescent lights. A bit of nature was exactly what he felt he needed. To the west, the snow-capped Rocky Mountains looked inviting.

"Be nice to head up there and forget everything, wouldn't it?" Rose said.

Crowley laughed softly. "Just what I was thinking. All this stuff about gassing cities, genocide, new world orders, it's... I don't know, it's mind-bending."

"I'd rather live in a cabin in those mountains and never have to think about any of this again. Except that my sister's missing."

Crowley took a deep breath. "Yep, that's the key factor."

"Look at that damn thing," Rose said, staring off past Crowley's shoulder.

He turned to see the giant blue mustang sculpture, its red eyes surveying the land beneath its flailing front hooves. It reared up menacingly, black mane flying in the wind.

"It's truly weird," Crowley agreed.

Rose shook her head. "What's it even doing here? What is any of this stuff doing here? It's all so... so..."

"Blatant?" Crowley offered.

She turned to him. "Yes! So bloody in your face, like these Illuminati or whoever they are just enjoy rubbing everyone's nose in it. All those billions of dollars poured into this strange, ostentatious display. What else can it be but some kind of temple and bolt hole for the super rich?"

Crowley smiled. "Starting to buy into the conspiracy theories, are you?"

Rose allowed herself a laugh, shook her head again. "How

can you not when it's all just in your face like this?"

"And this is where the big statue of Anubis stood," Crowley said. He pointed to the ground where the statue had been according to Mike. "You think maybe having that was a step too far?"

Rose pointed to the giant blue mustang. "Compared to that?"

"Good point."

Crowley kicked at the ground, walked around the area. It was mostly gravel, but a circular slab of relatively new–looking cement occupied the center, presumably where the statue had been mounted.

He crouched, looked more closely. The new disc was encircled by older cement which had designs carved into it. "Look", he said, pointing.

Rose joined him. "The same wavy lines as the marks in the bone room back in the Black Pyramid!"

"Yep. And this cement is new. Didn't Lily say something about moving it from there to America?"

Rose looked from the designs on the ground to Crowley and back again. "You think whatever they're looking for was stored there, then moved here?"

Crowley nodded. "And hidden under the statue of Anubis."

"But then the statue had to be moved and they moved whatever was under it too?"

"I think so," Crowley said. "But moved it where?"

"You think this was where they hid the Anubis Key? Whatever the damn thing actually is?"

"Possibly. Or maybe they hid directions here, some information about how to find the Anubis Key." Crowley exhaled in frustration. "Who knows? But we've missed something here, and presumably Lily did too." He felt around the cement, ran his fingers through the gravel at its edge, then sat back, annoyed.

"Did you expect a secret trapdoor or something?" Rose asked, one side of her mouth hooked up in a smirk.

He grinned at her. "Did you?"

"I am a little disappointed there isn't anything."

Crowley stretched and shook himself. "There's nothing here. Come on, let's go pick up the rental car."

"And then what?"

"I guess we head to the Denver Museum like Mike

suggested. See if anyone there remembers talking to Lily." Rose's eyes were narrowed, looking past Crowley. He turned to see what had caught her attention.

A tall, familiar looking young man was staring at them.

"Isn't that the guy who was traveling with Lily?" Rose asked, her voice almost a whisper.

"Most definitely. He's seen us."

The man had indeed seen them. In fact, Crowley thought, he had been heading towards them all along. Crowley braced himself, drew a deep breath, ready for a fight. The young man saw Crowley's posture, and the look in his eyes, and raised both hands, palms out.

He stopped a dozen paces away, hands still raised. "Please, we need to talk. I need your help."

"Don't trust him," Crowley said quietly to Rose. Then he raised his voice. "Where's Lily?"

"That's what I want to know too. I thought she might have come back here, to this spot." He shook his head. "I don't know how much you know, but you're looking on the ground here because there used to be an Anubis statue, right?"

"Maybe," Crowley said guardedly.

"Lily was into Anubis," the man said. He looked at Rose, took another couple of steps forward, but stayed out of fighting range. "There's a strong family resemblance. You're her sister." It wasn't a question.

"Did she talk about me?"

The man nodded. "A little bit. Not much."

Rose stared for a moment, expression unreadable. Then she said, "How were you and Lily separated?"

"We argued on the plane. Then again at the airport and we split up, supposedly only to cool off. Then I couldn't find her again. I think maybe she deliberately dumped me."

"Really?" Rose asked. "Lily spent a long time at the airport. How could you not find her? And where have you been since? She was here a week ago, right?"

The man's face twisted in frustration. And, Crowley thought, maybe a little guilt. Or regret. "I had a... meeting," he said. "I had to see some people. It distracted me for a while and now I'm trying to pick up where we left off."

Crowley surged forward and grabbed him by the collar. He twisted the shirt material, made the guy yelp in surprise and probably a little pain. "You'd better start making sense, buddy.

Stop prevaricating. This is about the Anubis Key, isn't it?"

The man nodded, his unshaven chin rough against Crowley's knuckles. "Lily's not the only one after it, but it's not what..."

A shot rang out and the man's head jerked suddenly to one side as a bullet took him in the temple. He was dead before he hit the ground.

"Run!" Crowley yelled.

He and Rose bolted, zigzagging left and right, hunched half-over to reduce their target size. Crowley spat a string of inventive curses, trying to stay between the unseen shooter and Rose as they ran. Bullets pinged and whined off the ground and nearby vehicles, then they dove between two large SUVs.

"Which way?" Rose asked, eyes wide. Her skin had paled to gray.

Crowley wanted desperately to know who was shooting at them, but he didn't dare a look back. He pointed. "That way, at the end of the row, is a car hire place. I pre-booked us a car. You go and get it and bring it back this way."

"And what are you going to do?"

Crowley grinned. "Lead them on a chase. Pick me up at Blucifer."

"Jake, I..."

He didn't want to give Rose time to prevaricate. "Green Star Rentals! Go!" He pushed her in the right direction and then jumped up and ran the other way, just high enough to attract the shooter.

The enemy was good. The window of a nearby car exploded in a shower of glass. He ducked and ran on, dove around the car and sprinted away from the shot. He desperately hoped Rose had accepted his plan and was currently running for the rental car. He also hoped there wasn't a line or some officious employee who would drag out the process.

The shooting had stopped for a moment and Crowley assumed the attacker was trying to find a better position, a new angle to see him again. He took a deep breath and ducked across one row. Three rapid shots popped, echoing through the open space. Then he was between cars once more. The windscreen right above Crowley's head exploded in a shower of tiny glass cubes and he yelped. He would give anything for a weapon, to be able to return fire.

He hissed between his teeth, took a sighting on Blucifer,

rearing up into the sky, and bolted across another gap, stepping left and right. The bullets came quicker this time and Crowley felt one rip through the sleeve of his jacket, the heat of its passing searing his skin, but he was fairly sure it hadn't hit him.

A family of five, three children wide-eyed and their parents pale, were hunkered down by a trolley-parking bay. They tried to hide behind their luggage.

"What's happening?" the father asked Crowley as he skidded up next to them.

Crowley cursed. He couldn't risk drawing this family into the firefight. "Active shooter!" he said. "Stay where you are, he's going the other way."

As Crowley moved to look, the mother yelled, "Shouldn't you stay down, too?"

"Can't, sorry!"

Without explaining, Crowley jumped up and ran again. The air was eerily quiet, no shots ringing out. His back crawled as he imagined bullets tearing into it at any second. Could he dare hope the shooter had lost sight of him?

He moved more slowly, glancing back the way Rose had gone, but he was too far away to see her. So he scanned the rows and rows of parked cars looking for the shooter. If not for the angle of the sun, he would have died that moment, but he glimpsed the reflection of the scope a split second before the shot and dove to the side. The bullet tore through the hood of the car he fell behind, gasping, adrenaline surging through him. How much longer could this go on before airport authorities got involved?

He assumed the shooter had logged his position and direction, so he stayed low and kept moving. After twenty meters or so, he turned ninety degrees, heading towards the shooter's last position. The best defense was a good offense and he was tired of being the duck in this game of target practice. He hurried along, triangulating roughly the shooter's best position. He regularly dropped to the asphalt and looked under the cars, trying to spot the attacker's feet. And then there they were. Black combat boots and black cargo pants. Given the black canvas jacket he had spotted briefly a moment before, he was sure this was his guy. The man was moving obliquely away from him, clearly trying to get ahead and be in line when Crowley next appeared. He hadn't expected Crowley to come to him.

Crowley gritted his teeth. It was a fair expectation. Who the hell approached a well-armed active shooter, gunning specifically for you? He swallowed, cut across another row and moved again, low and fast. His back and legs burned with the effort of running hunched so low, his heart hammered with exertion and adrenaline.

Two more rows over, the shooter stopped moving. Crowley risked a look through the windows of the two rows of cars still between them and saw the man resting on the hood of a green sedan, settled in awaiting his shot. He was still looking the direction Crowley had been going. Now or never, Crowley thought. He moved another few meters away, then slipped between the cars and came around behind the shooter. The man was twenty paces away, looking in the wrong direction. Crowley ran on feet as silent as he could, but the man sensed him and spun. Then Crowley was on top of him. As the rifle swung up and around, Crowley delivered a solid punch to the man's gaping jaw. He staggered, the rifle barked and flashed, heat burning past Crowley's forearm. Tough bugger, he didn't go down. Crowley batted the weapon aside, and hit him again. This time he fell, stunned.

Crowley grabbed the rifle and dropped the mag out, sent it skittering across the asphalt, and ran for Blucifer. As he neared the giant blue mustang, Rose roared up along the row of cars, eyes wide in concern over the wheel. He waved her down and she popped the passenger door for him to jump in.

"Go!" he said, and the tires squealed as she floored it.

Crowley twisted in the seat, saw the attacker rise groggily between the parked cars. He lifted an automatic pistol into view and popped off several quick shots, but they all went wide. The man was clearly still too stunned to shoot straight.

"Are you okay?" Rose asked.

Crowley pulled up his sleeve to check where that one shot had grazed him. A very slight wound, but almost no blood. He spared a moment to wrap a handkerchief around his arm, then patted himself down, taking a moment to assess for any pain. Just aching muscles and the dying surge of adrenaline. "Yeah. I'm okay."

Rose stared at the road ahead. She pulled out onto the highway, and headed toward Denver. Regardless of the seeming calm, Crowley kept an eye out for pursuit.

"Close one," he said after a minute, for want of conversation.

"That man." Rose's voice hitched. "Just murdered like that."

"Yeah."

"And nearly us too!"

Crowley took deep breaths, steadying himself. "Nearly. You did good getting the car so quickly."

"What has Lily got herself into?"

What indeed? Crowley wondered. And an unasked question hung heavy in the air between them. Had Lily already met the same fate as the young man?

"So where next?" Crowley wondered aloud. "We're a bit out of leads. Where might Lily have gone after the airport?"

"Assuming she left the airport."

"Yes, assuming that."

"There's that Egyptian mummy exhibit at the Denver Museum of Nature and Science," Crowley said. "Worth a try. We might find some other experts there too, and perhaps they'll have suggestions of things we can follow up."

CHAPTER 29

The Denver Museum of Nature and Science was unimpressive from the outside. Blocky and industrial, pale brown, it looked more like a warehouse than a place of knowledge and learning. But Rose knew better than to judge books by their covers. As they entered, unsure of what they were expecting to find, she fought against the rising certainty that they had hit a dead end. The young man, jerking dead from Crowley's grasp in a sudden and violent attack, had disturbed her deeply. And she could see in Crowley's eyes that it had affected him too. He was no stranger to death and killing, not unaccustomed to violence, but setting was everything. In the theater of war, death was a given and while it was a shocking, it was also expected. She imagined he would react entirely differently in that environment. The unexpected nature of the young man's demise, the public and disdainful impact of it, had her and Crowley on edge. And though she surged with grief every time the thought arose, she couldn't imagine Lily still alive. How could her sister have avoided a similar fate if that man's life had been snuffed out so easily? So openly?

With no other direction presenting itself, they made their way up to the mummies exhibit. They paused at the entrance and read from a placard there.

"Mummies: New Secrets from the Tombs" is a rare glimpse at a collection of mummies from The Field Museum in Chicago, many displayed for the first time. Using modern technology and noninvasive research techniques, scientists avoided the hazards of unwrapping the fragile specimens and uncovered a wealth of new discoveries. Medical scanning, DNA sampling and advanced computer modeling revealed a storehouse of natural and cultural information with extraordinary detail.

"That's pretty incredible when you think about it," Rose said.

"They won't even take them from the tombs soon." Crowley grinned. "Maybe they won't even go to the tombs. Just scan them from outside with a drone."

"Sitting in a basement somewhere, with a nice cup of tea on hand?" Rose asked.

"Maybe!"

They wandered through, looking at displays. Large glass cases contained all manner of wrapped bodies and sarcophagi. Colorful wall displays explained the history of their archeology, shelves held canopic jars and models of heads. One section described how they used technology to rebuild the faces of long decayed people, recreating what someone looked like two thousand or more years ago.

Along with the expected Egyptian exhibits, there were preparations for the afterlife practiced by the ancient Peruvian cultures of Chinchorro, Paracas, Chancay and Nazca. Their methods apparently predating those of Egypt by 2,000 years. They looked at a Predynastic mummy from Egypt, one of the oldest in the world, apparently mummified naturally in the hot, dry sand about 5,500 years ago. The display suggested that some scholars believed this natural process gave the ancient Egyptians the idea for artificial mummification. There were animal mummies, considered offerings to the gods and pets for the afterlife. A crocodile, a cat, a baboon, birds and a gazelle. A walk-in tomb featured fragments of real stone sarcophagi and an intricately painted coffin. Rose stood for a long time looking at two women, wrapped in linen and enclosed in painted coffins, wondering at the lives they might have led. She took time to admire a scale model of an Egyptian temple, amazed by its detail.

Crowley sighed, turned in a slow circle. "This all feels like we're on the right track," he said. "But we need something concrete."

"A real lead." Rose agreed with the sentiment, assuming she pushed aside her concerns that they were already too late. She needed to act as though Lily were still alive, because otherwise the whole thing was pointless. And Lily might be alive, it wasn't beyond the realms of possibility. If nothing else, she owed it to Lily to keep focused as if her sister were still living and able to be found.

"I'll show Lily's picture around to the museum staffers," Crowley said. "See if anyone recognizes her."

"Okay, good idea." Rose pulled her picture of Lily from her bag, a different one to the half-profile Crowley had. "Take mine too, see what you can find. I'm going to keep looking around in here."

Crowley reached out, took the photo. "You okay? I mean, besides the obvious?"

"Yeah. I'm struggling, I don't mind admitting that." She sighed. "Perhaps I just need a break, but we're not likely to get one any time soon. The trail is getting colder by the minute."

Crowley took her hand, squeezed it gently. "I get it. Relax here, as much as you can. See if you can spot anything that might have caught Lily's eye. It might give us a new lead. I'll ask around. Be back in ten or fifteen minutes."

"Okay."

"Then perhaps we need to give ourselves a rest. Go and get a proper meal, find somewhere to stay tonight and get a good sleep. It's pointless to run ourselves ragged."

Rose smiled. "You're probably right."

"Of course I am. I'm always right."

She grinned crookedly. "Don't do that. You're all right all the time you're not being a dick." She leaned forward and quickly kissed his cheek to show she was joking.

He absently put one hand to where her lips had touched him and she experienced a moment of regret. She didn't want to give him any mixed signals. They had to focus on Lily. "You got it, Ms. Black," he said. "No more dick. Just one hundred per cent Crowley." He smiled, and turned away, heading for the entrance to the exhibit.

She watched him go, then continued to browse. Her own fascination with history and archeology was reason enough, her interest piqued by every item, every snippet of information. But the added relevance of her sister's interest made Rose ache to understand everything. Surely there were answers hidden in these academic phrases, these cold and clinical explanations. Some deeper meaning that would give her insight into her sister's passions and help Rose find the missing woman.

She reached a display with four canopic jars, the funerary storage vessels that held the vital organs of the deceased after the mummification process. Of the four in this display, each was inscribed with a different stylized head: a human, a falcon, a baboon, and a jackal. A jackal! Rose's breath caught, finally recognizing something with at least a tenuous connection to Anubis. Surely if Lily had been here, this would be an item that captured her interest. It was the only representation of Anubis Rose had seen thus far.

She looked around to find Crowley, to show him, but he wasn't anywhere she could see. No doubt trawling the other parts of the exhibit with Lily's picture. She smiled softly. He was a good man, a genuinely caring man. He bent over backward to help her. She would never take that for granted.

She spotted a museum docent eyeing her suspiciously, the museum-issued shirt wrinkled and strangely oversized on the woman's short form. Rose smiled, thinking perhaps this guide would have more information about the display, about the jackal-inscribed jar. She opened her mouth to speak but the woman turned on her heel and hurried away.

Rose frowned. Odd, she thought to herself, watching the guide's wide butt whip out of sight around a corner. Shaking her head, Rose went back to inspecting the display. She read the signage, made a circuit of the glass case. Nothing there caught her interest beside the canopic jar itself. She needed to know why these four jars were marked as they were. What was the significance of the jackal design? She looked around again for a museum staffer, wondering if the one who had run off might have returned, when both her upper arms were seized in painful grips. She jumped, struggled, but the two uniformed men were giving her no quarter for escape.

One grimaced as he tightened his grip. "You need to come with us."

CHAPTER 30

Rose sat in a tiny office in the back corridors of the museum. Her jaw ached where she ground her teeth in frustration. Her wrist stung, chafed by the handcuff gripping it too tightly, the other end secured to the back upright of the straight-backed chair she sat on. Those goons who grabbed her weren't police, just museum security. They had no right to detain her, certainly not to physically restrain her. They had taken her bag away and left it on the desk outside the room she had been locked in. Anger seethed through every fiber of her, and no little fear. After what had happened to her sister's friend, what might have happened to Lily herself, Rose knew a lot of her anger was a cover for her terror. And where was Crowley? Was he oblivious to all this? Was he locked in another office somewhere else? She decided not to mention him unless someone else did, just in case he was still under their radar.

Through the tiny window in the door she saw one of the security guards talking with a man in a suit. The suited man glanced at the door and grinned. He said something else to the guard then came into the office. He closed and locked the door behind him, then sat facing her, a narrow aluminum desk between them. He remained silent, impassive. Rose sneered inwardly. She wanted to demand to know what was going on, demand he unlock the handcuff painfully securing her to the chair. She wanted to remind him his men weren't any kind of police and all of this was highly illegal. At least, she assumed it was. Did different rules apply in America? Regardless, she realized he was playing a petty power game, waiting for her to talk first. Stubbornness was one of her best skills. She forced herself to relax and stare at him. They remained that way for what felt like an age.

Finally the man lets out an exasperated sigh. "My name is Hargrave."

Rose nodded, kept silent.

Hargrave clicked his tongue in annoyance. "So, you're back, eh? Which one did you plan on stealing this time?"

Shock washed over Rose. She knew she had never been

here before, and for a micro-second she had felt a thrill of relief. He had the wrong person. But of course, he thought she was Lily. Stand them next to each other and the differences were legion. See each of them a few days apart and no one could tell the difference, it seemed. That only added to her anger. But she chose to play dumb.

"I don't know what you're talking about."

"Don't waste my time. I'm more than happy to involve the police, but frankly, all I really care about is the jar. Assuming you haven't already sold it on the black market, you can return it and I'll forget the whole thing. I'm a reasonable man, and I hate paperwork."

"Return the jar?" she asked, trying to buy time to think.

"Yes. Simple as that." Hargrave raised a warning finger. "And I'll be able to tell if it's a fake. Don't think you can trick me."

Rose realized she had to buy space with a little honesty. "I don't know what you're talking about." As Hargrave opened his mouth to speak again, anger glittering in his eyes, she added, "You want my sister."

He barked a laugh, and then flashed a pitying smile. "You don't really think I'll believe that, do you?"

Rose drew a deep breath, calmed herself in order to speak slowly and clearly. It wouldn't help if they got into a shouting match. "I know how this sounds. My sister is missing. I'm trying to find her and I believe she was here five days ago, maybe less." Hargrave's insistence on the theft and Rose's culpability removed all doubt that Lily had been to the museum. There was some hope in that. At least she had made it out of the hellish airport.

Hargrave shook his head. "I don't believe you. One of our docents recognized you as the woman who asked a thousand questions about the jackal-headed canopic jar... the one that disappeared later that night."

Rose frowned. "The jar is still there. I was just looking at it moments ago."

"That's a reproduction, to keep the display intact." He paused thoughtfully. "How did you manage it? Hid inside an office and slipped in after hours, I suppose. But to avoid all the security measures? Impressive."

Rose sighed, shook her head. "It wasn't me. It was my sister, Lily. I really need to find her, she might be in danger.

Look in my bag, out there on the desk. I've got pictures."

Hargrave's brow furrowed. He turned and went out into the front office. He returned with her bag, locking the door behind him again. It disturbed Rose that he kept locking them in. He put the bag on the small table between them and sat down again.

Rose used her free hand to reach into the bag, then sighed, remembering that Crowley had the pictures. "Actually, my friend has the pictures I was thinking about," she said, reluctantly admitting she wasn't in the museum alone. "He was asking around about my sister, to see if anyone here remembered her."

Hargrave rolled his eyes. "Your friend has them. Of course. And you're going to stick to the sister story?"

Rose wished she had some photos on her phone or something. Why hadn't she thought to do that, in case the hard copies were lost? It was infuriating. "It's true! We both want the same thing, to find my sister!"

Hargrave shook his head. "I'm going to give you..." He glanced at a clock on the wall. "Ten minutes to change your mind. If you are willing and able to return the jar, we can move on with our lives. If not, we'll involve the police."

CHAPTER 31

Denver Museum of Nature and Science

Rose stared at Hargrave's retreating back, shock making her tremble. Or was it rage? In all honesty, probably equal measures of each. Maybe she could convince him to look back at CCTV footage from the museum. They must have plenty of records. He could compare her and Lily and see for himself that they looked alike, but not the same. Then again, CCTV might be grainy; this guy might simply refuse to see it. He claimed to want to avoid involving the police but was reluctant to resolve the situation otherwise. She struggled at the cuff attaching her to the wooden chair, but it was too tight to slip out from. And securely fastened to the back, between two horizontal bracing bars. No way to slip it off the leg or anywhere else. Rose growled, low in her throat, angry and upset.

His threat hung heavy in the air. Ten minutes. She paused, thoughts tickling at her mind. She forced herself to sit still for a moment, took a couple of long, deep steadying breaths. Why was he so eager to make some kind of deal with her? What paperwork would there be for him if the police were called? She assumed he would be interviewed and it would be the cops doing all the paperwork. A smile ticked one side of her mouth briefly. He was trying to play her, calling her bluff. If someone had really stolen something from a museum, the police would be called as a matter of course. She suddenly found that she didn't trust Hargrave at all. Something wasn't right.

In any case, she certainly couldn't produce the stolen canopic jar, so there was no trade to be made anyway. Clearly Lily had taken the relic, but what for? Rose would give anything for a chance to study the thing in detail, maybe figure out some of Lily's thinking that way. Perhaps the replica in the museum exhibit was accurate and there might be details she couldn't see from the display case.

But what if all this was paranoia? Maybe Hargrave really just wanted a simple life and was trying to protect himself from the chaos of a police investigation. She really didn't want to deal with the police, didn't need that complication. Who knew what might happen then? She also worried that her Asian features might complicate any dealings with American law enforcement. Stories were all over the news lately and she didn't like any of them. Perhaps she'd be fine, especially with her English accent, but she didn't want to find out.

Either way, whether Hargrave was playing her or really about to call the police, it wouldn't go well for her. And where was Crowley? She needed to get away, get back on Lily's trail.

She gasped in surprise as the door banged open and Hargrave stood there, eyes dark with anger. It had only been a few minutes, five at most.

"Right, I'm not playing anymore." Hargrave strode forward, planted his hands on the desk and loomed over her. "Where is the jar you stole?"

"I told you, I didn't…"

"Did you sell it? Who bought it? Was it Gray or Bell? What do they want with it?"

Rose gaped, the machine gun questions making it hard to think.

"What does the mark on the bottom mean?" Hargrave was yelling now, leaning forward, spittle flying from his lips. "Do Gray or Bell know the meanings?"

Rose was overwhelmed by the intensity of the questions, but something hovered in her hindbrain. Something familiar. A memory sparked, the capstone from Denver Airport flashed into her mind. Gray and Bell were the surnames of the Grand Masters listed either side of the set square and compass Masonic logo. She could see the words clear as day in her mind's eye.

Claude W Gray Snr, Grand Master and Benjamin H Bell Jnr, Grandmaster.

Her eyes widened at the memory and Hargrave barked a sound of triumph.

"I knew it! The bastards! What are they up to?" Hargrave's hands trembled with rage. He pulled open a drawer on his side of the small desk, grabbed out a notepad and tape dispenser.

Rose watched, puzzled and frightened, as he tore pages from the notepad and taped them over the small window in the door. Puzzlement turned to deeper fear as he locked the door again and turned back to her. He reached into the drawer once more and drew out a box cutter, used his thumb to slip the blade out. It glittered in the overhead fluorescent light.

Rose tried to lean back, but the chair blocked her as Hargrave leaned over the table and moved the blade in a slow figure eight in front of her face. "From this moment on, I'll accept nothing but the truth from you. No more games, no more stories. Spill it."

Something in his eyes left Rose in no doubt that he would gladly cut her. She was out of options. "All right! All right. I'll tell you everything."

Hargrave relaxed a little, but remained wary. The blade stayed threateningly between them.

Rose took a deep breath, swallowed, tried to think straight. "It's connected to the airport here."

Hargrave scoffed. "Well, yes, that much is obvious."

Rose racked her brain, tried to figure any connections that might be convincing. She remembered Mike and his wild conspiracy theories about the strange and disturbing murals. Theories which, in fact, appeared less wild by the minute. The image of the small cart inscribed on the floor came to mind. The letters *AU AG*. "They're having trouble with the formula," Rose said suddenly, her mouth dry, heart hammering.

"That was no formula on the bottom of the jar," Hargrave said. "No more games!"

"I don't know what it was, or even if that's why they wanted it."

Hargrave's eyes narrowed. He shook his head, stood up from the table as he thought, his eyes drifting up to the ceiling momentarily.

It was the chance Rose had been waiting for. Hoping for. She sprang to her feet, grabbed the upright of the chair she was cuffed to, and whipped it up and around. It smashed into Hargrave's head with a sickening crack, the vibration feeding back into her hand, shocking her wrist. Hargrave grunted in pain, blood flooded one side of his face as he dropped to one knee. He put out a hand to steady himself, struck out blindly with the box cutter in the other. But Rose was already moving around the small table. She hefted the chair high and brought it crashing down on him once more. It slammed across the back of his head and his shoulders, the wood splintering and splitting in half a dozen places. Hargrave collapsed like a sack of rocks, blood trickling onto the pale floor tiles. As Rose bashed the chair against the floor, finishing the cracks, someone tried to open the door from outside, found it locked. Rose freed herself from the chair, the cuffs hanging loose from her wrist as whoever was outside began hammering on the door, calling

Hargrave's name. Rose looked around, eyes wild, and realized she was trapped.

CHAPTER 32

Denver Museum of Nature and Science

The banging continued, heavy thuds against the door. Rose stood with her feet planted wide apart, looked left and right. She felt like a caged animal, impotent and scared. The man's voice outside yelling for Hargraves rose from concerned to desperate.

"Open the door! Let me in now! Hey!" More crashes sounded in the room outside, like the man was trying to kick the door in. The wood flexed and bulged, the frame creaked as wood began to give way.

Rose crouched, grabbed the box cutter from the fallen Hargraves. He groaned and shifted on the floor and she realized she was relieved to see that. She had feared she might have killed him, though he deserved no less for threatening her with a blade. She stood again, box cutter raised and prepared to defend herself. Then the man outside yelled again, but this time he sounded concerned. She caught the distinctive sound of fist meeting flesh and the door banged once more as something heavy hit and slid down.

Rose strained to hear, then Crowley's voice came through the wood. "Rose? You in there?"

She shot forward and unlocked the door, pulled it wide. A security guard, groaning through bleeding lips, fell into the room and she hopped back. Then she rushed forward and gathered Crowley in a fierce hug.

"Let's get the hell out of here," he said.

She went to step over the unconscious security guard, but paused, rummaged through his pockets. She found a set of keys and tried several before one fit the handcuff lock. With a sigh of relief she cast the manacles aside and they hurried out.

"I couldn't tell where you'd gone," Crowley said as they jogged along. "I asked one of the staff and she looked contrite, cast a glance this way. Next thing I know, I see that guard hammering on the door and I figured only you could be at the center of that kind of drama."

Rose let out a laugh, partly relief. "I thought I was in serious trouble. He was going to cut me."

"Why?"

"Turns out Lily stole something from here. I'll explain later. But there's a replica." She ran for the exhibit but two burly museum guards stepped out in the corridor ahead of them and sneered. Rose skidded to a halt.

Crowley grabbed her arm and hauled her back. "Let's just get out of here."

Sirens sounded in the distance, getting unmistakably closer.

"That's not good," Crowley said. "They'll pull up out front and that means we can't get to our rental car."

"So what do we do?"

"Well, I'm not in any mood to try to explain things to the police. Let's find an emergency exit and leave the car behind."

"Oh, man," Rose said. "We're never going to able to rent another car anywhere in the world the way we're going."

Crowley led them around a corner and they saw a fire exit at the end of a short corridor. They ran to it and looked out the window nearby.

"This is the back of the building," Crowley said. "Good."

He hit the bar across the door and it burst open, the claxon of fire alarms bursting out immediately. They were only on the first floor and hammered down the stairs, found another door at the bottom and ran out into a light rain being carried on a cool breeze. Rose had never been happier to be outside.

"Which way?"

Crowley pointed and they ran. They rounded the building and found themselves in a wide green park. Down a short slope and across a cement path, and Crowley pointed again. "Head for those trees, I guess."

The grass was slippery from the rain, but not treacherous. As they headed towards the trees, Rose caught the echoes of distant shouts and the sirens sounded as though they were right behind. Past the trees a narrow cement path wound off across the park and they followed it, feet slapping.

Someone behind yelled, "There they are!" and Crowley cursed loudly.

They redoubled their pace and emerged into a narrow road. Dozens of cars were parked nose to the curb on their side. Opposite lay a rough footpath, then a high, thick hedge.

"Stay with me, don't pause!" Crowley said and Rose wondered what harebrained scheme had come to him. Before she had time to consider it much more, he ran to the hedge and crouched, fingers laced together. "Up and over!"

She gave him a frustrated look, but didn't dare stop. In two strides she reached him, put one foot in his hands and he boosted her up and over. She crashed into the top of the hedge, felt a solid wall somewhere inside it, but didn't stop to investigate. Ignoring the spikes and scratches, she rolled over and dropped down the other side among thick trees. As she turned to look, Crowley himself came flying over the top like some crazed ninja. How he had gained such momentum she couldn't even guess, but it made her smile.

"They went over the top!" someone yelled.

Another voice shouted, "Then follow them!"

Crowley gritted his teeth. "Run!"

They dove between the trees, jumped a low ditch and then both skidded to a halt, eyes and mouths wide. An enormous elephant stood before them, looking almost as surprised as they were.

"What the hell..?" Crowley muttered.

Then Rose remembered the map she'd looked at to guide them to the museum. "Er, Jake? We've just jumped straight into Denver Zoo."

"I guess we should be thankful we didn't land in the lion enclosure."

Rose took a deep breath. "Let's go. Move nice and slow."

Crowley took her advice, sidestepping away. "I know rhinos and hippos are bad news, but how dangerous are elephants?"

She shook her head. "I don't know. And I don't want to find out."

Crashing sounded through the trees behind them and a voice shouted, "Freeze!"

"Leg it!" Crowley said, and they bolted.

A gunshot rang out, bark burst off the tree by Rose's ear, but her cry was drowned out by the sudden and deafening bellow of the elephant. The ground shook as it charged. Rose risked a glance over her shoulder and saw two men, neither police nor museum security guards. But they had bigger problems to worry about as the enraged beast barreled at them and raised both front legs in attack. The men each rolled in opposite directions and the elephants huge, round feet slammed into the ground where they had been moments before.

Then Rose rounded a tree and lost sight of the confrontation.

"We must remember to send Dumbo there a thank you

card," Crowley said. "Here, up you go!"

They had emerged into a wide sandy area with gray stone walls along one side. Beyond the wall was a building with large glass windows and a sloping roof. To the other side, a large muddy-edged pool of murky water and beyond that a crowd of wide-eyed tourists. Crowley was pointing to the rocky wall.

Again he boosted her up, then scrambled up behind. They ran along, clambered up the next section of wall, higher than the previous part. That brought them within almost reaching distance of the sloping metal roof of the building behind. Not waiting for Crowley to lift her again, not needing his help, Rose ran and jumped. She caught the edge of the roof, hauled herself up, and turned to check Crowley was still with her.

He was smiling as he dragged himself onto the slippery sloping metal. "Impressive! Now watch your step, this wet roof is deadly."

She couldn't argue with that. They cautiously made their way along it, away from the elephant enclosure. They still heard the enraged creature trumpeting in fury; several others in the wide open space and two in the water had turned to look. The beasts all began lumbering towards the cries of their friend and Rose spared a thought for the two suited goons. She hoped they would be smart enough to go back the way they had come and not shoot the innocent creatures. Then again, bets were still odds on favorite for the elephants, this many against two men with pistols. And who were those guys anyway? Associates of Hargrave, she presumed. And with that she lost all sympathy for them, given they had shot at her and Hargrave had threatened to cut her. She hoped they were both stomped to death under giant elephant feet. Some natural justice meted out.

"This way," Crowley said. He had found a drainpipe and they shimmied down.

Rose was glad to have her feet back on solid ground, on the public paths of the zoo. They jogged along, quickly making space between themselves and the enclosure.

"Let's hope no one recognizes us," Crowley said. "We'd better just find our way out."

They hurried past rhinos and hippos and saw the large buildings of the main entrance up ahead. They joined a group of people all heading for the exit and Rose was about to allow herself a sigh of relief when she saw a group of at least five or six policemen come running up on the other side of the gates. She ducked back, Crowley beside her.

"So damn close!" she said.

Crowley pursed his lips, thinking. Then he said, "They're not after me, I don't think. Which means they're just looking for a woman of Asian appearance, right?"

"I guess, unless those security guards at the museum or the goons in suits have radioed them. Those guys saw us running together."

Crowley looked left and right, then smiled. "This way."

"Where are we going?"

"These places never let you leave without passing through at least one gift shop. Follow me."

A few minutes later, and several dollars lighter, Crowley and Rose emerged from the zoo gift shop in entirely new outfits. Changing in a café toilet had been easy enough, but the choices had left them both looking faintly ridiculous. Crowley wore oversized khaki shorts and a jacket with about a thousand small pockets in it. He looked like a parody of Steve Irwin. He had an *I Heart Denver* trucker cap on, pulled low over his eyes. Thanks to slightly misguided efforts at multiculturalism, Rose wore a bright red and green sari and had a silk scarf emblazoned with parrots pulled over her head and around her face like a niqab. It was an insulting pastiche of cultural appropriation, but it left little of her to be recognized.

They waited for a sizeable group of people to come along, then heard a man in a tour guide jacket calling, "Bus leaves in ten minutes!"

A dozen or so people jumped up from a couple of café tables they had pushed together and headed for the exit. Crowley and Rose fell in behind them and a few minutes later they were past the police and hurrying along East 23rd Avenue toward downtown Denver. When they were well clear of the zoo, they allowed themselves a laugh.

"Let's find a hotel and catch our breath," Crowley said.

CHAPTER 33

Crowley and Rose slipped into a McDonald's and changed back into their regular outfits once they were a good distance from the zoo, but they kept the disguises in case they needed another incognito exit.

"I'm really not sure how incognito we were back there," Rose said with a laugh.

"True, but we didn't look like us." Crowley looked at the menus above the busy serving area. "This stuff is barely food, but I'm hungry. Let's take a moment."

They ordered burgers and fries, and tall cups of over-processed post-mix cola, and sat at a corner table. They had their back to the wall and could see both entrances to the restaurant. Crowley was pleased to have a chance to rest and eat, to catch their breath, but they needed more than a few minutes. Fatigue dragged on him again. Rose put on a brave face, but she had to be as tired as he was. As he ate, he poked around on his phone and found a simple but suitable looking motel about ten miles from the Denver city center.

When they'd finished their meals, they hailed a cab and had him drive them out to the Red Lion Inn & Suites. It was a brick building in two-tone orange and white brick. It had a restaurant, good-sized, clean rooms, gym and pool. Way more than they needed. But it felt entirely anonymous and that helped to ease Crowley's anxieties.

"I think maybe we should get a shared room," he said. At Rose's raised eyebrow, he added. "If these people are after us, especially given how easily they killed that guy at the airport, I don't like the idea of us separating."

"Fair enough," Rose said. "Let's get a twin."

Crowley pursed his lips. He wanted to push, to suggest a queen bed, but knew it would be foolish. He booked the room and they locked the door behind them.

"I need a shower," Rose said, and headed straight to the bathroom.

When she emerged, fully dressed again, she slumped down on her bed, stared at the ceiling. "So what now?"

Crowley had been thinking about that. "I wish we knew what Lily learned from that canopic jar she stole."

"Or what she plans to bargain for with it."

Crowley hadn't thought of that. "Interesting. You think she's trying to set up a trade for something else? This Anubis Key maybe?"

Rose shrugged into her pillow. "No idea, but maybe. Or perhaps the jar itself is a clue about the Key." She glanced at Crowley, her eyes heavy with concern. "Honestly, it's our only clue, right?"

"I guess so."

She sat up, pulled her knees into her chest and hugged them. "Maybe we should go back to the airport and poke around."

Crowley considered that. "I think there's certainly more to be learned there," he said eventually. "It's just too bizarre a place and we barely scratched the surface."

"I think it's what's under the surface that matters."

"Yeah, you're probably right. But I'd rather avoid the place unless we have hard evidence Lily's there. Or some better idea about what to look for. Where to look."

Rose sighed. She took her phone out and began searching through websites.

Crowley moved to sit beside her. "What are you looking for?"

"Seeing if there are any images of that stolen canopic jar, but there aren't. No mention even of the theft that I can find." She searched again, different terms. "And there's not even any information about that particular part of the museum's display. It's too specific, I suppose."

Crowley fished out his phone. "I wonder if Cameron can hack the museum's computer system and search for information on it."

Rose looked up, eyes bright. "That's a good idea! Museums keep inventories and detailed records. If he can hack those it'll be great."

Crowley dialed the number. "Let's see."

As the phone rang, Crowley had a sudden lurch of guilt that he hadn't even thought to check the time difference. He glanced out the window at the darkening sky, tried to do some quick mental arithmetic, but Cameron answered.

"Jake! You must be psychic, I was just about to call you."

"Ah, not too late?" Crowley was relieved.

"Nah, man. I've never been one to go to bed early, you know that. What do you need?"

"What were you just about to call for?"

Cameron laughed. "You first. How much are you going to abuse my good will this time?"

Crowley grinned. He missed his old mate. How long, he wondered, before Cameron wouldn't be able to help himself and had to come out into the field again. Crowley wondered if his pal's leg would be up for it. He was still guilty at effectively getting the poor man shot last time. "I was wondering if you could hack the records of the Denver Museum of Nature and Science. We need the notes on a particular exhibit."

"No problemo. I can probably do that. Give me the details."

Crowley told Cameron as much as he could about the display and the collection of canopic jars. Rose threw in extra information that he relayed and added that one jar had been stolen and that might be in the records too. Rapid tapping stuttered over the line as Cameron typed up the notes as they were related.

"Okay," he said, when Crowley ran out of details to share. "You'll have to leave that one with me."

"And what do you have for me?" Crowley asked.

"I've finally hacked into 'Iris Brown's' credit account. She's covered a lot of territory in a short period of time."

Crowley grinned. "He's got your sister's credit card details," he said to Rose's questioning expression. "Go on, Cam, I'm putting you on speaker." He tapped the button and Cameron's voice came through, tinny, but loud.

"Five days ago, she was in Denver, as you already know."

"What specific purchases here?" Crowley asked.

Cameron named a rental car agency at the airport, a restaurant, and the Denver Museum of Nature and Science. "None of that is particularly helpful I imagine, given what you just told me. Seems you're ahead of this stuff."

"We are. So where did she go next?"

"There's a string of petrol and food purchases south along the interstate highway system, through New Mexico and into Arizona."

Crowley and Rose exchanged a confused glance. "Where could that be leading?"

"The last purchase being at a place called Dragoon," Cameron said. "That's in Arizona, and happened three days ago."

Crowley frowned. "Where the hell is Dragoon, Arizona?"

"Near Tucson."

"That doesn't really help, mate. I'm as English as you are and not looking at a map."

Cameron laughed. "You ever heard of Tombstone? Gunfight at the O.K. Corral, Wyatt Earp, Johnny Ringo, and Doc Holliday?"

"Sure, I've seen the movie. Isn't that near the Mexican border?"

"Sure is. And it appears to be in the middle of nowhere."

"Why would Lily go there?" Crowley wondered aloud.

Rose shook her head, shrugged. "Hardly seems in keeping with the theme of things so far."

"And it beats the hell out of me," Cameron said. "But the good news is, her next stop is much more interesting."

"That right?" Crowley said. "So where are we going next?"

He could hear the amusement in Cameron's voice. "Vegas, baby!"

Chapter 34

Rose stared straight ahead as they drove west on Interstate 70 toward the Rocky Mountains. The peaks and ridges, dappled with white snow against the steel gray sky, were mesmerizing. She wished the circumstances were different so she could enjoy the experiences more. Last time her life had been threatened for her strange, back-covering birthmark. This time she was worried about her sister and murderous unknowns were on her tail. And Lily could already have fallen prey to them for all she knew.

They had decided to forego the twelve-hour drive to Dragoon, Arizona and head directly to Las Vegas in hopes of shaving some time off Lily's lead. Flying would certainly have been faster, but the airport seemed an unnecessary risk. She wondered if this third rental car would survive or end up wrecked or abandoned like the others. She stole a glance across at Crowley, his face passive as he drove. She'd be lost without him and that bothered her. She would be forever grateful for his help, but preferred to think she could do all of this without him if necessary.

And maybe she could. Sure, she didn't have Cameron as a contact, but a lot of the leads and information came from her own associates through the museum and her own research. Though she and Jake did make a formidable team. Truth be told, he wouldn't be nearly so effective without her. Maybe she should stop thinking about how much she needed him and remind herself that they needed each other. But that set off a chain reaction of thoughts she wasn't prepared to face and she quickly looked out at the view again, eager to shake them off.

They had driven in a companionable silence for a long time when Crowley said, "I just can't figure out why Lily went nearly all the way to Mexico. Surely it's not a hotbed of the Anubis Cult."

"I've been thinking the same thing. There must be a reason. We've learned so far that she's damned focused and determined. She wouldn't take a break for sightseeing. Let me see what I can dredge up."

"Good idea."

She fired up her phone again and reclined the seat a little, settling in for some detailed research. She pulled a notepad and pen from her bag to keep track of anything she discovered. After only a minute or two, she said, "I don't suppose she'd visit the JH Smith Grocery Store and Filling Station."

Crowley laughed. "Well, she might. You know, for groceries or fuel. Is that relevant?"

"It's the first place listed on the 'Things to Do in Dragoon' website. Along with the local cemetery, Texas Canyon, and an art gallery."

"Dragoon pretty proud of its tourist attractions then?"

Rose gestured with the phone. "It would seem so."

"I wonder if the art gallery has any Egyptian artifacts," Crowley said.

Rose looked up the gallery website and perused the images. "It looks like Southwestern artwork for the most part. Let me search a bit more specifically. She opened a new browser window and began looking up various terms along with 'Dragoon Arizona'. She tried Egypt, Egyptian, Anubis and got no relevant hits. She tried regional stuff, like Cairo, Darshur, Denver, the Denver museum, anything that might cross-reference with their search or anything they'd uncovered so far. Still nothing. On a whim, she tried mummy and immediately got results.

"The Thing," she read out, then barked a laugh. "Best horror film ever made."

Crowley frowned. "What?"

She stared at him in disbelief. "You haven't seen *The Thing*?"

"A horror film?"

She was a little bemused by his lack of recognition. "Yes a horror film! John Carpenter's *The Thing*. Kurt Russell, Wilford Brimley, Richard Dysart?"

Crowley stared at her, slowly shook his head.

Rose pointed, nearly shouted, "Look at the road!"

Crowley swerved back into his lane, grinning a little manically. "Sorry about that." He glanced over again and she gestured angrily at the road ahead.

"Eyes front!"

"Okay, okay."

"But seriously, I can't believe you haven't seen *The Thing*."

"Never even heard of it."

"Man, it's truly the greatest horror film ever made. We have to rectify that situation and watch it soon." Rose couldn't help laughing, shook her head.

"But why did you bring up *The Thing*?" Crowley asked.

"Because I saw it here." She tapped her phone. "But not the 1980s horror film."

"What then?"

Rose turned her attention back to her research. She smiled subtly. She enjoyed these bursts of passion she occasionally elicited from Crowley; he was often so taciturn otherwise. So pragmatic. She really didn't know all that much about him, and wanted to know more. But that came with complications.

"It's a roadside attraction in Dragoon," she said. "It's called The Thing."

Crowley harrumphed. "Disappointing." He flicked her a grin, then looked forward again.

"They claim," Rose went on, "that it's an Egyptian mummy found somewhere in the southwestern US."

"Bollocks!" Crowley said. "A mummy found there? That's ridiculous."

Looking at the website, Rose found herself doubtful too, but the claim was bold as brass. Then again, a lot of places made bold and entirely fictitious claims, especially if they were hard up for tourist dollars and there wasn't much other industry in the region. The place was clearly a tourist trap. "I agree," she said to Crowley. "It's almost certainly codswallop. But there's no harm in checking. I'd hate myself if I ignored even the most tenuous lead and it turned out to be important."

"So you want to change direction and go to Dragoon after all?" Crowley sounded as though he was entirely reluctant to do that, and Rose had to agree.

"Not yet," she said. "Hang on." She found the phone number and called, bracing herself for a conversation with a complete kook.

It rang a few times and then, "The Thing, Kelly speaking, how may I help you?"

Rose smiled. That had to be one of the more unusual receptions she'd ever received. "Hi, Kelly, I hope you *can* help me. I'm trying to track down a missing person and I know she was in your neck of the woods recently." She gave the date they had learned from Cameron of Lily's visit to Dragoon from her fake credit card. "Her name is Iris Brown. She's half-Chinese, short black hair, but English, so she has an English accent. Does that ring any bells?"

"Sounds pretty specific," Kelly said. "But I wasn't working that day. I maybe could pass the information along to Burt, he was working then. Maybe he can give you a ring?"

"Thank you, that would be really good of you." Rose read out her phone number and heard the scratch of a pencil as Kelly wrote it down. "While I'm on," Rose said, "can you tell me about The Thing?"

"Oh, The Thing is truly wonderful, dear. It's a sight like you wouldn't believe. A wonder of the world, a thing utterly unexplained!"

Rose stifled a laugh at the woman's sudden switch into her sales patter. "But what is it?"

"Oh, honey, you really need to see it for yourself."

Rose knew from the websites she'd already looked at before calling that the thing was supposedly a mummified mother and child. One story said it was purchased around 1950 for fifty dollars, another said it was found in the desert nearby. Numerous theories had sprung up, but Rose hadn't dug too deeply before calling. "Well, if ever I get down that way I certainly will come to see for myself," she said. "Out of interest, do you guys have any artifacts related to Anubis?"

A moment of silence hung in the air, then Kelly said, "I'm sorry, a new what?"

"No, no. Anubis. Ancient Egyptian god of the underworld. Has the head of a jackal?"

"Oh no, nothing like that. But you really should come and see all the wondrous things we do have."

"Thank you, I'll surely try. And if you could get Burt to call me about Iris Brown, that would be really helpful."

"I will. I hope you find her. Bye for now."

"Bye." Rose hung up, disappointed. She should have known the call would be as good as pointless, but a part of her had hoped it might suddenly crack things wide open. She grew tired of running across the country, picking at one tiny, useless clue after another. It felt like they were on a treadmill, going nowhere fast. "How much further to Vegas?" she asked.

Crowley laughed. "This land is nothing like England. A good eight hours, I'd say. You might as well get some sleep. I'll wake you when we're there."

CHAPTER 35

Las Vegas

Night had fallen by the time Crowley cruised the rental car slowly down South Las Vegas Boulevard, commonly known as the Strip." He admired the sights which were strangely so familiar, even though he had never seen them in person before. American culture permeated the English-speaking world like water through canvas. It was impossible not to be exposed to it, particularly via movies and television. And given the nature of those mediums, there was little more visually enticing than the Strip. He had seen it a thousand times, from the 60s or 70s onwards. He'd enjoyed it from afar in dozens of films and now he found himself driving along it. The sensation was a little surreal.

They passed the pirate ship of Treasure Island, brightly lit and wrapped in ropes of white light. Everything was brightly lit, countless bulbs and LEDs and neon tubes. Crowley couldn't imagine the amount of power this single street would suck out of the grid every hour. He drove by The Mirage's famed volcano, wide, squat and brown, sitting in its lake of fire. It stood dormant at that moment, but ready to spring to life. Then Caesar's Palace, with its faux-Roman architecture, impossibly tall columns topped with enormous triangular pediments. Up ahead and to the left, the Paris Casino, with its replica of the Eiffel Tower lit up in golden light, and a huge hot air balloon, vertically striped with bright blue neon, wrapped with crisscrossed gold bands.

"Look at that," Rose said, her voice quiet with wonder. She was looking out of her side of the car, across the street at the dancing fountains of the Bellagio. Lit gold and white, they burst up and arced, crossed each other and made rising and falling waves with their incessant jets.

They passed the epic cross-shaped MGM Grand, its facade of green and glass standing out even among the other sparkling and dancing lights. Moving images along each side advertised a forthcoming David Copperfield show.

"Holy crap," Crowley said, laughing under his breath. "Look at this one!"

New York New York dominated their view, a behemoth of a recreation of the city's skyline, a pale blue lit Statue of Liberty standing high over them as they drove by. Liberty looked down on the tourists swarming the pavements, wide-eyed and grinning, snapping photos and losing dollars. Dozens of costumed characters paraded around, sequins and giant feathers, rainbows of color and acres of bare, tanned flesh. Numerous shysters and hucksters shilling for business. "Porn slappers," agents who advertised prostitution, milled along the strip wearing brightly colored T-shirts emblazoned with logos and phone numbers.

GIRLS GIRLS GIRLS
GIRLS DIRECT TO YOU IN 20 MINUTES
PLEASURE CLINIC

"Where are the women advertising the male hookers?" Rose asked, half-amused, half-appalled at the brazen displays of decadence and debauchery.

"You make a good point," Crowley agreed. "I just think women would naturally be more discreet about the whole thing. I don't doubt there are plenty of male sex workers busy in this town."

Rose smirked. "Every variation of gender for any kind of taste and persuasion, eh?"

"Undoubtedly."

Shrill cries rang out from passengers in the bright yellow cars of the New York New York roller coaster high above. The loops and whorls of red track swept around over the roofs of the fake skyline, a swirling, complicated pattern.

They drove by the Excalibur, looking like a giant child's play castle with its tall white crenelated turrets and bright red, blue and yellow colored roofs, then left the crush of the busiest part of the Strip. As they moved along, the spaces were wider, the crowds less dense, and up ahead they saw their destination. The massive black pyramid of the Luxor Casino.

Its glassy, jet surface danced with reflected light. A brilliant spotlight beamed up from the capstone, an enormous Sphinx lying out front surrounded by golden light and palm trees.

"Classy," Rose said sardonically.

Crowley laughed. "Can't argue with that, but, you know…" He gestured back over his shoulder at everything else they had seen so far.

"True," Rose said. "I don't think the word 'ostentatious' appears in any Las Vegas dictionaries."

"Or garish, tasteless, crass." He flashed her a grin. "The list is pretty long, I think."

"I think so, too. Man, what a place. It's so horrible, but just so incredible too. So enticing. And in the middle of the desert!"

"Insane."

A street-side obelisk, with the word LUXOR in lights, loomed up ahead. Behind it, the massive sphinx guarded the entrance to the casino.

"This, though," Crowley said, jabbing his chin towards the huge black pyramid. "After so recently seeing the real thing, it's..." He searched for the word.

"Take your pick from the list we just made," Rose said. "Or try tacky, kitschy, ugly. It's just plain cheap and nasty, really."

"Brummagem," Crowley said with a grin and Rose laughed.

"Right."

He pulled up beneath an overhang and a valet hurried to park the car for them. The man gave them a ticket which Crowley slipped into his wallet. They entered the casino and both paused, stunned by the immensity of the place, jammed with pseudo-Egyptian decor. The walls sloped up towards a point, obviously mirroring the external structure of the place, myriad glowing balconies looking down on them. There were entire buildings inside the place, an IMAX cinema, obelisks and giant carved pharaohs in stone thrones. Crowley grimaced, thinking it was no doubt all fiberglass and chipboard.

They went to check in to the hotel and the receptionist told them there were very few rooms lefts. Only a few small doubles remained, no twins. Crowley avoided Rose's eye and said that would be fine. He gave the name James Crow. He mused on the fact that he hadn't used that particular pseudonym for a long time. The identity seemed like a lifetime ago.

Rose raised an eyebrow as he signed the form, but didn't say anything. Was she interested in the new name, or annoyed about the situation with the room? He decided to default to the former. After all, there was nothing they could do about the sleeping arrangements.

He grinned. "I'm allowed to have a few secrets."

They headed up to their room, slightly perturbed about the motion of the elevator as it moved at a 45-degree angle, following the pyramid shape of the hotel. They entered the room and Rose stared for a moment at the one double bed.

"You heard the clerk," Crowley said. "It's all they had. Is it a problem?"

"Not for me," Rose said. "But I was hoping there might be a fold-out sofa or something. You're going to be uncomfortable on the floor."

Crowley couldn't prevent the wave of frustration, though he knew she owed him nothing. He simply couldn't get past the fact that before they *had* been growing so close, and then she'd cut him off after the Landvik situation. Gone cold, utterly.

"I'll be okay," he said, determined not to be a dick about it. "I've slept in a lot worse places than a hotel room floor."

Rose smiled, put a hand briefly to his cheek. "Thanks."

"What happened between us?" he asked. As her face began to shape into outrage, he quickly said. "I don't mean any presumption, I wouldn't expect us to share a bed. But there's a distance here that didn't exist after we got back from Lindisfarne. In the hospital in Edinburgh with Cameron, things were... good, you know? I'm not expecting anything, really. I'm just confused about what happened after that. You've never explained why there's suddenly this new remoteness between us."

Rose opened her mouth, eyes narrowed, like she was about to finally reveal some deep truth. Then she let it go, her eyes widening again and she plastered on a smile. "We're too tense. This is Vegas. Let's dress up and go have some fun."

Crowley frowned, shook his head slightly. He didn't want to push her, but something was up and he needed to know what. Partly for his own peace of mind, even his own ego, but also because he was worried about Rose and what she was hiding from him. And why.

"I need a break," Rose said. "We both do. For one night, let's not think about Lily, Anubis, or anything else." She smiled and it was genuine. She gave him a sly wink.

Crowley refused to read anything more into that than exactly what she'd said. He knew his own needs and biases were likely to make him think too much of simple gestures, but he had to admit it sounded like a good idea. Blowing off some steam would do them both good. Though he was puzzled by her sudden change of demeanor. Was she keeping something from him to protect him? He could only nod.

Rose grinned and planted a kiss on his cheek.

CHAPTER 36

Crowley woke to a thumping headache and refused to open his eyes. A groan escaped him as he turned over on the hard floor and pressed his face into the pillow. The carpet was nice enough, and he genuinely had no issue sleeping on the floor. It would probably do his back a world of good. There were plenty of extra pillows and blankets too. But despite all that, he felt awful. And it was entirely self-induced. His stomach churned, he desperately needed to pee, but refused to rise just yet.

Through the maelstrom of ache and self-pity, he tried to recall the night before. They had certainly blown off some steam. Rose had been right, they both needed it. Vague images passed over his mind's eye. Gambling, laughing, drinking, even dancing at one point in a club somewhere. More drinking. There had been a moment too when they held each other tightly during a slow song, and Rose had said something that he hadn't quite caught. He'd asked her to repeat it, but the alcohol was back under control and she shook her head, smiled, gave him a quick, hot kiss on the lips.

"Not now," she'd said, and then the music had struck up again and she'd laughed and twirled away. They ended up back at the hotel casino and Crowley smiled, patted the pocket of his jacket on the floor beside him. Sure enough, there was a thick wad of bills in there. He'd struck a sweet winning streak late in the night and pulled down a few thousand dollars. Then they'd quit while they were ahead, to the scowls of the dealer.

They had come up to the room and Crowley had very little recollection of any details. In fact, after the big win and deciding to call it a night he couldn't even remember riding the elevator or arriving at the room. He lifted the blankets and willed his eyes to unstick for a look. He still wore his pants and shirt from the night before, just his jacket, shoes and socks removed.

He frowned. The light was too bright and he had clearly been the perfect gentleman. He groaned again as he sat up and looked across to the double bed. The sheets were disheveled, but the bed was empty.

The bathroom door opened just enough for Rose to poke

her head out, clouds of steam swirling around her bare shoulders. "Morning! I was about to wake you."

"You're perky," he said, his voice thick and gravelly. He cleared his throat as she laughed at him.

"You're not!" She disappeared from the door, then quickly returned wrapped in a thick, fleecy robe. "Get in there and have a shower, shave, all that. I'll order up a big room service breakfast. Treat ourselves."

Crowley forced a grin. "We can afford it."

"We sure can. I can't believe how much you won last night."

"It'll keep us going for a while." He stood, winced against the extra throb in his head, but tried to ignore it. "It was a good night, wasn't it?"

Rose put her hand, hot from the shower, against his cheek. "It really was, Jake. Go clean up."

Crowley had to admit the hot shower was a good idea. When he emerged in clean clothes, the room was redolent with the aromas of coffee and bacon, and his stomach growled. He sat with Rose, who had waited for him, and they silently devoured the generous portions including eggs, toast, buttered mushrooms and hash browns. After a silent ten minutes, Crowley sat back with a sigh, patted his stomach.

"Man, that's better."

Rose dug around in her bag, then produced a packet of analgesics. He took a couple gratefully, swallowed them down with the last of his coffee.

"Fully operational again?" he asked.

Rose grinned. "Like a completed Death Star?"

"What?"

She sighed. "I really have to get you in front of some books and films. Your pop culture education is sorely lacking."

He shook his head, smiling. "Whatever. So, we've got the Grand Canyon tour today."

"We have. The last purchase on Lily's credit card was that tour, so I booked the same agency, same tour."

"Good idea."

Rose stood, brushed herself down. "I just need to use the bathroom, then we'd better get moving."

As the bathroom door clicked locked behind her, Rose's phone rang. Crowley saw the number was from Dragoon, Arizona. It must be the roadside museum calling back. He took up the phone, answered it.

"You the folks wanted to know about a lady called Lily came through here?"

"That's right, we're trying to find her. She's missing."

"Well, that surely is bad news."

"It is," Crowley agreed. "Can you tell me anything about what she did there? You talked to her?"

"I did. Had a brief chat but wasn't able to help her."

Crowley frowned, wondered how best to ask the right questions that might trigger the right memories. "What was she specifically asking about?"

The old man hummed down the line as he thought. "Well, she asked about the origins of The Thing. She specifically wanted to know if it had any connection to a man named Kinkaid."

Crowley scribbled the name down on a napkin stained with egg yolk. "Who's that?"

"I have no idea, and I told her that, too. I told her the mummy was donated anonymously years ago, and without any account of its origin. It's a mystery, and no mistake."

"Can you tell me anything about it?" Crowley asked. "Is there anything at all that's not a mystery?"

"Well, I can tell you what I told your missing friend. We don't actually know anything, but rumor has it that the mummy was found somewhere in the Grand Canyon."

The trails converged again, Crowley thought. That's where they were going anyway, without any more information than they had the day before. "Okay," he said. "Thanks very much for calling. I appreciate it."

"You're welcome. I hope you find your friend."

"So do I. Thanks again. Goodbye."

"Take care now, and God bless."

Crowley hung up as Rose emerged from the bathroom.

"Who was that?" she asked.

"I'll tell you on the way. Let's go."

Crowley and Rose stood on the sidewalk outside the casino with about a dozen other tourists, all waiting for the tour bus to arrive. Crowley's head was beginning to clear and he listened casually to the conversations around him. Everyone was excited about the Grand Canyon, some first-timers, others extolling its virtues from previous visits as if they were the tour guides. One guy, somewhere in his fifties, with a paunch and a know-it-all face, was busily explaining geological phenomena to a group of three young women who were clearly not interested. One even rolled her eyes and turned her back, so the man moved around to be in front of all three again, completely oblivious. The three girls laughed and shook their heads at each other.

"That guy could mansplain at an Olympic level," Rose said, face creased in a frown.

"And here's me thinking the golf was a boring Olympic event to watch."

Rose grinned at Crowley. "Hey, at least there are some people into golf."

Crowley watched the man still gamely explaining things the three girls didn't want to know. "I bet if they televised this there'd be guys who thought it was great viewing."

"MRA meetings?" Rose wondered.

"Redpill TV!" Crowley said and they both laughed.

The man turned to look at them, some moment of self-awareness perhaps. He had one eyebrow raised.

Crowley smiled at him. "Those girls were thoroughly fascinated by the depth of your knowledge; look."

The man turned back to see the girls had quickly moved away and stood huddled together, giggling. The mansplainer harrumphed and folded his arms just as the tour bus pulled up. The guide, a short, pot-bellied guy with an unkempt beard, glasses, and a fanny pack strapped across his doughy midsection, stood on the steps as the door hissed open and welcomed them all in a loud, croaky voice. He seemed oblivious to the early hour and his passenger's bleary eyes.

"Come aboard, grab a seat, I'll tell you more about the tour on the way there."

Crowley and Rose boarded and Crowley watched the three girls wait for the man who had bored them to choose a seat before they got on the bus. Once he had sat down, they came on and chose a spot as far from him as possible. The man saw Crowley watching and shot him an acid look. Crowley raised his palms and shrugged, but couldn't help chuckling. Some people.

The guide introduced himself as Giles and started to explain the journey and how long it would take. He droned on with weak jokes and boring anecdotes, which Crowley tuned out as he let his eyes close and his head rest against the seat back. For all the improvement in his condition since he had awoken, he still felt as though he could sleep for a solid week if given half a chance.

He realized he had dozed off when Rose jabbed him in the ribs with an elbow.

"We're just pulling into the Hualapai Indian Reservation," she said.

Giles was still waffling and Crowley looked up as he said, "And don't forget to keep an eye open for the lost Egyptian city!"

Crowley and Rose exchanged a glance. "Let's wait till everyone's off and ask," Crowley said. Once they had parked up and everyone had disembarked, Crowley and Rose stood to leave last. Giles smiled patiently as they approached.

"So what was that about the Egyptian City?" Crowley asked.

Giles laughed. "It's just a local legend, but if you want to hear the story, go to the   Grand Canyon Skywalk office and ask for Shepherd."

"Shepherd," Crowley said. "That a first name, last name, or nickname?"

Giles shrugged. "All I knows is the man is old, crotchety, and easily offended. Don't piss him off."

CHAPTER 37

Crowley and Rose moved away from the bus and both stopped dead, staring. The Grand Canyon yawned before them, epic in scale. Crowley had never been before, had only seen it in photos and on TV. To be standing before it, he felt less than insignificant. A speck in the universe, an ant on the face of Everest.

"Wow," Rose breathed.

"You've never seen it before, either?"

"No. It's amazing."

The rock faces were orange with the early sun, striations of light and dark topped with rolling domes and deep fissures. In places, the cliffs sloped down, or sliced into the space of the canyon like knives. In other places the walls were sheer drops, inconceivable distances. After they had stared for a few minutes, Crowley pointed.

"The Skywalk is that way."

A building of brick and orange fascia with gold-tinted windows stood right on the edge of the canyon not far away. On the far side of it, an arch of orange metal and glass reached out into space above a sheer canyon wall that dropped out of sight into depths unknown.

"Oh, hell no," Rose said in a whisper.

"We only have to talk to someone inside," Crowley said, hoping he was right. He had no real fear of heights, but a structure like that seemed to him to be tempting fate. He was a history teacher, not an engineer. He had trouble dealing with this kind of human denial of nature.

They entered the building and found themselves, not surprisingly, in a large and well-stocked gift shop. Rich, savory smells drifted to them from a nearby café. The only person in view was an old man behind the ticket counter. Crowley walked over, smiled warmly.

"Is Shepherd here?"

"Shepherd?"

"Yeah, I was told he was the person I needed to talk to."

The old man smiled. "That right? Well, if you want to see

him, you'll need to buy a ticket."

Crowley grimaced, then looked out of the large windows towards the Skywalk arcing out into nothingness. A lone old man strolled along it, a Native American in a security guard's uniform. Crowley gave a curt nod. "Two tickets then, please."

"Jake!" Rose said, alarmed. "I'm not sure about that!" She pointed.

Crowley had already seen it. Not only did the walkway curve far out into thin air, its floor was clear glass. "It'll be okay," he said, as much to himself as to Rose. "Come on."

He took the tickets from the old man and they headed out. Rose looked doubtfully at the transparent deck hanging over the sheer wall, but took a deep breath and stepped onto it. Crowley followed, a strange vertigo causing his stomach to lift and turn over as he walked seemingly in the open air. The canyon wall fell away from them, the rock-strewn bottom impossibly far below.

"Wooo, I feel like I'm flying," Rose said, spinning in a circle with her arms out to either side.

"You're enjoying this now?" Crowley couldn't help laughing. "I'm not well enough over my hangover for this kind of activity."

"You can't deny the experience is surreal."

And he had to admit it was. A warm breeze blew over the glass sides of the walkway and ruffled their hair, birds wheeled high above, the incredible landscape stretched away from them in every direction, even down.

"I wonder if Lily came here?" Rose said as they reached the apex of the arch. She put her hands on the railing and leaned forward, looking into the vanishing distance.

"Perhaps she's somewhere down in the canyon even now," Crowley said.

The security guard pacing the skywalk, apparently watching out for cameras, which were strictly forbidden, began his walk back towards them from the far side.

As he approached, Crowley said, "Excuse me, are you Shepherd?"

The guard shook his head. "Shepherd is inside. The man who sold you tickets."

Crowley couldn't help but laugh, and Rose joined him. "Scoundrel!" she said

They took a last look at the breathtaking views, then made their way around the arch and back inside. Shepherd grinned at them from behind his counter, his skin deeply wrinkled, long iron-gray hair pulled back in a ponytail tied with a leather lace. "I never said I was working on the Skywalk," he said. "Only that you'd have to buy a ticket if you wanted to talk to me."

"You just conveniently left out the bit about it being you," Crowley said.

Shepherd let his shoulders lift and drop as he let out a cackling laugh. "What is it you want anyway?"

"We're looking for my sister," Rose said. "Her name is Lily, but sometimes she goes by the name Iris." She held out a photo for Shepherd to see.

The old man scratched his chin. "I remember. Lord, you look a lot alike. I talked to her just a couple of days ago. She wanted to know all about the Lost City."

Chapter 38

Crowley and Rose enjoyed the sights for a couple of hours until Shepherd was able to take an early lunch break. He said he'd be happy to chat with them in exchange for a free lunch at Guano Point.

Crowley had looked into that while they waited and discovered a strange history. In the 1930s, a boater passing on the Colorado River far below in the bottom of the canyon had discovered a guano cave. For the next twenty years unsuccessful attempts were made to mine the nitrogen-rich guano for fertilizer. Then, much to Crowley's amazement at the existence of such a body, the U.S. Guano Corporation heard there was more than one hundred thousand tons of guano in the cave, so they bought the property. They spent $3.5 million to construct a tramway system to extract valuable bat waste. An aerial tramway was built from the mine to what was now known as Guano Point, with the cable head-house built on land leased by the Hualapai Tribe. The cableway then crossed the river, a distance of 7,500 feet, some 2,500 feet high.

But by 1959, in a bit of bad luck for the U.S. Guano Corporation, all the cave's resources had been exhausted. The original prediction of one hundred thousand tons turned out to be closer to one thousand tons. And the bad luck was compounded when, shortly after this discovery, a U.S. Air Force fighter jet crashed into the overhead cable system and permanently disabled it.

An intricate leaning structure of wooden beams, mostly the cable head-house, remained in place as a monument to the entire endeavor and Guano Point got its name and subsequently became a tourist attraction with the Guano Deli, where visitors were exhorted to "dine on the edge of the canyon."

Once Shepherd's relief arrived and took over the ticket sales at the Skywalk, the old man led Crowley and Rose to a battered old Jeep and drove them out to Guano Point, which wasn't far away.

Crowley bought everyone barbecue chicken and they sat at an outside picnic table watching a trickle of tourists make their way along the narrow trail atop the steep dropoff and up onto the Guano Point overlook. An eagle, its wide wingspan black against the orange and tan canyon sides, wheeled past far below, but still high above the canyon floor and the shining brown ribbon of the Colorado River snaking through.

"Quite a history to this place," Shepherd said as he sucked chicken meat off the bone. Crowley thought the old man looked a little like a plucked chicken himself, all skinny, wiry limbs and sharp movements.

"We read all about it," Rose said. "Amazing really."

The old man chewed slowly and thoughtfully. "I was here, you know. When the mine was still operating. Only a kid, of course."

Crowley smiled, wondering what changes the man might have seen in his life. Probably not always for the better. "So what can you tell us about the lost Egyptian City? It seems a strange thing to even suggest here."

Shepherd chuckled. "Don't it just?" He sniffed, took another bite of chicken then nodded, almost to himself. His voice took on the lilt and musical tones of an inveterate storyteller. "It started in 1909. A front page article in the Phoenix Gazette told of an expedition sponsored by the Smithsonian Institute. That expedition uncovered a vault filled with Egyptian artifacts."

"That's kind of my business," Rose said. "But I've never heard of it."

Shepherd gave her a crooked smile. "Few have. It's the stuff of conspiracy theorists now. The Smithsonian denies that any authentic Egyptian artifacts have been found anywhere in North America. Some claim it's a cover-up."

"Why would they do that?" Rose asked.

Shepherd shrugged. "I don't know, but I have a theory. The scientific community is slow to change. If you make a discovery that's too far out of the norm, you're ridiculed, even blackballed. The Smithsonian might not have wanted to subject itself to that, especially a hundred years ago, when its reputation wasn't as well-established as it is now."

"Well, I can agree with most of that," Rose said thoughtfully.

"The other possibility is they discovered something they didn't understand, or something they thought needed to be kept a secret." Shepherd gave them another grin before tearing into another chicken leg. "That's my favorite theory," he said around the meat in his cheek.

Crowley was skeptical, but decided to play along. He was becoming used to how pointless his skepticism often turned out to be. "How did they find it?" he asked.

"Well, the story goes that a man named Kinkaid discovered it."

A jolt passed through Crowley as he recognized the name as the same one Lily had inquired about. He glanced at Rose and the look on her face said she'd thought the same thing. It was the first solid connection between all these wild loose ends they were trying to round up.

"Kincaid, eh?" Crowley said, trying to prompt Shepherd to reveal more if he knew it.

The old man's voice slipped into storyteller tones again. "Yep. G E. Kincaid. He was traveling alone down the Colorado River, prospecting for minerals. In a remote area, he spotted, from a great distance away, unusual stain patterns in the sedimentary formations of the wall, nearly two thousand feet above the river bed. When he reached the area, he found a series of steps that started just above what was then the level of the river. They ran about thirty yards to a rock shelf and beyond it, a cave. He noticed chisel marks and decided to explore. He saw enough to know he was on to something big. He took a few artifacts, made his way back to civilization, and contacted the Smithsonian."

"So, what did they find?" Rose asked.

"The story goes that an expedition led by a Professor Jordan of the Smithsonian went with Kincaid back to the site he'd found. And in there they discovered a whole underground city. The cave, which couldn't be seen from above or below due to the shape of the canyon wall, led back to a massive main chamber, with passageways radiating out from it all around. I could sketch it for you."

Rose dug in her bag and produced her notebook and pencil. Shepherd hunched over the page, holding the pencil in a strange overhand grip, his face close to the paper, tongue playing at the corner of his mouth. When he sat back, they saw he had drawn the river, with a passage leading into the rock, a cross-passage at right-angles, then the passage led on to a large circular room with thirteen more corridors evenly spaced around it.

"It looks like a sunburst," Rose said.

"It does," Shepherd agreed. "Apparently, the Smithsonian found loads of rooms inside. Storerooms, armories, granaries, a dining hall, crypts holding rows of mummies. An entire small city of stuff."

"That's crazy," Rose said.

Crowley had to agree with her. How could even the Smithsonian keep something like that quiet for all this time?

"That's not even the craziest part," Shepherd said, his grin back in place. He clearly enjoyed spinning these yarns and Crowley had to wonder how much the wily old guy was playing them, winding them up for a free lunch and some entertaining sport.

"It gets crazier?" Rose asked, eyebrows high.

"Outside of one chamber they found a series of hieroglyphs they'd never seen before. Inside, the air was strange. It had what Kinkaid called a 'snaky smell.' He claimed their lights wouldn't penetrate the blackness. It was as if the air had substance." Shepherd sat back, quietly sucking on a chicken bone as he watched them take in that strange and hard to believe tidbit. Before Crowley could draw breath to challenge it, Shepherd pointed the cleaned bone at Rose and said, "Your sister was really interested in that, for some reason."

Rose said nothing, only nodded thoughtfully. Crowley watched her instead of Shepherd, realized something in that last bit had affected her quite deeply. Maybe some connection she had drawn between the old man's story and Lily's quest for something beyond death. The Stygian blackness Shepherd had described had all the hallmarks of something supernatural enough.

Shepherd sniffed again, sat forward to take more chicken. The man had the appetite of a teenager. "Anyway," he said around a mouthful. "One of their researchers died trying to explore that room."

"How?" Crowley asked.

"Don't know. Went in and never came out again, I think. They sealed it up."

They sat in silence for a moment, then Crowley shook his head. "No offense, but do you honestly think this could be in any way real? Any of what you've told us?"

Shepherd considered, lips pursed, before finally replying. "Yes. I do. Considering the sheer size of the canyon, plus the inaccessibility of most of it, it's not at all unreasonable to believe there are systems of caves and passageways that have gone undiscovered. And don't forget that Kinkaid emphasized that the cave was impossible to spot from above or below."

"Don't people take helicopter tours through the canyon?" Rose asked.

Crowley nodded, pleased with her thinking. He hadn't thought of that.

"Parts of it," Shepherd said. "But not everywhere. And there's a limit to how far down they're willing to go. So many of the gorges are narrow, and the winds strong and unpredictable. It's not safe. And not only that, but large parts of the canyon are off-limits, even to park staff. Claims of unsafe caves and dangerous waterways. There are a lot of areas, big areas, that no one is allowed near. Can it really be that dangerous compared to other parts?"

"Well, it could," Crowley said.

Shepherd smiled. "It could, sure. But I don't think it is."

"Is it possible that Kinkaid misidentified it?" Rose asked. "Maybe it was an Anasazi cliff dwelling, something like that?"

Shepherd shook his head. "You know your stuff. But no, it's unlikely. The Anasazi built beneath overhangs, but they didn't live in caves or tunnel into the stone. And Kinkaid specifically mentions finding bronze age weapons inside, in pristine condition." The old man's eyes narrowed and he looked around, lowered his voice. Crowley thought it a bit melodramatic considering no one was paying them any attention.

"There is a part of the canyon," Shepherd whispered, "where the prominent features are given Egyptian names. The Tower of Set, Tower of Ra, Horus Temple, Osiris Temple, Isis Temple. And, what's more, this is a huge area, and it's one of the forbidden zones I was just talking about. One of the ones even off-limits to park personnel. You ask me, I think there's something there the government, or somebody, wants to hide."

Rose took a long slow breath, thinking. Crowley couldn't decide how much this old man really believed, and how much he enjoyed as drama. He obviously loved to tell a story, but how much was fiction?

"Do you have any theory as to where, exactly, the city is located?" Rose asked.

Shepherd sighed. "I've tried for years to figure it out. There are problems with minor parts of Kinkaid's account. Maybe he got some names wrong, maybe he changed a few details to protect the location. But my money is on the Haunted Canyon region. That's what I told your sister too."

He let that sink in for a moment, then bobbed to his feet with surprising agility. "Anyway, I thank you kindly for the lunch and I hope I was of some assistance to you. But I must get back to work and I have an errand to run first. You can catch a shuttle back to your tour bus whenever you please, but have a look around here first. It's quite a place."

Crowley stood and shook the old man's hand. "Thank you, we really appreciate your time."

Rose shook his hand too, echoed Crowley's sentiments. Shepherd smiled, and strolled away to his jeep.

They sat down and watched him, keeping quiet, then Crowley said, "Quite a story."

"Especially that bit about the dark chamber where one of the party died. Or disappeared. My sister would definitely be interested in that."

"Yeah, I think that could well be what Lily was looking for."

"So what next?" Rose asked.

Crowley grinned. "Next stop, Haunted Canyon."

CHAPTER 39

Luxor Hotel and Casino, Las Vegas

When they got back to the Luxor Hotel, Crowley rang Cameron.

"What's up, buddy?"

Crowley smiled. "You sound chipper for… what time is it there anyway?"

"Time?" Cameron asked. "What even is it? I was hoping to hear from you again. I'm glad you haven't been shot or anything. What do you need?"

"Well, your concern warms my heart. I need you to snoop through some conspiracy theories and crazy talk and see if you can root out any seeds of truth."

Cameron groaned. "Oh, man. Information I can deal with, crazy talk is not my specialty."

"But you'll do it for me, right?"

"What is it?"

Crowley laughed at Cameron's resigned tone and relayed the key points of Shepherd's story. "So what it boils down to," he concluded, "is that we need to know the most likely location of this actual Lost City, starting with the Haunted Canyon area Shepherd mentioned."

"If it even exists."

"Yeah, if it exists," Crowley admitted. "I think there's something to it, even if it's been blown out of all proportion by the retellings of the story. I bet there's something, even if it's just some weird caves. We need to know and we need to go there."

"Okay. Leave it with me. I'll start digging."

"You're worth your weight in gold, Cam."

Cameron laughed. "I'll eat extra doughnuts in case I ever need to cash myself in." He hung up without another word and Crowley smiled as he slipped his phone back into his pocket.

"We need to get back out there under our own steam," Rose said. "We can't have tour guides or park staff know that we're snooping about."

"True, but I'm too tired to drive through the night. Let's get a good rest here and we can head off early tomorrow. Hopefully Cameron will come through with some directions by then."

"Yeah, you're probably right. You think we'll catch up with Lily in the Haunted Canyon?"

Crowley shrugged, shook his head. "No idea. But I do think we're more likely to get some solid leads there than anywhere else we've looked so far. You want to head up to the room?"

Rose gave him a sidelong glance, seeming to measure his intent. He winced internally. If nothing had happened last night, drunk and footloose, it was unlikely that anything would happen now. But he wished she would talk to him. Something was eating at her and he wanted to help.

"I feel like moving around, not being cooped up," she said.

"Okay. You want to wander through the casino?"

"Sure."

As they walked, Crowley let his gaze roam over the grandiose décor. The Egyptian gods and architecture seemed foreboding now, oppressive. Not so much cheap and tacky, but as though they had a weight of intent. Maybe portent.

"I wonder why Lily decided to stay here," he said.

"That's an odd question," Rose said. "Why not stay here?"

"Well, it's not one of the nicer casinos. It's at the south end of the strip, away from the action. If she was only interested in learning about the Lost City, why not stay in a more affordable hotel off the strip?"

Rose looked around, frowned. "That's a good point, actually. But this one is very much her theme."

"If she's really that into Egypt, the real history, it seems to me she wouldn't think staying here was cool."

Rose considered that a moment. Eventually she said, "That's true, I suppose. The Lily I know would probably roll her eyes at this décor. But who knows? Maybe she just wanted to have a bit of fun."

"Although I wonder if there's something more here. Are there any Egypt-themed exhibits currently running?"

Rose shook her head. "Just the Human Body and the Titanic."

Crowley stopped short, something tickling at his memory. His brow creased in thought.

"What is it?" Rose asked.

"The Titanic. It rings a bell." He thought harder, then it came to him. "That's right! I once heard a tale of a cursed mummy that brought death and disaster to everyone who possessed it as it made its way out of Egypt and on to England.

Finally, an Egyptologist purchased it and arranged for it to be shipped to the States. On board..." He grinned at Rose.

"The Titanic?" she ventured. She gave him a mocking look. "Really? A cursed mummy sank the Titanic?"

Crowley grinned. "May I remind you that we're currently on the hunt for a lost Egyptian city in the Grand Canyon?"

"Touché," she replied.

"Maybe Lily knew about that legend and she stayed here to check it out more. Two birds and all that? Perhaps we should check it out, too."

"Might as well," Rose said. "We've nothing better to do."

Crowley gave her a sly look, deciding to push his luck. "We had fun last night, even though I ended up on the floor after all. We could always, you know…"

Rose looked at him levelly, eyes slightly haunted. She opened her mouth, her expression like she was about to say something serious, then shook her head. "Not now, Jake."

He wondered what she might have been about to say before she changed her mind. He sighed. "Okay then. But I wish you'd talk to me."

"I will. But for now, let's go."

They headed over to the exhibits and paid their admission. Inside the Titanic exhibit were numerous artifacts from the sunken ship, in glass cases and on tables, each labeled with whatever details were deemed relevant. As they wandered through, signs and videos told the story of the ill-fated voyage. Letters and articles gave names and faces to the dead, the weight of history and humanity entangled. Crowley knew the story well, he'd taught aspects of it numerous times, but it was only when he saw the actual, physical articles that the history came off the page and into his heart. These were real people, this was a real event. It was too easy to think of history like stories, no more than a tale to be told. But that was the beauty of history. It happened, it shaped everything that came after. These people lived this story in every cold, wet detail.

Rose took some time to admire an impressive replica of the grand staircase. Glossy wood swept down from either side to a final central descent, brass edges glittering on every step. A bronze statue of a toga-clad boy holding aloft a torch stood at the bottom. "Imagine it," she said quietly as Crowley came to stand beside her. "Imagine the people, gliding up and down there. Imagine the dresses!"

He kept silent. Eventually they moved on.

In one display, visitors were invited to press their hand against a block of ice for as long as they could, in order to understand what the passengers felt when they plunged into the icy water.

"Challenge you?" Crowley said, with an impish grin.

Rose smirked. "Sure. Let's see what you got, soldier boy."

They counted to three, then each planted a palm flat to the ice. Both acquitted themselves well, but Rose finally gave up with a muttered curse, whipping her hand away and rubbing her palm vigorously against her leg to warm it up.

To prove a point, Crowley kept his hand there for several more seconds, smiling at her, before slowly removing it and wiping it gently on his jacket to dry it.

"What are you?" Rose asked, brow creased. "Some sort of Buddhist monk?"

He grinned. "Not exactly."

Her frown deepened. "What's that supposed to mean?"

He wiggled his fingers like a stage magician. "An enigma wrapped in a mystery, that's me."

She slapped his shoulder. "You're a bellend, that's what you are."

They both laughed and Crowley was pleased the mood was genuinely lightened from the discomfort before. They were comfortable with each other, relaxed good friends, even if they might never be anything more. Much as Crowley wished there could be more, he was glad of the friendship and wouldn't do anything to jeopardize it.

He pointed. "Check it out."

The exhibit space was capped off with a large section of the Titanic's hull. They entered the room, kept dark to recreate the night the ship went down, with only enough concealed lighting to allow them to see the artifact. It gave Crowley a chill to consider that night, April 14th, 1912, the sudden panic and alarm in the darkness.

As they admired it, Crowley noticed an employee standing in the corner, keeping an eye on things. He wondered how much the staff might know of the exhibit's history. He saw no harm in asking.

He nudged Rose and they approached the employee.

"Hi there."

The woman smiled. "Hello." Her name badge said Janet.

"This is quite the exhibit here," Crowley said.

"Fascinating, isn't it?" Janet said. "One of those moments in history that almost everyone in the world knows something about. Everyone's heard of it."

"How much more do you know?" Crowley asked.

"What do you mean?"

"Well, there are a lot of stories surrounding the main event, aren't there? The cursed mummy story, for example. You heard about that one?"

Janet laughed softly. "I have, actually. That, in fact, is quite a story."

CHAPTER 40

Rose and Crowley exchanged a glance and Crowley shrugged. Rose smiled, then turned back to Janet.

"Can you tell us about it?"

"I can. I really enjoy this story, in fact. It all starts with the Princess of Amen-Ra, who lived some 1,500 years before Christ. After she died, she was laid to rest in a deep vault at Luxor, on the banks of the Nile, in a beautiful wooden coffin. There she lay in peace for centuries, until, in the late 1890s, four young Englishmen, rich and self-important, visited the excavations at Luxor. They were offered an ornately fashioned mummy case. Of course, it contained the remains of the Princess of Amen-Ra." Janet lowered her voice. Clearly she'd told this story often enough that she'd added theatrics to the retelling.

"The young men all wanted it and drew lots to see who might win the honor of the purchase. The one who did parted with several thousand pounds and had the coffin delivered to his hotel. A few hours later, he was spotted walking out into the desert and was never seen again."

Crowley grinned. He loved tales like these, but never believed them as fact. "This is shaping up like a classic," he said.

Janet smiled. "We've barely started. Of the three remaining young men, the ones unsuccessful in the purchase, one was accidentally shot by an Egyptian servant, his arm wounded so badly that it had to be amputated. The third man returned home to learn that the bank holding his entire wealth had collapsed, and the fourth suffered an illness so severe that he lost his job and was reduced to selling matches in the street."

"That really is a litany of bad luck," Rose said, unable to hide a half-smile. "You think this is all true?"

"Certainly," Janet said. "But is it a curse or coincidence? Bad luck? I wouldn't make a call on that."

"But the coffin is still in Egypt at this point," Crowley said.

"True, but it was owned by the man who disappeared into the desert and, somehow, eventually arrived in England. Apparently it caused other misfortunes on its way, but they're not recorded. What is known is that it was subsequently bought by a London businessman. However, after three members of his family were injured in a road accident and his house nearly lost to fire, the businessman decided he believed the stories of its curse and donated it to the British Museum."

Crowley laughed softly. "That's not entirely altruistic!"

"Perhaps not. Especially as, according to the stories, as it was being unloaded in the museum courtyard, the truck mysteriously fell into reverse and trapped a passer-by. As two laborers were carrying the casket up the stairs, one fell and broke his leg. The other, until that point in perfect health, died two days later, for reasons unknown."

"Okay," Crowley said. "This body count is really racking up. Surely none of this can be true."

Janet held up one finger, smiling. She clearly did enjoy this story. "It's when the coffin containing the Princess was put on display in the Egyptian Room that things really got bad."

"This isn't all bad enough already?" Rose asked.

Janet began counting occurrences off on her fingers. "Night watchmen frequently heard hammering and sobbing from the coffin. Exhibits in the room were strewn about at night. One watchman died on duty. Others simply quit. The cleaning staff refused to go anywhere near the Princess. The final straw, apparently, was that a museum visitor threw a dust cloth at the face painted on the coffin, and then his child died of measles soon afterward."

Crowley scoffed. "That's the most tenuous connection yet! Surely that can't be attributed to the Princess."

Janet laughed. "Maybe not. But the museum authorities had had enough and the reputation of the curse was costing them business. They had the Princess of Amen-Ra taken to the basement where they decided it could do no further harm. But in less than a week, one of the people who moved her was seriously ill, and the man who supervised the transfer was found dead on his desk.

"This was all too good, of course, for gutter journalism to ignore. The papers had a field day. One photographer took a picture of the Princess's coffin and the face on it came out in the photo as a hideous and distorted horror. The photographer, they say, went home, locked his bedroom door, and shot himself."

"Oh man," Crowley said, really beginning to enjoy things now. "I want to see the movie of this. Why isn't there a Hammer House of Horror film about this story?"

"More to the point," Rose said, "what does any of this have to do with the *Titanic*?"

Janet smiled. "Let me wrap this up. After the events I've relayed so far, the museum sold the mummy to a private collector. There were more deaths, more misfortune, and the new owner hid the thing in his attic. Enter Madame Helena Blavatsky, well-respected occultist. The private collector asked her to lift the curse and, on entering the house, she immediately felt the evil presence and searched for its source. Without the owner's help, she found her way to the attic. She informed the new owner that there's really no such thing as an exorcism, that evil can't be removed, and that he must get rid of the Princess and her casket.

"Of course, after all the brouhaha before, no British museum would touch it. Finally, the new owner found a brave and skeptical American archaeologist who paid well for the Princess of Amen-Ra and arranged for its delivery to New York. The American came along to England and prepared to accompany his prize home on a new White Star liner making its maiden voyage."

"Let me guess," Crowley said. "The *RMS Titanic*."

"Indeed. And on April 14th, 1912, the Princess of Amen-Ra took her greatest toll yet, carrying 1,500 souls to their deaths in the icy depths."

"And that was the end of the Princess, too, then," Rose said. Crowley thought she sounded disappointed.

"Well," Janet said. "That's not the end of the tale. Some say the American collector managed to bribe the crew of the *Titanic* to put the mummy in a lifeboat, from where she was smuggled on board the Carpathia, the ship that picked up the survivors from *Titanic*. And that the Princess of Amen-Ra was safely delivered to New York."

"She just doesn't quit, does she?" Crowley said.

"Nope. And in America, she brought further tragedy to any who handled the coffin. So eventually she was shipped back to Europe on the *Empress of Ireland*. And guess what?"

"That ship sank too?" Rose ventured.

"It did. With the loss of 840 passengers. But somehow, the mummy was saved again. Now no one would hold her and she was quickly put aboard the Lusitania, headed back to Egypt."

"And that one sank too?" Crowley asked.

Janet grinned. "Torpedoed by a German submarine. And no

one knows what happened after that."

Crowley clapped his hands together softly. "Well, I did enjoy that yarn. Thanks for sharing."

Janet nodded good-naturedly. "My pleasure."

"I know this is a silly question really," Rose said. "But is there any truth to it? Any artifacts that might have been the source of the legend?"

"Well, there are so many problems with the story," Janet said. "First among them that there was no Princess Amen-Ra. The men who are credited with concocting the legend probably got the idea from a display at the British Museum of the Priestess of Amen-Ra."

"That's what I was thinking while you told the tale," Rose said. "I've seen that one; it's still on display."

"There is one other legend that links Egypt to the sinking of the *Titanic*, though. Supposedly, a group of passengers were enjoying drinks and cigars, when one, a spiritualist and self-described Egyptologist, began telling the story of a discovery he had made. A Book of the Dead containing a curse so foul that to speak it aloud meant certain death."

Crowley and Rose exchanged a quick glance, something cold creeping through Crowley's gut as he did so. Suddenly the good-natured exchange seemed to have a sinister undertone. He saw that Rose was thinking of the spell too, the one Lily was so keen to learn about. "Did the man say what the curse actually was?" Crowley asked.

"Well, according to the story, no one took it seriously and, after a few drinks, they persuaded him to recite the curse. That night, the ship sank, with only one of the group surviving to tell the tale. The survivor said that, as soon as the man uttered the curse, all the candles in the room went out, and the place went dark. An impenetrable darkness that turned the air foul and strangely thick. He immediately fled from the room, leaving the others behind.

"The *Titanic* went down as the man ran from the room and, though he survived, the others were never seen again. Did they go down with the ship or were they lost in that darkness? The survivor swore the words of the curse were burned into his memory, but he vowed never to recite them. And some people suggest that the curse which was spoken was taken from the coffin lid of the Princess of Amen-Ra. Or the Priestess, depending who you talk to."

"An impenetrable darkness that turned the air foul and strangely thick," Rose repeated quietly. She looked at Crowley and he nodded. Those words had disturbed him too, so similar to Shepherd's yarn.

"It's a great story," he said, to lighten the mood.

"And it's the second time this week someone has asked me about the legend," Janet said.

Rose quickly dug in her bag and showed a picture of Lily. Janet leaned forward to see and said, "That's her." She looked more closely at Rose. "In the low light in here I hadn't noticed the resemblance. You must be family."

"She's my sister," Rose said.

"Well, I hope everything is okay."

Rose smiled, a sad, small thing. "So do we. She's missing."

"Oh. I'm sorry to hear that."

"Is there anything Lily said that might help us? Anything she might have mentioned to you?"

Janet pursed her lips in thought. "She asked about the lost city in the Grand Canyon but I wasn't able to help her with that."

"We've been following that lead already," Rose said. "Thank you."

"Although I remembered something about the lost city after she had gone," Janet said. "It might not be helpful. But if you find Lily, tell her to look into a man named Seth Tanner."

CHAPTER 41

Rose enjoyed the sensation of workout she got from the rough trail. The hot sun beating down, the warm breeze blowing up from the canyon bed, all contributed to a feeling of action. Doing something positive at last, even if it may well prove fruitless. She shifted her backpack into a more comfortable position, heavy with trail rations, water, rope, a few other essentials. Crowley carried a similar load. The Tanner Trail was categorized as "primitive," and received little maintenance by crews and few patrols by park rangers. That only made her appreciate it more; the remoteness and wildness suited her mood. It was recommended only for seasoned hikers, being steep, rocky, with little shade, and the only water source the Colorado River far down below. But she and Crowley were both seasoned outdoors people. She glanced across and saw a slight smile playing across Jake's face. He was enjoying the exercise and fresh air, too.

"This started as an ancient Anasazi and Hopi route to the Colorado River," Rose said. "It's called the Tanner Trail now because Seth Tanner was a friend to the Navajo and Hopi, an explorer, guide, and prospector. He improved the trail so he would have better access to his copper mine. I read up about it last night once we decided this was the most likely next step."

Crowley grinned. "Exactly why I didn't read up about it."

"What?"

"Because I knew you would, then you'd tell me about it."

She punched his shoulder, pleased to elicit a wince. "You make me sound like a swot."

"Well, you *are* a bit of a Hermione! But I enjoy the way you relate history, so it's good." He looked over, smiled reassuringly. "I mean it!"

"Do you realize you just made a pop culture reference?" Rose winked at him, then turned serious. "Anyway, most people think this trail, leading through Tanner Canyon, is where García López de Cárdenas became the first European to encounter the Grand Canyon." She looked out over the vast expanse falling away below them, the striated rock walls, distant rounded cliffs and peaks. "Can you imagine being the first to see this?"

"I'm pretty excited being the… whatever I am. Four hundred fifty-ninth millionth or whatever."

"True. Historians think Tanner Canyon was used as an old horse thief trail. The rustlers would bring the horses this way from Arizona into Utah, then change the brands on the horses en route. Then they'd cross the Colorado River and drive the horses out through the Nankoweap Trail up onto the North Rim. That's why it used to be called Horsethief Canyon."

Crowley laughed and Rose knew he was impressed with her recall again. She enjoyed showing it off, but especially for him. "Museum brain in action," he said.

"You know it. But there's a good treasure story attached to this place too."

"Is there?"

Rose found herself breathing hard from talking and walking the rough trail. "Let's break for a sip of water."

"Sure."

They sat against warm rocks, sipping sparingly from the canteens, looking out over the impressive expanse before them.

"Long Tom's treasure," Rose said. "It's actually a terribly sad story. In 1910 'Long Tom' Watson discovered papers in an abandoned cabin that he realized were written by outlaws. They described a hoard of stolen gold hidden in a cave behind a seasonal waterfall. A couple of years later, Watson began a search of the area. He found nothing and, after two years of searching, gave up in the spring of 1914."

"That's not much of a story," Crowley said.

"So let me finish! He finally returned home along the Horse Thief Trail from Morgan Point, and along the way he spotted a waterfall. He hiked to it and found a cave behind, and in the cave he found a stash of gold nuggets!"

Crowley laughed. "Always the way. You look for something for ages and only when you finally give up do you find it. That's not a sad story though. Sounds like a happy ending."

"Well, it's not ended. As Watson was leaving with his treasure, he slipped and fell, and broke his leg. He couldn't carry anything and had to concentrate on getting out alive. He crawled to the nearby Buggelin Ranch. When he'd recovered from his injury, he tried to go back and get his gold, but couldn't find the waterfall. He ended up committing suicide."

Crowley stared, a look of horror on his face. "Bloody hell.

That's an awful story."

"Told you."

They put their canteens away and took to hiking again.

"So do you really think the Egyptian City could be somewhere along this trail?" Rose asked.

Crowley shrugged. "I wish that employee at the Titanic exhibit could have told us more than Tanner's name in connection with the legend. But it's the only lead we've got. Still, look around. With everything we know so far, this is as likely a place as any."

Rose had to agree with that. "And I wonder if there's a connection between the city and the legend of Long Tom's treasure. These things often overlap and blur together."

Crowley considered. "I suppose it's possible. But Long Tom's treasure cave was supposedly behind a waterfall, you said. There's no mention of that in the legend of the Egyptian city. At least, not that we've heard."

"Or perhaps the waterfall is BS," Rose suggested. "Something to throw people off the trail."

"Or it just wasn't mentioned. Or maybe not there. You said it was seasonal, right? So people wouldn't see it every time. Sometimes there'd just be a cave mouth, high up a canyon wall."

Rose sighed, some of her earlier enthusiasm draining away. "It's all such wild speculation."

Crowley pursed his lips. "Then again, according to your story just now, Long Tom committed suicide after finding treasure. I mean, I can understand the despair of finding treasure but losing it again so unjustly, but maybe it was connected to the mummy's curse?" He laughed, threw Rose a bright grin.

She frowned. She didn't find the idea funny at all, especially when she considered they were no closer to finding Lily, alive or dead. Crowley's smile faded and they walked in silence for a while. After another thirty minutes or so, they came to a deep gorge above the Colorado River. Rose paused, scanned the lay of the land. "Remember how the entrance to the lost city was described as high above the riverbed?"

"Yeah," Crowley said. "You think this is a likely spot?"

"It's the only place we've come to that might fit the description." She moved to the edge to peer over but Crowley grabbed her arm, pulled her back.

"What are you doing?"

"I don't want you to be another muppet tourist falling to

your death in the canyon."

Rose was partly annoyed, but also slightly charmed by his genuine concern. But she wasn't a child. She shook him off. "I'm being careful. You're such a grandma."

Crowley scowled, but couldn't help a smile escaping. "Just…"

"Be careful?"

"Yeah." He sighed.

They walked along as close to the edge as they dared, staying near each other, ready to catch. Rose ignored the slight sensation of vertigo from the vertiginous drop right under her feet. She didn't like being this close to certain death, but their search was too important.

"Don't forget the legend says the cave can't be seen from above or below," Crowley said. "I'm not sure what we're looking for."

"Me either." Rose deflated, stepping back from the edge. "Perhaps we should have hired a helicopter."

Crowley stood, hands on hips, looked around critically. "You know, I think we're onto something here. We just need to come at it from a different angle. Now we've had a closer look, I think maybe coming back in a chopper is a good idea."

"Shall we head back and see about that?"

"I think it's the only option left to us now."

They turned to retrace their steps when Rose stopped, stared at the ground just before them. An eroded line snaked across the trail and down over the edge.

"What's so interesting?" Crowley asked.

Rose pointed out the miniature valley across the trail. "The story of Long Tom's treasure? The seasonal waterfall. It would be a dry bed outside the rainy season."

Crowley stepped up beside her, then crouched to look at the indentation in the trail. It was full of loose rock and dust, but a good couple of meters wide, maybe half a meter deep at the center.

Rose looked back up the trail, followed the declining lay of land. "I think that would probably look like a waterfall at the right time of year," she said. "Falling right over the edge here."

Crowley remained non-committal, but Rose ignored him and moved to the edge of the canyon. "Hold onto me."

Crowley leaped up, hurried over. "Wait a minute!"

"Don't be a grandma, Jake. Hold me."

He grabbed her by the belt and bent his knees to brace himself. "I don't like this!"

She leaned out, peering over the lip of rock. "Ha! I see a ledge, just like in Kinkaid's account. You remember?"

Crowley pulled her back. "I remember. But please, be careful!"

"We need to climb down there and check it out."

Crowley dropped to his belly and scooted forward to look over. He shook his head. "We need to come back with equipment and a plan."

"We both brought rope."

"That hardly constitutes equipment and a plan!"

Rose took a deep breath to contain her excitement and trepidation. Was it really possible they had found what they were looking for? Everything indicated they had. She got down on hands and knees, peered over the edge again. There were lots of handholds. "It's not that far. Put a rope around me, I'll climb down and check it out. You can pull me back up if I get into trouble."

"Are you serious?" When he saw she was, he held up both hands in surrender. "Okay, okay. But I should be the one to climb down."

"What, because you're the man? I'm just a weak and feeble woman, incapable of this manly stuff?" She saw the swift wince of contrition pass over his face.

"That's not what I meant, of course you're capable."

"You don't have to mother me all the time, Jake. Besides, I wouldn't be able to pull you back up."

Crowley let out a deep breath. "This is a bad idea. It's too remote, and not worth the risk."

Rose pointed over the edge of rock. "The city, if it exists, is in a remote location. Otherwise it would have been found already. At some point, we're going to have to take some risks. Besides, what if Lily's down there right now, in need of help?" As soon as that thought had occurred to her, she was convinced and knew she would go down with or without Jake's help.

Before he could stop her, she shrugged off her backpack and slid on her belly, feet first over the edge. Crowley barked her name, panic in his voice, but she was committed. She found a toehold, let herself go further back, then a handhold, then she was away, down towards the ledge of rock below.

CHAPTER 42

Tanner Trail, near Grand Canyon Village

Crowley shouted her name again. She heard the scuff of gravel as he rushed towards her. His hand swept through the air just above her as he made a grab for her. She scrambled down quickly out of his reach.

She gritted her teeth, ignored Jake cursing her stubbornness, and kept climbing. But a fear had set in, trembling in her knees. Already her grip was weakening, her arms shaking. She was strong and a capable climber, but fear started to morph into panic as she realized how stupid she had been, how impetuous. For a brief moment, her frustration at this wild goose chase, her worry that something awful would happen to Lily before she had a chance to mend the relationship, had overwhelmed her and pushed her to reckless action.

Now common sense began to prevail once more. Rose's stomach turned to water, the trembling increased in her arms, as she became keenly aware of her own mortality. Aware of just how far the drop to the canyon floor was from her position, precarious like a fly on the rock face so high up. Although a fly could grip and her grip was failing. The toehold she had last found, that seemed so certain moments ago, felt too small for her booted foot, the handholds uncertain. Cold sweat made her fingertips slippery, rivulets of sweat trickled over her wrists, down the center of her back. She took a long shuddering breath, knowing she shouldn't look down, but she had to know how far it was to the ledge.

"Rose!" Crowley's voice was firm, authoritative, but she heard the fear underlying his brave façade. "Climb back up, Rose!"

She ignored him, looked down. The ledge, which had seemed so close to her excited eyes before, was suddenly tiny and a long way off. Unable to avoid the compulsion, her gaze drifted out, down to the canyon floor, where the dark, serpentine waters of the Colorado twisted through the parched landscape. A tiny sound of horror escaped her. Dizzy, she closed her eyes and tried to control her breathing. A rushing sound, like crashing waves, filled her ears. Her pulse pounded, too strong, too fast.

She felt it in her chest, but in her neck too, in her temples. It would be so easy to just let go.

And with a bright flash of shock and panic, she was alert again.

Crowley's voice came to her as if from a great distance. "I'm lowering the rope. Rose, look up!"

The rope, a big loop at the end, dropped over the rocks and slithered towards her, making a scuffing sound as it slid across the rocks.

"Is a noose the best idea?" she asked, and let out a laugh that was entirely too high-pitched. Too manic.

Crowley's voice remained calm. Concerned, but the fear was gone. He was in operational mode now, doing what needed to be done. She needed to match that, and she knew she could. "It's a bowline knot," Crowley said. "So it won't cinch up... never mind that, just put your bloody arm through it."

Rose realized he was right. There was no time for pep talks or banter. She had put herself in a ridiculous situation and all that remained was to get out of it, quickly. She secured her grip with her right hand, let go with her left, and reached for the rope. As her fingers brushed the bright nylon material, her footing gave way. The stone beneath her right foot crumbled, her leg shot straight down, then her left gave up its toehold on the tiny rock it was wedged against. Air rushed past her as her stomach lifted while her body fell. The rough cliff face shredded her clothes, scoured her skin. She had no time to scream, fingertips scrabbling for purchase, before a powerful jerk bounced her and pain shot through her shoulder.

Her fall was arrested and she realized she managed to hook her arm through the loop as she fell. Just. What felt like a precipitous drop had only been a couple of meters. To add insult to humiliation, she could clearly see the ledge below now and there was nothing there. No cave, not even a crack in the orange rock face. Angry and embarrassed, she found secure footing and a strong handhold and got the rope looped around her chest, secured it beneath her armpits.

She looked up and saw Crowley's face, concerned, eyes wide, looking over the edge. The sun behind him made him seem to glow. "You okay?" he asked.

"Pull me up, Jake."

The way back up was painful as she tried to assist Crowley as much as she could. But she spent more time banging her knees against the rocks than she did finding secure footholds. As Crowley braced and grunted, hauling her up, she collected new abrasions on her face and arms. By the time he pulled her over the edge, thankfully, blessedly, back on solid flat rock, it was all she could do to hold in her rage. How could she have let her emotions overcome her like that? Let her make a fool of herself like that in front of Crowley? And why did she care what he thought? It was all too much to unpack and explore and she let out a roar of frustration.

Crowley stepped back in shock, then quickly came forward again. He reached for her. "You're okay."

She sucked quick, shallow breaths. "Piss off, Jake. We should head back."

Hurt passed over his face, but she ignored it, turned to walk away. But the pain and exhaustion overwhelmed her, sank her in a wave of relief. Her knees buckled and Crowley shot forward, caught her before she faceplanted on the hard rock. He pulled her close and the dam broke. Terrified at how closely stupidity had just lead her to certain death, fear for Lily's well-being, frustration at every dead end, every ridiculous, pointless clue, it all flooded out. She turned her face into Crowley's chest and sobbed.

He held her tight with one arm, gently stroked her hair with his free hand. "It's all right. You're all right."

She found comfort in his strength, knew she was strong too, but was nevertheless grateful at that moment for Jake's stability. But a quiet, private voice wondered if she really was all right.

CHAPTER 43

Crowley felt terrible for Rose, but a sense of relief pervaded his concern. While she had made a thoroughly stupid mistake out there on the trail, she hadn't died. When it came to it, her cool head had prevailed even if she had had to melt down afterward. And that was where the relief lay. He thought perhaps she had needed that outlet, the steam valve blowing on her emotional pressure cooker. All this was hard enough for him but, just like before with the Landvik stuff, it was personal to Rose. She had no way out of it, her sister's life at stake. Given that nothing worse than scratches and bruises had occurred, he was glad she'd had the chance to blow out.

He found a place for them to stay and plan, the Mosayru Lodge in Grand Canyon Village, near the south rim. It was a solid two-story adobe-style building on the outside, but inside had all the trappings of the classic hunting-lodge. Cedar paneling on the walls reflected soft light from antler chandeliers, deer heads protruded from the walls. There was a huge common room, packed with opulent armchairs and couches and a big fireplace crackled in a deep, gray stone hearth.

Their room was simple but comfortable with two large single beds and a desk, TV, clean bathroom. Crowley had given up wondering if they might eventually share a double bed. All things in time. Once they were checked in, Rose excused herself to clean up. She yelped with delight on seeing the big tub in the bathroom.

"I'm going to soak in here for a while!"

Crowley smiled. That would no doubt feel good. "Sure thing."

He laid back on one of the beds and let himself drift in and out of a light doze for a while until movement brought him around again. Rose sat on the edge of his bed.

"Can you help me?"

He coughed to clear his throat, thick from dozing, pulled himself into a sitting position. She wore a heavy toweling robe, her smooth legs visible from its hem, slim feet bare. "Of course, what do you need?"

She smiled uncertainly. "Now, no funny business, okay? I need you to check some wounds."

Crowley steadied himself. "All right."

She paused, then dropped the robe off her shoulders. She wore a smooth black bra underneath, no lace, but a provocative cut. Her skin was smooth and lightly tanned, her shape enough to make the breath catch in Crowley's throat. He shifted uncomfortably to a more suitable position.

There were long grazes up the left side of her flat stomach, under both forearms and across her left shoulder. "Here," she said, pointing to the shoulder.

Mustering all his self-control, Crowley leaned forward for a better look. It was a nasty abrasion, leaking plasma in a few places where she had managed to take off most layers of skin. She held up a make-up removal pad and a bottle of disinfectant.

Crowley took the items and cleaned a few last bits of sand from the wound carefully while she hissed between her teeth.

"Stings?" he asked.

She nodded, looking past him, towards the windows and the wan late afternoon light spilling in.

"You have a dressing?" he asked. "Or I can get one."

"Here." She held out some first aid kit gauze and micropore tape. Crowley put some soothing cream onto the clean wound, then dressed it neatly. He looked down at her stomach, but she quickly pulled the robe up and closed it.

"I did that. It's just hard to see my shoulder well enough to do it one-handed, you know?"

"Of course."

"I did my arms and knees too," she said. She sounded almost apologetic.

Crowley smiled, tried to let her know with that look that he was okay with help she needed, or whatever space. "Cool."

She leaned forward, kissed his cheek, long and lingering. Her lips were hot. "Thank you, Jake."

He forced a weak smile, unsure what to say. The silence between them stretched as they watched each other. Crowley lost himself in her large eyes, imagined running his hands over that smooth flesh she had so recently covered up. He couldn't help himself picturing it.

The silence threatened to grow uncomfortable, then Rose drew in a breath through her nose. She kissed his cheek again, quick and almost perfunctory this time, and the moment passed.

"Let's get dressed and go downstairs for something to eat," she said.

Crowley nodded, wondering if he might need a cold shower first. "Good plan," he said instead.

Fifteen minutes later they sat side by side in one of the large leather couches by the gently crackling fire. Only two other people shared the common room with them, an elderly couple facing each other over a dark, scratched wooden table, playing backgammon. The couple murmured to each other, but were too far away to be overheard.

Crowley sipped the tea they had ordered and grimaced. "American tea."

Rose looked down at her cup with an expression of mild insult. "Yeah. You wouldn't think it would be so hard to get right." She picked up a pastry, dusted with bright white icing sugar and took a large bite. She smiled as she chewed. "These though. These they get right."

Crowley's phone vibrated in his pocket and he pulled it out. "Cameron," he said, after glancing at the screen. "What's happening, my brother from another mother?"

Rose frowned, half-laughing, shook her head. Crowley gave her a *What?* look, and grinned.

"Jakey-boy," Cameron said. "Everything okay with you guys?"

"Yeah, pretty much okay but we could really do with some good news from you. We're in a cul-de-sac right here."

"Well, I'm still working on possible locations for the entrance to this lost city of yours. There are just so many variables. We have no way of knowing which details are authentic and which are false. Right now I could give you at least a dozen locations scattered over various sections of the canyon."

"The Grand Canyon is a good 450 kilometers long," Crowley said.

"Right. So you see the problem. However, this Seth Tanner fellow is interesting."

Crowley let out a sound of frustration. "We tried the Tanner Trail today. Amazing, breathtaking. But a complete dead end."

"Hmmm. Well, I think there's maybe more there," Cameron said. "I'd really like to find out what Tanner knew that led the natives to blind him."

Crowley sat up from his slump in the couch, suddenly interested. "Wait, what?"

"You didn't know that?" Cameron said, clearly surprised. "Then again, it's not something you'd find in a Wikipedia entry."

"Hey," Crowley said, choosing not to ignore the insult to his research efforts. "Sit on something and swivel!"

"Well, if you don't want to know…"

Crowley laughed. "Of course I do. Spill it." Rose leaned forward, gave Crowley a questioning look. He smiled. "Hang on, old Cam might have got a lead for us. Go on, mate."

"Okay. Well, late in his life, Tanner went exploring in a remote part of the Grand Canyon. Apparently, he stumbled across a place that he shouldn't have been."

"What kind of place?"

"That's just it!" Cameron's frustration was clear in his tone. "I'm not sure, but it's a safe bet that whatever it was, it was either sacred, dangerous, or both. So much so that the Hopi blinded Tanner so he'd never be able to find his way back, or lead anyone there. And what's more, they threatened to cut out his tongue if he ever told anyone. That's got to be something worth us finding out about, right?"

Crowley thought about it. Sacred and deadly certainly could describe the Egyptian city, should the thing really exist. And they had to operate on the assumption that it did. But how did any of this help, without knowing more? "So did he take the story to his grave?" he asked.

"Not that I've found so far," Cameron said. "That's not to say he didn't, but a copy of his journal turned up a few years ago. It's now in the collection of the Pioneer Museum in Flagstaff. It appears no one has found it important enough to report on its contents, much less digitize it and put it online."

"If he was blind, he'd have had a hard time writing in a journal," Crowley said.

"But he could have dictated to someone else, if he did manage to keep his tongue. I'm just saying it would be worth a look."

Crowley had to agree with Cameron there.

"If there are any hints in there about where he went," Cameron said, "I might be able to use those to make sense of the lost city clues I've found so far. Maybe determine which are false trails and which might be worth your time following up. "

"We might as well take a look," Crowley agreed. "We've nothing better to do at the moment."

"Do I detect a note of judgment in your voice?" Cameron

joked.

"Frustration, mate, that's all."

Cameron's voice grew serious. "Don't get complacent, Crowley."

"Like I ever do!"

"I'm not kidding. Let's not forget what happened in Denver. Your false identity has kept you off their radar for the moment, but if the lost city is truly what they're after, you're bound to encounter them sooner or later. They won't be leaving this alone or dragging their feet. And I guarantee you, if they're willing to kill over it, this is about more than some antiquities."

A sense of dread crept over Crowley. "In other words," he said, "don't sit around waiting."

"I wouldn't."

"You're right. Thanks, mate. Leave it with us. I'll get back to you as soon as I can."

"Be careful!"

"We will." Crowley hung up the phone and stood decisively.

"What did you learn?" Rose asked.

"I'll tell you on the way."

She frowned. "On the way where? Where are we going?"

Crowley grinned, took her hand to pull her up. "To steal something."

CHAPTER 44

Pioneer Museum, Flagstaff

It was dark as they pulled up the rental car a couple of hundred meters from the Pioneer Museum. Rose sat in the driver's seat, left the engine running.

"You're sure about this?"

Crowley was sure, and a bit excited to be doing something proactive again. "Piece of cake. I'll be ten minutes tops."

He slipped from the car, pulled the hood of his dark gray sweat top up, and hurried away in the night. Darkness fell as Rose killed the car's headlights, but he heard the engine continue to purr. By the thin light of a sliver of moon, he made his way along to the Pioneer Museum. It was a small, two-story building of pale pumiceous dacite stone which, according to Rose, had been harvested from an explosive eruption of Mount Elden about half a million years before. The building had several tall narrow windows on each level, a high porch in the center of one long side and a steep tan A-frame roof. The building was used as a hospital until 1938, servicing the county that used to be called Poor Farm.

The place was far from impressive, and not well guarded, both of which worked in Crowley's favor. But, though no one seemed to be about, he remained on high alert. Cameron's reminder that dangerous people might be on the same trail as he and Rose was fresh in his mind, making him nervous. After the frightening events at Denver airport, he had not really thought too hard about where those people might be, but that could prove to be a fatal mistake. They had tracked him and Rose once and would almost certainly be attempting to do the same again. And Crowley wasn't too arrogant to think that he and Rose had learned anything those people couldn't. It wasn't so much a case of if they caught up again, as when.

Not wanting to use a flashlight and draw attention to himself, he waited in the shadows, letting his night vision take over. He stared at the small, unassuming building, wondering where he might need to look. Once he felt that his vision was as good as it was going to get in the dark night, he crept around the back. He soon found a back door and spotted the simple alarm system. He moved along the wall, staying in deep shadow, to get a closer look at the tall, white-framed windows. He smiled. As he had suspected, none were alarmed. After all, this wasn't the sort of museum that had a collection of valuable antiquities. It was a local interest place, the value in the history it recorded, not the items it held.

He pursed his lips, looked from the door to the windows. He could disable the alarm if necessary, but what if security was genuinely lax? He tried the back windows one after another and, after two disappointments, the third one rattled in its frame. It wasn't latched. He pushed it, but though it shook, it didn't budge. He spread his feet, braced himself, and got a better position with the heels of his hands against the top of the lower sash. He pushed again and this time it shifted up quickly, releasing a shrill squeal that shattered the silence. Crowley winced, ducked involuntarily against the sound. After a moment, he looked around, but still there was no one in sight, no other sounds but night birds.

He clambered in, leaving the sash up. No need to make added noise or slow himself down should he need to leave in a hurry. He stood in a dim room and looked around. As expected, no fancy security system, motion detectors, or even cameras. Security exit lights gave off a dull glow that allowed him to easily find his way without a flashlight.

He began a quick but thorough exploration of the first floor. Glass cases, glass-topped tables, bookshelves heaving with the small minutiae of life in the region for the past couple of hundred years. There were some period dressed manikins, each with small placards talking about life in the pioneer days. None of it was about Seth Tanner, so none of it held his attention.

He made his way upstairs to continue looking on the second floor, wincing at the creak of the wooden steps. His search of the web on the drive here hadn't turned up a single mention of the journal, much less where in the museum it might be found. Not for the first time, Crowley was impressed by Cameron's skills at turning up something most people didn't know existed. He really needed to find a way to properly thank his old pal. Sure, Cameron enjoyed the distraction, but he deserved something more solid by way of recompense. Crowley decided that maybe when all this was over he would shell out for a fine bottle of single malt scotch and go to visit his friend, maybe treat him to a fancy Indian meal too. Cameron liked a good, hot curry.

Crowley looked around the second floor, which wasn't much different to the first. What if the journal wasn't on display at all? Perhaps it was stowed away with other sundry bits and pieces, waiting to be rotated out at some point in the future. Or maybe it wasn't deemed interesting enough to be put out at all. It could be buried in some back office somewhere. Or worse. Did this museum have a basement? What if he'd come all this way only to fail?

His concerns were allayed, however, when he spotted a simple exhibit devoted entirely to Seth Tanner. There were a few black and white photos, one showing Tanner in his middle years, the others as an old man. Even with the dim security lights, it was too gloomy to see any real detail. Crowley clicked on the small flashlight he had brought, cupping the light with one hand to shield its glow. In one photograph, the elderly Tanner stared back at the camera through milky orbs, clearly blind. Crowley was mesmerized by the image. The old man sat with his hands resting on his thighs, barely bent by age. He had a lined forehead, bald to the top of his head, but his hair thick and collar length from the top and down the back. He had a thick, white beard, and an intense expression despite the obvious blindness. He stared, unseeing, directly at the camera, his presence strongly disquieting for no particular reason Crowley could define. He winced at the thought of what the natives had done to the old man, and why. How had they blinded him?

When Cameron had told the story, Crowley had imagined something somehow brutal, like they had put his eyes out with knives or arrows. He chided himself for the unfair stereotype of barbarism. Those white, haunting eyes filled Crowley with a dread he didn't care to dwell on, nor did he want to dwell on how the blindness had been effected.

He took a step back and shone his light across the exhibit. A brief bio of the explorer, a map of the Tanner trail, and a glass case containing some personal effects. He moved to the case to look more closely. A hand-held pickaxe, a compass, and a journal book. He grinned. That had to be it.

He cursed when he realized he'd left his lockpicking tools in his messenger bag in the car with Rose. He didn't want to push his luck going back for them now. He looked around and found a small toolkit stashed in one corner, a half repaired chair upside down beside it. He rummaged in the toolkit and came up with a flat-ended screwdriver. It would have to do. He slipped on gloves to avoid leaving fingerprints and began prying carefully at the display case just above the small lock. He worked at it for several seconds, wincing as the wood cracked and split, but managed to pop open the lid without leaving too much obvious damage on the outside of the cabinet.

He took the journal and gave it a quick scan. Lots of hand-written notes and drawings. He pocketed the small leather bound book, then looked down at the open display case. Inspiration dawned. He hurried down the hall to an office he had passed on the way along this level. Through the open door, he'd spotted a shelf sagging from the weight of too many books, some of them quite old. Hurriedly, he chose an old, leather volume roughly the size of Tanner's journal and took it back, put it inside the glass case. He figured it wouldn't stand up to close scrutiny, and the broken lock would be a dead giveaway if it was discovered, but it would pass casual observation. He pressed the lid back down and the wood sat quite neatly thanks to his careful work with the screwdriver earlier. It might go unnoticed for a little while, and that would be good enough.

He headed back to the stairs, then froze at the top of them. From below came the sound of someone moving around. Someone clearly trying to be quiet. The screwdriver was his only weapon. He drew it, held it in a downward grip, and retreated to the other side of the banister at the top of the stairs. He crouched and hid in velvet shadows.

After a moment the silhouette of the figure came into view through the balusters, carefully mounted the first step, and began to slowly ascend. Crowley tensed, ready to spring. And then relaxed.

"Rose, what are you doing here?"

She let out a soft "Oh!" of surprise and jumped, nearly fell back down the stairs. "I didn't even see you. Or hear a thing."

"I've got experience at not being seen or heard when I don't want to be. But what are you doing here? I was just heading back."

"You've got it?"

"Yes. Will you answer the question! Do I need to be concerned?"

Rose joined him at the top of the stairs and he stood to meet her eye.

"A car drove past where I was parked, one of those freelance security firms. The driver gave me a long look as he drove past, really slowly. So I thought I'd better move on."

"Sounds reasonable," Crowley admitted. "But why are you here?"

"Well, you needed to know where I parked. I didn't want to risk calling or texting you. What if your phone vibrated at the wrong time?"

Crowley sighed. He supposed that was a good point. "Fair enough. Anyway, I've got the journal so let's get out of here."

They hurried back down the stairs and Rose headed for the window he had opened. He was pleased she'd had the foresight to look for that and follow him in. She might not have been moving quite as stealthily as he could, but she was smart and came at these things the right way. He had to give her credit, she could become a formidable operative with the right training. She was already super fit and could kick serious butt.

They gave each other a quick smile and Rose went ahead of him, climbing out of the window. As she dropped cat-like to the soft ground there was another sound outside and Crowley froze. A dark shape emerged from the shadow of a nearby tree.

"Stop right there."

CHAPTER 45

"Put your hands up where I can see them."

Rose raised her hands slowly, palms out. "It's okay, I'm not armed."

Crowley quickly, silently, moved into the deep shadow under the window sill. Their only advantage would be if this guy thought Rose was alone. Thankfully, she hadn't glanced back when challenged, and Crowley credited her smarts again. She worked well under pressure. He carefully peeked over the white wooden sill.

Rose stood with her hands in the air as a man with a flashlight approached. Crowley tensed, his thoughts going immediately to American policemen and their Wild West, shoot first mentality. He let out a sigh of relief when a quick glance reassured him this was no police officer. The man wore khakis and a t-shirt that read *BECK SECURITY*. His paunch hung over his belt and his knees were close together, aging ankles pronating in. He had to be a least fifty and in pretty poor shape. The guy would be hard-pressed to run more than twenty meters at Crowley's estimation. A pepper spray sat in a holster on his belt, but no gun. He held a radio in his free hand as he roved the flashlight up and down Rose. Crowley ground his teeth as the man leered and slowly looked her up and down again. This would be no problem though.

"Run!" Crowley whispered, softly enough that only Rose would hear.

She didn't hesitate, took off away from the startled security guard. The overweight man froze a moment in surprise, then yelled for her to stop. A second later he lumbered after her. Crowley gathered himself, tensed. As the guard passed the window, Crowley jumped out and tackled him quickly to the ground. The guard squealed like a stuck pig, thrashing randomly, as Crowley slipped around behind him and locked him in a chokehold. The man coughed and gagged twice, tried gamely to drive his elbow back into Crowley's ribs. A glancing blow made Crowley wince and he shifted position, locked his legs around the man's hip and straightened his knees a little. The guard stretched out flat, his back arching against Crowley's chest. Crowley got a better position with his arm under the guard's chin and secured his free hand behind. He tightened the elbow across the guy's throat and the guard's struggling quickly weakened and in a few more seconds he fell limp, unconscious.

Crowley crawled out from the under the man's bulk. "Sleep tight!" he said, as the guard stirred restlessly, and ran. He caught up with Rose as she slowed ahead of him. Their car was parked in shadow just another twenty meters away.

"Let's book!" Crowley said. "I'll drive."

Rose flipped him the keys and in seconds they were away.

As Crowley drove, slowing to legal speeds once he hit the highway, he handed Rose the journal.

"What have we got?" he asked. "Let's hope it's worth it."

Rose used her small flashlight to see and thumbed through. "Mostly boring stuff, to be honest. Man, his handwriting was pretty poor. There's talk about landmarks, some rough maps, cryptic notes about spots where he might dig. By the phrasing I think he's making notes he can decipher but that anyone else wouldn't understand."

"Maybe scared someone would find the journal and beat him to some good mining."

"I guess."

"Maybe flip to the back," Crowley suggested. "Unless Tanner dictated to someone else, he probably didn't do much writing after the natives blinded him. Let's see what happened right before that."

"Good point." Rose turned to the back, flipped backward through some blank pages. "He's less careful here, some maps and sketches." Then she gasped. "Wow!"

"What is it?"

She held the journal up so Crowley could see it without taking his eyes completely off the road. In large, rough scrawl was one word: *BLIND*.

"So that particular legend would appear to be true," Crowley said. "See what comes before it."

Rose turned back a few pages, scanned, read slowly. Then she let out a small laugh and read aloud. "Ahiga came by. Says I was seen coming back from the cave."

Crowley's heart skipped a beat. He glanced over to see Rose smiling.

"Says the council won't like it," she went on, "and I should leave. Asked what was so special about the cave. Ahiga was quiet for a long time, then said 'the dark god lives there'. Superstitious nonsense."

Crowley glanced over again and Rose looked up, grinning. "Do you think the cave is the city?" she asked.

Crowley shrugged. "Regardless, it sounds like a promising lead. But it's worthless unless he gives directions to this cave in question."

Rose held the journal up for him to see again. "You think this map might be good enough?"

CHAPTER 46

Haunted Canyon Region- Grand Canyon

The sun beating down was hotter than it had been last time they were in the canyon, but still not too bad. They had taken the precaution of bringing a lot of water and new climbing gear from a brief stop at a surplus store on the way in. After getting back to the hotel the night before, Crowley had photographed the journal and sent all the information to Cameron. He and Rose had fallen into their separate beds and slept like the dead. By morning, new messages from Cameron made them both happy. He had combined the map and details from the journal with the information he'd already amassed and confirmed a location in the Haunted Canyon area.

How accurate do you think this is? Crowley had messaged.

You doubt my skills, bawbag? Cameron had immediately pinged back.

Crowley laughed, sent his thanks, and now they found themselves at the foot of a high cliff, hoping Cameron's skills were indeed up to the task.

"There's definitely a ledge up there," Rose said. Her voice wavered with hope and the preparation for disappointment.

Crowley couldn't blame her for that. Her last experience in the canyon had been bad. "In Cam we trust," he said with a grin. "Come on."

They began the climb, working together well, taking care with well-placed pitons. Crowley sincerely hoped they were in the right place, as any disappointment now would be the end of the road. He saw no other way forward if this proved a dead end.

"Look here." Rose, a little above and to the right of him, pointed to a crack in the rock. "Fresh handhold chiseled here. Evidence someone has climbed recently."

As she moved on, Crowley followed and looked for himself. It was unweathered. She had a point. He allowed himself a little more hope.

"I wonder if it was Lily," Rose said from above.

"We can hope."

Sweating, but exhilarated, they finally reached the ledge and crawled up onto it. It was fairly large, several meters deep, and a small cave entrance yawned darkly right in front of them. Crowley looked up at the canyon wall, arching out, casting the ledge in shadow.

"This would definitely be hard to see from above or below," he said.

Rose couldn't keep a smile from her face. She pointed up. "Look there. And there."

Crowley followed where she indicated, saw several small indentations in the cliff edge high above. A rippled edge to the rock and slight discoloration from the stone either side. "That certainly looks like the erosion of a seasonal waterfall," he said quietly.

"Let's go." Without waiting for him, or even looking to see if he followed, Rose hurried into the darkness.

Crowley quickly followed her in, taking a deep breath and letting his caution rise higher than his excitement. He understood Rose's need to find Lily, but they had been shot at too much for him to think this encounter would be violence-free.

"Slow down," he said softly, as kindly as he could. "Bad guys might be here, too. Let's not give ourselves away."

Rose paused, glanced back at him. Then she nodded. Crowley fell into step beside her and they moved cautiously forward, guided by the light of a single small flashlight, half-shielded by Crowley's hand.

The passageway was neatly hewn from the stone, flat-floored and roughly arch-shaped, some four meters or so high and about as wide. As they moved along, it narrowed to around three meters. Crowley glanced back to the brightness of the entrance, growing smaller behind them.

"Side passages," Rose whispered.

The passages branched off at about forty-five degrees to the right and left, and the main passage continued on.

"Which way?" Crowley asked.

Rose shrugged and turned left. Crowley flashed his light along, checked both sides of the new corridor. Along each side were a number of oval-shaped wooden doors. Rose glanced at him, eyebrows raised. Crowley smiled, tried the first door. It opened onto a room about the size of an ordinary living room in a modest modern house. The wall between the room and the passage was a good meter or more thick, ventilated by round air spaces only a couple of centimeters in diameter. The passage and the room were chiseled or hewn as straight as could be laid out by any engineer.

"This place is incredible," Rose said. "You really think it's old?"

"I do," Crowley said, realizing she shared his thoughts. What if the place was relatively new, not the ancient lost city of legend. It was entirely possible. "Only exploration will tell us that, I guess."

They checked a number of other rooms, some as big as ten or fifteen meters square, but otherwise all similar. The ceilings of many converged up to a center point. As the passage continued on it bent slowly to the left until Crowley estimated they were at a right-angle to the main passage they had left. Eventually the side passage ended, with the largest rooms either side. The other similarity the rooms shared was that they were all empty.

After another five minutes they had established that the side passage to the right was symmetrically identical.

"So many rooms," Rose said. "What are they for?"

"If this place is a lost city, I guess they could be living quarters." Crowley did some quick calculations. "If we assume several people per room, what we've seen so far could accommodate hundreds of people. More than a thousand, maybe."

"So I guess we need to go deeper to find anything more interesting."

Crowley lifted his flashlight beam to see ahead along the main passage. "I suppose so. Let's go."

Their feet scuffed and echoed dully off the stone as they moved cautiously onwards. Before long they emerged into a much larger space. Again Crowley explored it with his light. Rose gasped.

"This is just like Shepherd described. I can't believe it's real."

"It is. And it's huge!"

The room was circular, the ceiling arching high above in a smooth dome. Evenly spaced around the room, thirteen passages radiated out like sunbeams, exactly like Shepherd's description, each one a dark mystery.

Crowley strained his ears to listen, tried to guess which might be the right way. But silence pressed in on him.

"I guess we try a few?" Rose said.

They started to the left, checking quickly but carefully along the neatly carved corridors. They came across various chambers, carvings of Egyptian deities, hieroglyphs.

"Okay, this is starting to look a lot more like a lost Egyptian city and not some modern excavation, after all," Crowley said. "I'm more than a little weirded out here."

A few scattered artifacts littered various spaces, but they got the feeling that there was once a lot more. Several empty alcoves adorned the walls, rooms had scratch marks on the floors where things that must have been quite heavy had been dragged around.

"This place has been pretty soundly looted, I'm thinking," Rose said.

"Yeah, I think you're right. Hard to imagine what people might have found here when it was first discovered."

They moved around the chamber and when they reached the passage heading directly opposite the one they had entered by, Crowley reached out to stop Rose walking further. He crouched, looking closely with his flashlight.

"Partial footprints," he said. "Here in the dust. More here."

They searched more closely, before Crowley stood. "Based on the size of the prints, I thinks it's two men and one woman."

Rose took a deep breath, clearly trying not to get too excited. She placed her booted foot alongside one of the smaller prints. "Lily and I wear the same size." She took her foot away and her print neatly matched the other in length and width.

She didn't say more but it was obvious to Crowley where her hopes lay.

"Come on," he said. "But let's be quiet."

They moved along the passage and soon came to a strange drop off on one side that led to a large, rounded chamber. It was a several a meter fall to the circular floor, but two copper hooks extended from the near edge.

"You think some sort of ladder was attached there?" Rose asked.

"Yeah, probably," Crowley said. "As it's rounded, I wonder if it was a granary." He pointed his flashlight down, picking out reflections of shining silvery metal. As he played the light around, they caught sight of a number of yellowish stones, each engraved with a head or face of some sort. "Worth anything?" Crowley asked.

Rose smiled. "Impossible to say without a closer look and I

don't think we should waste time climbing down there."

"No. Certainly not now anyway."

They carried on, spotting the occasional stray footprint here and there, but the passage floors were fairly clean. After another fifty or so meters, they emerged into another large room. Evenly spaced along the curving back wall were numerous life-size statues, each standing in its own alcove. Each a representation of an Egyptian god. Horus with his hawk's head, Ra with a large sun disc. Isis and Osiris. And at the end of the row, jackal-headed Anubis. All beautifully carved, detailed and enameled or lacquered with bright, shining colors. The hall itself shone, carved out of a hard rock resembling marble. Between them and the statues were tables laden with tools of all descriptions, all seemingly made of copper.

Crowley picked one up, turned it over in his hands. "If this place is as old as we suspect, this is pretty amazing."

"The copper?" Rose asked.

"Yeah. These people clearly knew the art."

On a bench running around the workroom lay charcoal and other materials no doubt used in the process. Slag indicating the smelting of ores littered the benches. There were urns and cups of copper and, possibly, gold, beautiful in design. The pottery showed more of the enameling evident on the statues. On several pieces and on the walls and tablets of stone were numerous mysterious hieroglyphics.

Crowley and Rose moved around the tables and approached the statues. As they drew nearer they saw that each alcove had a door behind its occupant. Crowley checked the two nearest and discovered they were false, simply carved artistically into the stone wall.

He cast a nervous glance at Rose.

She shook her head. "No, no, no. We can't have found all this to only meet a dead end now." She hurried to the end of the row, to Anubis. "If anything, this one surely…" She pushed in behind the statue and put her shoulder to the carving of the door. It didn't budge.

Tears in her eyes, she stepped back out into the littered chamber and cursed eloquently. Crowley was quite impressed by the range of her vocabulary. He paid closer attention to the door behind Anubis and his eyes narrowed. The door looked different from the others. He slipped into the space and had a closer look with his flashlight. A tiny crack ran around the carved outline.

He quickly checked the alcove beside Anubis and this one had no similar fine crack.

"What is it?" Rose asked, hope quavering in her tone.

Crowley didn't answer. He went back behind Anubis and pushed against the carved door. It didn't move. With a strength born of frustration, he threw his shoulder into it. It made a cracking sound, a scrape, then swung open. He smiled at Rose. "Looks like you just didn't have the weight for it. We haven't reached the end of the line just yet."

CHAPTER 47

Crowley and Rose moved forward cautiously, listening hard, their flashlights once again masked with cupped palms. They emerged into a huge empty room, the ceiling rising high above them to a point like the inside of a pyramid. Against the far wall was an intricately carved Sphinx head, twice the size of a large person, its mouth open. Beyond the mouth was darkness, a passage continuing on. Without need to discuss it, they walked through the mouth and came out into another large room, bigger than the previous one.

"This place is immense," Rose whispered.

"It is. And long-abandoned, it would seem. But also long since looted. What could your sister want here? What have others missed?"

He shone his light around the walls and saw tiers of shelves with urns, stacks of old, tarnished weapons, scraps of leather and furs, degraded and mostly rotten. The urns and cups on the lower tiers were crude, while on the higher shelves the artifacts were finer in design, showing a later stage of civilization.

"It's like a history of artisanal skill," Crowley said.

Along the two long walls of the room, fifty meters or more each, were small divisions like cattle stalls. Old wooden bed frames, broken or run-down, could be found in some. Crowley pointed them out, then gestured to the old weapons up the front end. "A barracks?"

Rose pursed her lips, looked around. "Yeah, you're probably right. But there are no other doors leading out. Have we reached the end of this place?"

"Bloody disappointing if we have. But it can't be."

Rose frowned. "Why not?"

"Couple of things." Crowley pointed to the dusty floor. "For one, we didn't see a single footprint heading back toward the entrance. Nor did we encounter anyone or find any trapdoors."

"So we must have missed something." Rose moved back to the entrance, brows creased together. "Maybe a side passage or something?"

Crowley scratched his chin, frustration gnawing at him. "I think there's something we're missing right here. Why would the soldiers be quartered all the way at the back, unless..."

Rose turned to face him, eyebrows raised. "Unless they were guarding something important."

"Right. Otherwise, they'd be nearer the front wouldn't you think?"

"Well, that's entirely speculation, but yeah. It makes a kind of sense."

"Let's look around here more closely. See if there's another concealed door or something."

They spent a good ten minutes poring over all the shelves and tables in the huge space, looking for anything that wasn't simply aged junk. Eventually Rose called Crowley over. When he joined her, she pointed to a huge urn, bigger than any others.

"Is it me, or is this off-center?"

Crowley shone his light over it closely, stood on tip-toes to see in the top. The interior was black and empty, but he spotted something else. "Look. Handprints on the lip." His light showed up the greasy marks, left in the dry, pale pottery. "You think maybe someone has moved it recently?"

Rose smiled. "Maybe. You try."

Crowley pushed and pulled at it, but nothing happened. Then he had another idea and turned it like a crank. It was heavy, stiff, but pivoted slowly with a muffled grinding sound. The section of wall behind it dropped out of sight.

"This whole place keeps rewarding the persistent visitor," Crowley said with a grin.

They stepped through, the urn slowly rotating back to its original position once Crowley had released his grip. As the urn turned, the door rose back up from the floor.

"I hope there's another mechanism on this side," Rose said, her voice rising slightly in concern.

Crowley looked quickly around, found a small wooden table nearby, broken like the rest. He grabbed a sturdy looking table leg and jammed it in the gap while there was still around a meter of opening left between the top of the rising door and the ceiling. The door stopped, the urn ceased its motion.

He smiled at Rose. "We can climb over there easily enough to get out."

As Rose began to nod, relief washing over her face, the table leg splintered with a loud, dry crack and shattered. The urn spun and the door slammed up and closed before they could move.

They stared in silence for a moment. "Or," Crowley said eventually, "we hope there's another mechanism on this side." He squeezed Rose's shoulder. "Don't worry. I don't think this place is designed as a one-way trap."

"You said yourself there were no footprints coming out the other way!"

He had already thought of that but was hoping Rose hadn't. Of course, she was too smart to miss a detail of that magnitude. "Then there's another exit," he said. "Either way, for now we have to keep on, right?"

Rose sighed. She turned her light to shine around the room they'd entered and gasped. It appeared to be some kind of crypt. It was one of the largest chambers they had found thus far, all four walls slanting back as they rose from the floor at an angle of about thirty-five degrees. On each wall were three rows of neatly hewn alcoves and on the shelf of each alcove stood a mummy. There were several small benches, each scattered with copper cups and pieces of broken swords. The mummies were all wrapped in a rough fabric and daubed with a kind of reddish clay.

They turned in a slow circle, playing their flashlights over the walls.

"Hundreds of them," Crowley said in a low voice.

"I wonder if they were all dignitaries or just the general population?" Rose said.

"Wasn't mummification reserved only for the most important?" Crowley asked. "It was a difficult and costly procedure, right? Not just for anyone."

Rose turned slowly, taking in the vast crypt. "So many important people. I wonder who they all were?"

"And is this the end of the line?" Crowley wondered. There were no obvious doors again, no passages leading away. "It's possible the guards were at the back to guard this room, if these mummies are all important."

"So where did everyone else go? Why no returning footprints?"

"Unless everyone who makes it this far ends up in one of those alcoves," Crowley said, deliberately playing up his voice to sound like a spooky Hammer film.

Rose slapped his arm. "This is no time for jokes, Jake. What the hell is this place?"

Something caught his eye and he pointed. "Look."

One of the alcoves on the bottom row, in the center of the far wall, wasn't like the others. While all the other alcoves were uniform and contained largely similar ruddy-brown mummies, this one contained an upright clay sarcophagus. It was designed in the shape of Anubis, and contained no mummy. They hurried over to it, and Crowley gave it a pull. It swung forward.

"Another door," Rose said.

Crowley grinned. "Let's see what's on the other side this time."

Chapter 48

The door swung gently closed behind them but there was no telltale click of a lock or catch. Though neither Crowley nor Rose paid it that much attention as they stared dumbfounded at the sight before them.

"This is the place that just keeps on giving," Crowley said.

They stood on a ledge of rock in a massive chamber. Faint slivers of light trickled down from some unseen source far above, just enough for them to see what lay in front of them. Dropping away from the ledge, only a few meters away, was a pit so deep they couldn't see the bottom. Crowley moved forward and pointed his flashlight down it, but the beam disappeared into darkness, showing nothing but vanishing abyss. A deep cold seemed to drift up from the impossible depths. But the pit, though terrifying, was not the awe-inspiring part of this chamber.

To their right, the figure of Anubis was carved in the wall, impossibly large. Every crease of fabric in his skirt, every line of muscle on his skin, was minutely rendered, the realism of the carving breath-taking. Anubis half-crouched from his position by the wall, one hand braced against his knee, the other arm outstretched, palm up, as if offering something. But from the tips of his fingers on the outstretched hand a narrow bridge spanned the gap of the bottomless pit.

"Well this definitely seems like the kind of place the Anubis Cult would be interested in," Crowley said.

In the gloom on the far side of the enormous cavern they could just make out the darker patch of a passage leading away.

Rose moved forward, clambered up onto Anubis's palm and took a step towards the bridge. Crowley spotted the ropes in the center of the structure and panic washed through him. He shouted Rose's name as he leaped up behind her and grabbed her arm. He hauled her back just as she cried out in surprise, the end of the bridge dropping sharply down under the pressure of her foot.

She landed in his arms and he staggered back, clutching her tightly. They were both breathing hard, the rapid hammer of her pulse apparent against Crowley's chest where he held her.

"Are you okay?"

She half-laughed. "You nearly dislocated my shoulder, but I'm glad you did." She looked around at the bridge, now innocently lined up with Anubis's palm once more. "What in the hell? I thought it collapsed or something."

Crowley shook his head. "It's not a bridge." He pointed to the middle, where a kind of pivot structure was built underneath the narrow wooden boards. From either side, disappearing into the darkness of the cavern high above, a taut rope stretched, thick and rough. The ropes looked old, but strong, each almost as thick as Crowley's not insubstantial forearm. "It's a kind of see-saw," he said.

Rose sighed loudly in frustration. "A scale." She pushed away from him, angry with herself. "Of course. Before the dead could pass into the underworld, Anubis weighed the heart of the deceased."

"And it had to be light as a feather," Crowley said. He looked her up and down, wondering if a little humor might be worth the risk to break the tension of her self-recrimination. As his eyes passed over her ass, she scowled at him. "You been keeping up with your diet?" he asked, unable to help himself.

Her expression of outrage magnified, but she couldn't keep a smile from tugging at her lips. "You're a bloody pillock, Crowley!"

He grinned, pulled her into a quick hug, kissed the top of her head. "You okay?" he asked, letting go again so as not to seem pushy. He just wanted her to know he genuinely cared.

She stared hard into his eyes for a moment, some deep emotion swimming in her expression, then she nodded. "I would have dropped to my death there if not for you."

"It's okay. You've got more on your mind than me, worrying for your sister. It's more real for you. I'm here to spot the little details." He raised his palms. "Hey, it's not like you haven't saved me before. We make a good team, remember."

She smiled softly, but looked away. "Yes, we do," she said in a whisper.

A moment of silence fell, one that threatened to become uncomfortable. Crowley interrupted it before it could. "So, what do we do?"

"We could pull a Nick Cage," Rose said, staring thoughtfully out over the dangerous teeter-totter bridge. "Roll something heavy across..." She trailed off when she caught his confused expression and looked at him in disbelief. "You didn't see the National Treasure movies?"

Crowley hissed between his teeth. "Can't stand Cage. The guy tends to overact."

Rose's mouth dropped open and she gave him the hand, palm up between them. "You're dead to me."

Crowley laughed. This woman was full of surprises and contradictions, but he was charmed by every new one he discovered. "Anyway," he said. "we don't have anything heavy enough."

They both stared, lost in thought for a moment as they grappled with the problem. Eventually, Crowley said, "All we need is for something to stop this end tipping down as we step onto it. Let's get old Anubis here to help."

Rose watched as Crowley pulled his climbing rope from his backpack. He tugged hard against the railing on one side of the bridge, testing its strength. It was solid enough. Quite a contradiction to a lot of the furniture and other fittings they had seen through the place so far. He looped his rope around it several times, pulled it taut, then took the trailing end back across Anubis's palm. Balancing carefully, he stepped from the god's carved arm over onto his knee, then wrapped the rope around the arm braced there. He made sure to wrap it slightly higher than the bridge railing, near the crook of the god's elbow, so the secure end of the rope would offer more support. He leaned his weight in hard, hauled the rope as tight as he could, wrapped it again. After several revolutions he tied it off with a secure bowline knot.

Rose looked dubiously from his handiwork to the bridge and back again as he hopped back over to rejoin her.

"You think that'll hold?" she asked.

"It's added security. I'll hold this end of the bridge up while you cross. That rope will be insurance. Then, when you get to the other side, you stand on that end to balance my weight."

"Good idea," Rose said. "Until you cross the middle point and we both drop to our deaths."

Crowley laughed. "Well, when I get to the middle, you step off and hold up your end while I cross the last half."

Rose thought about that for a moment. Then she said, "I'd rather trust the rope than my ability to hold you up. You go across first and I'll hold the bridge with the rope's assistance.

Then you can hold up the far side while I cross. I reckon you're strong enough to take my weight. I'm not sure I'm strong enough to take yours."

Crowley doubted her assessment. He thought she was more than strong enough to do it, but didn't want to argue the point. If she was happier this way, so be it. The rope would help both sides anyway; it wasn't especially high.

"Okay," he said. "Brace yourself and support the bridge."

Before he could think about it any more, and start to doubt himself, he stepped tentatively out onto the rough, dark wooden boards. The bridge shifted downward, the rope creaked. Crowley swallowed, his pulse immediately in his throat. He took a long, deep breath, kept his focus only on the far side. He heard a kind of thrumming in the huge ropes either side of the fulcrum point, saw them vibrating slightly in the dimness with his movement. The entire structure seemed to move, shifting left and right. A creak swelled quickly into a loud crack and Crowley bent both knees, grabbed the railings either side of himself. His pulse rate doubled again, sweat trickling down his back.

"Jake, you okay?" Rose's voice seemed very far away.

"I'm fine." He took another step and found himself between the heavy, ancient ropes. As he moved onto the far side of the scale he called back. "Put a little weight on your end, just in case."

"Okay."

Crowley kept moving, the gentle swaying triggering a strange vertigo he had never experienced before. The creaks and groans increased in volume and frequency.

"You're nearly there," Rose called out. He could tell she was trying to encourage him, but her voice wavered with nerves.

And then he was across. Solid rock had never felt quite so solid before. He turned, gripped the railings either side of his end of the bridge, ready to push down as Rose started on her side, then lift up as she crossed the center.

"Go for it," he called across, his voice echoing strangely in the huge, dark space.

Rose licked her lips, then stepped out. She didn't wait or move cautiously, but hurried directly across, hands running along the railing either side of her. Crowley flexed his muscles, his strength tested as he countered her weight. He was fairly convinced his rope brace would hold either them, but if they never had to test that, he would be happy.

In seconds Rose was across and she grabbed hold of him. He gathered her into an embrace and they held each other again, enjoying the comfort of each other's bodies. Rose opened her mouth to speak, but Crowley quickly held up a finger to silence her. He tapped his ear. Rose's face hardened as she realized what he had noticed. There were muffled voices drifting out of the passageway ahead of them. Far away, impossible to hear the words, but undoubtedly voices.

CHAPTER 49

The dark passageway curved gradually to the right as they moved forward, their flashlights off and tucked away. The gentle glow from the cavern behind reached a little way along but in no time they were progressing in pitch blackness. The voices grew slightly louder, two male voices and one female. Rose gasped slightly at the sound of the woman's voice.

Crowley put a hand to her arm, bringing them both to a halt in the darkness. "You think that was Lily?" he whispered.

"I think it might be," Rose said, her lips tantalizingly close to his ear, a tremble of excitement in her voice.

"Okay. But we need to be really careful now. We have no idea who she's with, how armed they might be. We can't give ourselves away."

Rose drew a slow breath and he sensed her nod in the dark. "You're right."

"When we can see anything, let me go first. You stay back. Your presence might be our best trump card, so let's not play you too early."

"Okay."

They crept forward again. A wavering orangey glow leaked towards them as they slowly rounded the long, curving passage. They stayed close to the inside wall of the curve, Crowley first, Rose close behind, one hand on his shoulder to stay in touch in the darkness. Then up ahead they saw people. Three of them, wearing headlamps. Two were large men, powerfully built, clad in black. They each had a pistol on their hip. Both wore sleeveless black t-shirts and each bore a shining brand of Anubis's head on the side of his bicep. Not a tattoo, but a burned-in brand, the scar tissue glittering slightly in the low light of the moving lamps. A few paces in front of them, a young woman. Even in the scant and moving light, Crowley saw the resemblance to Rose.

"It's Lily," Rose said in a tight voice. "And the Anubis Cult has her."

"Looks like they're making her show them the way."

Rose made a quiet sound of frustration. "I warned her away

from all of that occult nonsense. Now look where it's got her."

Crowley put a reassuring hand on her arm. "It doesn't matter now. We're here and if we're smart and careful, we can get her out of this."

They stole forward again as the three disappeared around a corner. Voices drifted back to them again, one of the males, stern and short-tempered.

Then Lily's voice, louder, frustrated. "I told you already. I don't know. This wasn't in my research."

Another man. "You think it's inside?"

Then Lily again, in a tremulous voice. "Yes."

Crowley shifted silently forward and peered around the curve of neatly carved rock. The three ahead stood in front of a large black door, sharp-edged square blocks of finely chiseled gray stone surrounding it. Then, with a start, he realized it wasn't a door at all. The blackness between the stones swirled and undulated, solid, like a thing alive. He recalled the story Shepherd told them, of the room filled with a strangling black cloud. Could this be what that old man had described? Could there be truth to those old legends after all?

As he watched, one of the armed cultists wrapped a bandana around his face and moved inside. It was bizarre to watch, as the black cloud didn't swirl around him but appeared to have tension. It flexed as he moved forward, and then popped back into place as he disappeared from sight.

Lily stared at the black doorway, not looking back at her remaining captor, who also gazed at the seemingly solid portal. Crowley figured this was his best chance. "Hang back, unless I need help," he whispered back to Rose. She nodded and Crowley sprang forward.

The cultist turned just before Crowley was upon him, his hand whipping impossibly fast to his hip. His pistol rose swiftly in the space between them and Crowley lunged forward to slap it aside just as the man pulled the trigger. The report was harsh, deafening in the confined space, the muzzle flash momentarily blinding. The bullet whined as it ricocheted somewhere, but Crowley didn't pause to think about it. He ducked under the man's gun arm, grabbing the wrist as he went, and came up sharply, cranking the man's limb as he rose.

The cultist yelped in pain, turning quickly to avoid a broken arm, but it was all the space Crowley needed. He grabbed the gun butt with his free hand and twisted it aside, sent it skittering away across the stone floor.

His vision crossed as he took a glancing punch across the temple from the man's free hand. He staggered sideways, but ducked and drove in before the cultist could capitalize on his hit. The man growled and Crowley stayed low, delivered one, two, three quick body blows. But the cultist was huge and seemingly armored in solid muscle. He grunted against the blows but didn't slow at all.

With a curse, Crowley leaped back, knowing it was time to play dirty. As the man pumped out a quick jab and then a heavy cross, Crowley narrowing dodged the first, half-blocked the second, taking another glancing blow for his trouble. But, though his ears were ringing, he had the position he needed and turned his hips over to deliver a shattering shin kick to the side of the cultist's knee joint. The heavy man howled as his knee dislocated and he collapsed sideways. Crowley whipped around a fast right and it cracked satisfyingly into the man's jaw and he dropped like a sack of rocks, suddenly silent.

Crowley stumbled back, shaking his head to dislodge the spinning lights of the man's blows, rubbing his aching knuckles. That guy had a face like granite. Crowley hoped his hand wasn't broken. It was certainly badly bruised.

He took a deep, steadying breath, and turned to find Lily backed up against the side of the passage, her mouth hanging agape. She did look a lot like Rose, but there were striking differences too. Lily's features were sharper, her face and figure less full than Rose. Where Rose was athletic and muscular, Lily was wiry. Lily's cheekbones were higher, her hair longer and tied back.

And she looked at Crowley in utter horror.

"It's okay!" he assured her. "I'm a friend."

Before he could say more or Lily could reply, Rose came running from the darkness and grabbed her sister in a tight embrace.

"Rose?" Lily said, stunned. "What are you doing..?"

The question was left unfinished as the first cultist staggered out of the thick black portal, one hand clutching his throat, gasping for breath. His other hand was withered and black, skeletal, just like the strange old man in Cairo. Whatever was inside the darkness, it appeared to have caused this cultist the same injury. But his choking was more serious. As he staggered to the wall, his face was slowly turning black as though dark ink filled his flesh. Through his streaming eyes, he seemed to vaguely register Crowley's presence in the instant before Crowley's fist met his jaw and he fell limply to the ground.

"Bloody hell!" Crowley shouted, shaking out his hand and wincing in pain. "What are these twats made of?"

The one he had fought first rolled over on the ground, groaning and reaching blindly for his smashed knee. Crowley stepped back, lined up a kick, and silenced him again. He smiled at his heavy hiking boot. "That's more like it."

Lily stared blank-faced, shocked, then embraced her sister. They both made noises of relief and joy.

As they hugged, Crowley looked down at the cultist he'd just kicked, then the other, blackened and still, almost certainly dead. The unconscious guy would surely make trouble eventually. Crowley crouched, got his hands under the man's bulk, and hefted him over, rolling him through the door into the blackness. It was a callous act, but a calculated one. They needed to protect themselves at all costs. With any luck, Rose and Lily wouldn't notice.

"Are you all right?" Rose asked. She pushed her sister back, looked her up and down, searching for injury.

Lily stopped her, held her chin to meet her sister's eye. "I think I'm okay. Why... How are you here?" She pointed to Crowley. "Who's he?"

Rose let out a heavy breath. "It's a long story but the short of it is we realized you'd gotten into trouble with the Anubis Cult."

Lily flinched at the mention of that name, looked away, down at the ground. She was visibly shaken, silent. As Rose went to speak again, Lily said, "It's true."

"How could you let yourself fall in with a cult like that?" Rose asked. "You're smarter than that, Lily."

Her sister scowled, then looked away again. "It's not that simple."

"Was it because of grandfather?"

Lily hesitated, then finally lifted her face to meet her sister's concerned gaze. "Yes. I wanted to bridge the gap between life and death."

Rose let out a disapproving sigh, but Lily forestalled her.

"I know it seems crazy, but that's not what matters now. The Anubis Cult is in league with even more dangerous people." She pressed her lips together, clearly reluctant to say more.

Crowley thought about the trail that had led them this far, the bizarre murals and encounters at the Denver airport. "The Illuminati?" He felt stupid even suggesting such a thing, but Lily nodded.

"You won't believe what they have planned. We've got to stop them!"

"How?" Crowley asked.

Lily pointed to the swirling black cloud filling the doorway not two meters away. "We have to find out what's in there."

CHAPTER 50

Lost Egyptian City, Grand Canyon

Crowley stared for a few seconds at the swirling blackness. His eyes drifted to the strange hieroglyphs carved around the doorway, then back to the darkness ahead. He shook his head and pointed at the cultist lying prone on the floor, whose face was a solid black mask. Crowley crouched, felt for the man's pulse and found none. He shook his head again at Lily and Rose's expectant faces. "Whatever that stuff is, it's deadly. How are we going to get in there?"

To his surprise, Rose smiled. "I've got it covered, Action Man." She pulled a gas mask out of her backpack.

Crowley arched his eyebrows. "What the hell?"

"Well, at least *I* remembered what Shepherd told us. I suspected some kind of hostile atmosphere. I grabbed it at the army surplus store while you were buying the new climbing gear. Figured it wouldn't hurt. Turns out I'm a genius."

Lily rolled her eyes and Crowley couldn't help but laugh. "Maybe you are." He was genuinely glad she had bought it, but chilled at the same time. The sight of the mask called to memory the eerie murals at the Denver airport. The Illuminati connection Lily had revealed made it all too real. He took a deep breath and reached for the mask, but Rose jerked it back.

"What do you think you're doing?"

Crowley paused, his hand still halfway out for the mask. "Well, we don't know what's in there. Or if this mask will even help. I mean, look at that guy." He gestured down at the dead cultist. "Let me be the one to go in. Please?"

"Your friend is right," Lily said, one hand on Rose's forearm. "Please, let him go. We only just found each other again." She smiled. "Well, you found me."

Rose looked from Lily to Crowley to the black doorway, then her shoulders fell. "Okay." She handed over the mask. "You'll want these, too." She handed him thick, rubber gloves. "Hopefully avoid the withered hands?"

Crowley slipped on the gloves and then donned the mask, the task familiar from tours of Afghanistan and Iraq, in training and in combat. He took a couple of deep, calming breaths, and turned to the doorway. He looked at the alien-looking curtain of black, his breath loud inside the mask, and thought that perhaps this was the stupidest thing he'd ever done. And he'd done a lot of stupid stuff in his life.

Before he could change his mind, he stepped through. It was like stepping into a warm swimming pool, only the water was as thick as milk. Or blood. The stygian cloud enveloped him. He had half-expected it to be painful, like a WWI soldier exposed to chemical warfare, but instead it was merely... creepy, like being caressed by a million tiny tentacles.

He stood just inside the door for several seconds, listening to the rasp of his breath, checking his senses, wondering if the blackness was affecting him. But he felt largely normal, uncompromised. His eyes began to adjust to the darkness and he saw swirls and shifts in the cloud, like it was thicker in some places, thinner in others. But overall it was dense and claustrophobic. The sooner he got out of it, the better.

The cultist he had rolled inside lay on his back, his skin jet like his friend outside. He was equally dead. Crowley stepped over him and made a slow circuit of the room, following the wall to his left, his fingertips sliding over the smooth, carved surface. The room was circular and obviously small, maybe only seven or eight meters in diameter. He noticed a band of unfamiliar hieroglyphs running around the wall at waist height, beautifully carved in intricate detail. If he leaned close enough they were quite visible despite the cloud. It was as if the surface of it was thicker, more opaque, than its internal structure. Another mystery of its composition he couldn't fathom.

When he reached the door again, he took out his phone and made another circuit, moving slowly and carefully in order to record the hieroglyphs on video. When he had finished, he put his phone away and turned to move toward the center of the room. Surely there as more here than a single line of hieroglyphics. After ten short, careful paces and he found himself standing in front of a golden pyramid two meters high. The dark cloud dulled its gleam, but still it was remarkable in its perfection. How much gold was in the thing, he wondered. Or was it merely a thin veneer of gold laid over a more common substance? Native rock perhaps. He wouldn't be able to find out unless he cut into the gold, and he wasn't about to damage something so remarkable. So flawless. That task would be best left to more capable and qualified archeologists.

But how could a golden pyramid create this alien black cloud? Did it emanate from here? His eyes drifted upward and he had his answer. The capstone of the golden structure was made of something solid and dark. An obsidian-like substance, impossibly black, and perhaps a quarter of a meter in height. It made a perfect miniature pyramid itself, equilateral on all sides and base, atop the golden host. As he watched, a single drop of water fell from the darkness above and struck the tip of the capstone. Where it hit, a thick, black tentacle of smoke twisted out and merged with the surrounding swirls, vanishing into the cloud. He stared, counting seconds in his head. When he got to twelve, another drop fell, another writhing black swirl joined the cloud. He counted, twelve again and another drop, another writhing tentacle of darkness.

"This is..." Crowley whispered, his voice unnatural in the mask. He didn't know what is was. "Alien?" he said, needing to hear the word aloud yet still unable to process it.

But what it was didn't matter at this juncture. What mattered now was what to do about it. The fact that it could so easily produce a poisonous cloud from single drops of water, spaced many seconds apart, made it not only inconceivable, but genuinely dangerous. Lily was correct. If the Anubis Cult, and the Illuminati, though it still felt odd to think of that group as real, knew the capstone was here, they wouldn't stop until they possessed it. He could not allow that to happen.

He shrugged off his backpack and sat it open on the floor by his feet. He dug around in his pack until he found a plastic bag. He reached up high, stretching to drape the plastic over the capstone. Biting his lip, bracing against the potential weight, he lifted the capstone off the pyramid, careful to touch only plastic. He took a sudden step back, surprised as it came away easily and had almost no weight. He set it down, found another plastic bag and wrapped it carefully. He tucked the two coverings around it as thoroughly as he could, then managed to get the small pyramid inside his backpack. It sat neatly on its base in the bottom and he shouldered the pack and was glad to leave the small chamber.

The air in the dim passage outside felt thin and cold, but an enormous relief after the cloying denseness of the cloud inside. He could only imagine that it might slowly dissipate now he had removed the capstone. He turned and put a gloved hand to the surface of it, pressing out from the carved stones of the doorway, but not emerging into the passage.

He realized Rose and Lily were both talking, exasperated as he ignored them. He turned, pulled the mask off. He grinned. "We've got it."

CHAPTER 51

Lost Egyptian City, Grand Canyon

"What have we got?" Lily asked, her eyes alive with curiosity.

Crowley set his pack down and carefully removed the small pyramid to show them. "Don't touch it," he warned.

Lily crouched, looked closely. "So that's the Anubis Key," she said in a soft voice.

Crowley described what he had seen inside the room, the way the thing reacted so strangely to the dripping water. Rose frowned throughout, concerned and, he thought, only half believing him. Lily's face was a picture of fascination, a small smile tugging at one side of her mouth.

"That's astounding," she said when he'd finished his recounting.

"We thought the Anubis Key was about summoning the dead," Rose said. "Or maybe some kind of spell to communicate with them. But something like this, out in the world, exposed to water? It seems it's actually for creating legions of dead! Is that why the Anubis Cult want it?"

"It's not like anything I've ever seen," Crowley said, still perturbed by the existence of the strange thing.

"So what now?" Rose asked.

Crowley wrapped the plastic bags carefully around the small black pyramid again. "It should probably be destroyed, but maybe we need to understand it first."

Lily looked uncomfortably at the backpack as Crowley secured it again, but remained silent.

Rose pursed her lips in thought, then said, "No good to drop it down a crevasse or anything like that. There's every chance the Anubis Cult might find it again." Her face brightened. "We could rent a boat and drop it into the ocean."

Crowley shook his head. "No way! After what I saw a single drop of water do to this thing, no telling what an ocean of water might do."

"I was thinking we'd wrap it thoroughly first."

"Too big a risk. Maybe, years from now, the wrapping gets compromised somehow and then... Who knows?"

"Seed it into a rain cloud," Lily said quietly, then looked

abashed. "Sorry, I'm still thinking of what the Anubis Cult, the Illuminati, might want with it. It's... It's a terrible thing."

"The only thing we know for sure," Crowley said, "is the Anubis Cult should absolutely not get their hands on it and, in the meantime, we absolutely should not get it wet. For now, let's just get it out of here."

Rose took off her pack, emptied out unessential things, then shoved Crowley's pack deep inside her own.

Crowley picked up a few items and put them back in on top. He glanced at Rose's frown. "Partly to wedge it in securely, to brace it against movement. But also to conceal it from a casual inspection. Imagine some busybody park ranger seeing us emerge from the cave and demand to know what we found in there." He shrugged, pushed the thought away. No need to create worries that would probably never come to pass.

"Can't be too careful," Rose said. Crowley reached for the newly combined pack, but Rose shook her head, slipped it onto her back. "I got it. Hardly weighs anything anyway."

"Okay," Crowley said. "Then let's get out of here."

They made their way quickly back along the curving passage, the way clear with both their flashlights and Lily's headlamp. They emerged into the huge, dimly lit cavern with the balance bridge and Lily laughed.

"I never thought of using rope like that. It took those two goons all kinds of effort to support each end and balance their way across."

"Brawn not brains," Crowley said.

"And yet you whupped that one guy." Lily looked him up and down with narrowed eyes. "Just what are you anyway?"

"I'm a friend, that's all."

Lily looked from Crowley to Rose and back, a smile playing at her lips. "A friend. Okay. If you say so."

"I'll hold this end," Crowley said, before the moment could get any more uncomfortable. "You two go first."

Rose quickly hurried over. The bridge shuddered and swayed, made more groans and creaks than it had before. Crowley felt the vibrations through the railing he held. Lily crossed next, carefully but quickly.

"Put some pressure on that end," Crowley said.

The women each leaned on one railing and Crowley started across. His end dipped sharply and something cracked. A section of wood under his left foot dropped, spiraled away into the darkness below.

He braced, hands to the railings either side, and watched his feet as he took one careful step after another. He had to outweigh both women by at least twenty kilos, but surely they were strong enough. Would it be too much? The ancient bridge was not holding up well under all the recent traffic. Crowley chose his steps carefully, tempted to run, but he feared one of his feet might punch right through a weak spot if he did. More creaks and groans sounded, more frightening cracks, quickly increasing in frequency. Then another sound came to him, one that turned his stomach to water. A rapid sawing and snap. Rose cried out in surprise, and the bridge vibrated violently. Crowley staggered and almost went to his knees as he looked up in horror.

"Both of you freeze!" Lily shouted. In one hand she held a knife that she had used to cut the rope Crowley had previously secured. In the other hand was a gun, pointed at Rose. Rose leaned heavily into the railing on her side, one foot on the bridge, the only thing preventing it from tipping Crowley into the abyss.

"What the hell, Lily?" Rose yelled.

The gun. Crowley ground his teeth, remembered disarming the cultist, the weapon skittering away across the stone floor. While he hoped Lily didn't spot him disposing of the cultist, which she surely had though she might have chosen not to mention it, she had secretly retrieved the pistol. What an idiot he was. He should have noticed that. And then he might have foreseen this. He took a step forward and Lily stared him down.

"Stay where you are or I kill her."

He stopped stock-still, hands up, mentally calculating how long it would take to cross the bridge. But he knew it would only take a fraction of a second for Lily to pull the trigger. She might miss; most people firing handguns under stressful situations did, but he couldn't take the chance. Clearly the woman had secrets.

"Walk out onto the bridge," Lily ordered Rose. "Balance it out for your friend there."

"Why are you doing this?" Rose said, but she complied.

Crowley felt his end rise and backed up a couple of steps. The bridge shuddered, groaned deeply.

"Give me the backpack," Lily said, her gun still aimed at Rose's back.

"Why are you doing this?" Rose asked again, turning to face

her sister. "Grandfather..."

Lily laughed harshly. Yes, Grandfather! I'm continuing his work."

"What are you talking about?"

Lily sighed melodramatically, shook her head. "You really are as stupid as he always said you were. Grandfather was an Illuminatus."

"What? No!"

Crowley heard the disbelief in Rose's voice, but he had already reached that conclusion the moment Lily turned a gun on her sister. Rose simply didn't want to believe it, though she was smart enough to know it couldn't be any other way.

"He worked all his life to bring about the New World Order," Lily said. "He was distraught he wouldn't live long enough to see it come to fruition. But his dying wish was that I would see it to completion. And I will! Now, give me the bag or you both die."

Rose hesitated, looked back to Crowley, then her sister.

Lily smiled, trained the gun on Crowley. "How about I shoot your boyfriend first and let you watch him bleed to death? Don't think I can't do it. I'm quite good."

Trembling, face a mask of fury, Rose complied. She removed the pack slowly as the bridge swayed alarmingly, and tossed it to Lily who dropped the knife and caught the bag easily.

Lily chuckled. "I could tell you had a thing for him. Does this mean you're finally over Liam?"

"You bitch!" Rose shouted, and Lily fired a shot at her feet. Rose danced back, the bridge trembled and creaked loudly.

Crowley kept one eye on Lily as he frantically looked for a way out. Some angle to use against her. But she had them well trapped on the rickety old wood. He ground his teeth in frustration.

"Let her go," he said, loud enough for Rose to hear but maybe not Lily. "We'll run her to ground again. We did once, already."

"I'd love to stay here and catch up," Lily said, shouldering the pack. "But I've got a lot of important work to do."

She reached into a pouch at her waistband and dug something out. "But here's a little parting gift. As the American's say, 'Don't say I never gave you anything.'"

She tossed the small, rounded thing out onto the bridge. It bounced twice and Crowley's mouth fell open in horror.

"Grenade!" he yelled.

Rose turned and ran toward him, then everything vanished in noise and fire and smoke.

CHAPTER 52

Lost Egyptian City, Grand Canyon

Crowley's ears rang from the noise and concussion, rock dust fouled the air, but he was alive and on something solid. He coughed, rolled over, every part of his body hurting like he'd been hit by a truck. Or launched through the air by a grenade blast. He rolled into a sitting position, rubbed dust from his eyes. The bridge was gone, an open abyss between him and the huge Anubis on the other side, reaching mockingly across the wide gap. But he and Anubis were alone in the huge cavern.

He yelled Rose's name. And again. Grief tore at him, shredded the breath in his lungs. He vowed to hunt Lily down and take her apart piece by piece until she gave him the name of everyone who had even heard the name Illuminati, and then...

"I'm down here." Rose's voice was weak, drifting up from the darkness. "But I don't know how long I can hold on."

Crowley scrambled to the edge of the bottomless drop, adrenaline surging as relief washed over him. In the wan light lancing down from above he could just make out Rose hanging down in the darkness. She clung white-knuckled to one of the thick ropes that had supported the pivot-point of the bridge, her forearms and legs locked around it in a death grip. She was coated in dust but for two tracks where tears had cleaned her cheeks. She had come to rest against the side wall of the cavern, far from either edge, some five or six meters below the edge. She was entirely out of reach.

"Hang on!" Crowley said, struggling to come up with a solution.

"Don't let me fall, Jake."

"I won't." He tried to calculate the length of the rope she clung to, imagined her using her feet against the cavern wall to run left and right, set up a swinging action to bring her towards the edge. But it wouldn't work, the rope was too short and would only swing her up too high. Then another idea struck him. "You hold tight, I promise I'll be back in a couple of seconds!"

"Where are you going?"

He grinned. "Don't go anywhere!" He turned and bolted off down the passage back towards the chamber where they had found the pyramid. He played the beam of his light around when he got near the portal, looking for the stuff they had emptied from Rose's pack to put his pack and the pyramid inside. And there it was! A coil of thin nylon rope for climbing. Strong and a spare, only ten meters, but it would be enough. It had to be enough. He grabbed it and ran back, uncoiling it was he went.

He was pleased to see Rose still there, eyes wide but determined. "You're going to have to work with me now," he said. "I know you can do this."

"Do what?"

He gathered the rope he had collected into a loose coil and began spinning one end of it. "I'm going to send this out to you, okay? You have to let go with one hand and catch it."

"I don't think I…"

"Yes, you can! I know you can. Grip tight with your knees and ankles, keep one hand locked, and catch it with your right hand. Ready?" Before she could protest again, he sent the rope sailing out across the gap. He was pleased to see it was just long enough to reach her, but Rose remained clinging to the large rope, unable to let go and grab for it.

He coiled it up again. "See how it reached you?" he said in a calm, encouraging voice. "You can do this. Grab for it this time."

Rose swallowed hard and grimaced. She shifted on the rope, squeezed her legs tightly, then tentatively held out her right hand toward him. He smiled, swung the rope, and sent it out again. She snatched at it, but it slipped past and dropped to Crowley's side of the abyss.

Rose made a noise of fear and frustration, but her fire was up. She scowled, shifted her position. "Again!"

Crowley wound up the rope, got it spinning, then cast it out again. This time she grabbed it and held on. "Attagirl!" Crowley said. "Now, here comes the difficult part."

"What do you mean? Just pull me in."

"I will, but it's not going to bring you all the way to the edge. Just hold on tight and you'll see."

Rose wrapped the nylon rope several times around her wrist and gripped it tight. Crowley braced his feet and began to pull. She moved across the cavern wall like a pendulum in slow motion, rising as she came, but arcing a couple of meters away from the lip of the abyss. She frowned as she saw the problem.

Eventually, sweating and straining, Crowley had her level

with the edge, still two meters from solid rock. "I don't have the strength for you to think about this for long," he said. "You need to let go of that big rope now and trust that I can hold you on this one. And you have to hold tight."

"Holy crap, Jake!"

"You can do it. *We* can do it! On the count of three, you let go of the big rope, grab both hands onto the nylon rope and hang on. I'll hold you and haul you up." Crowley's arms began to tremble with the weight already; he knew he didn't have the endurance for much longer. He hoped his plan wouldn't drag him over instead and they'd both fall to their deaths.

"On three or on go?" Rose asked.

Crowley laughed. "We'll do it as one, two, three, go. Okay?"

"Okay." Her voice trembled, but she was ready.

It had to be now before his strength failed. Crowley shifted back, braced his feet wider against the rough rock floor. He took a deep breath, locked every muscle in his body and shouted, "One! Two! Three! Go!"

On *Go*, Rose screamed in determination and let herself drop. He saw her free hand clutch and wrap into the nylon rope, then she was below the edge and every part of him jarred as her weight pulled the rope taut as a bowstring. He grunted and hauled, his feet skidded and shifted against the stone floor, and he was sliding toward the edge. He cursed, eloquently and extensively, dragging back on the rope and digging back hard with his heels. The edge got closer, one meter, half a meter, dust swirled up from his scrambling feet, then he finally arrested his forward motion. But it wasn't over. His shoulder and hands burned with the effort, his entire body trembled, but he grit his teeth and growled like a beast as he leaned hard into the rope, almost laying back flat against the ground. He pushed back one step, then another. Then another.

"Almost there!" Rose called up.

Crowley let out an incoherent shout and hauled back once more, then her hand and arm appeared over the rock edge. The tension went out of the rope as she pulled herself up and stumbled forward. He fell back, sat hard onto the ground, then she had fallen into his arms. He held her and she wrapped her arms around his shaking body. They both trembled violently, both gasping for breath. Slowly, Crowley's heart rate began to settle back down.

"You did it," Rose said in a slightly broken voice. "Thank

you, Jake!"

She kissed him, hot and shaking on the lips, then put her head against his chest again. He held her, thought only of regaining his breath and letting his strained muscles relax by increments.

After several minutes, Rose stirred against him. A soft sob escaped her. "I can't believe..." she said. "She's my sister. We didn't always see eye to eye, but I thought I knew her better than that."

"You're not the first to be fooled by someone close."

Rose shook her head. "This isn't the first time she's crossed me."

Unthinking, brain still reeling from the exertions, Crowley said. "Liam?" He realized he might have hit a raw nerve he had no business probing and glanced down at her.

Rose didn't look up, but nodded against him. "She stole him from me. He was good and kind and naïve, I guess. I knew he'd come back to me once he saw her for what she was. You know, saw that she was playing with him. I was prepared to talk about that, to give him another chance. But she talked him into going rock climbing."

"That wasn't his thing?"

"No. It's hers. Always has been. She's an adrenaline junkie for that stuff. But she knew it was the last thing he wanted. He was deathly afraid of heights, but she talked him into it anyway. Probably shamed him, questioned his manhood. That's how she is." The bitterness was evident in Rose's voice.

Crowley thought he could figure out the rest. "I'm guessing it didn't go well."

Rose shook her head. "He fell. He died." She looked up at Crowley at last, tears filling her eyes. "Since then, I haven't let anyone get too close to me. I just can't..."

She buried her face in his chest and he stroked her hair, cursing himself for every time he'd pushed her for an explanation. Like he had had any right to demand anything from her and would only have been dredging this stuff up every time. He remembered the story she had told of a girl she had been with, but she had also said she liked guys. Through none of that had he considered there might have been someone special. Someone really serious. What an idiot he was.

He had to say something, even if it was stupid. "For what it's worth, I don't find Lily all that attractive." He winced. He hadn't meant to say something that stupid!

Through her tears, Rose laughed, punched him in the chest. She sat up and kissed him again, lightly on the lips. "So, how are we going to get out of this now? I'm more than grateful you got me out of there, but we're on the wrong side and there's no bridge anymore."

Crowley's gaze traced the walls of the chamber, the rough and folded rock with many crevices and gaps. Pretty straightforward if they retrieved some more of the stuff they had left near the pyramid chamber. "I hate to say this," he said, "considering the story you just told, but I think it's going to take some advanced rock climbing."

Rose smiled sadly. "For me, that's not a problem."

CHAPTER 53

The sun broke the horizon as Crowley and Rose reached the top of the Bright Angel Trail and emerged at the south rim of the Grand Canyon. It had taken all of their skill to free climb their way out of the Anubis cavern, then a further challenging climb down from the hidden city. Arms and hands trembling from their efforts, they had hiked through the night to get back to the Canyon edge. The final leg, an exhausting trek up the steep switchbacks of the Bright Angel Trail, had taken nearly everything Crowley had left to give. After the efforts of hauling Rose out of the chasm, then everything that had followed, he wanted to just lie down and sleep for a week. His legs felt like water, his stomach growled with hunger. At least they had kept their canteens with them and had managed to stay hydrated.

Rose looked worse than he felt, but as they stood at the top of the trail, basking in the early morning sun washing over them, she allowed herself a smile. "Pretty glad we're in good shape, eh?"

"Hardcore." Crowley drank deeply from his remaining water supply then handed her the canteen. "Finish it up. We can refill soon enough now."

"I need to rest. Get some food."

"No time." Crowley grimaced at her dismay. "We have to catch up with Lily before she hands the capstone over to her Illuminati cohorts. She had, what, an hour head start on us? I'm convinced we've narrowed that gap at least partially. How fit is she?"

Rose made a rueful face. "She's in good shape. Does triathlons and stuff like that. Part of her obsessive nature, you know? Pushes herself."

Crowley squinted into the dawn light. "Hmm. Maybe we haven't closed the gap that much then."

"Except we were really pushing it. Lily thought we were dead, so she wouldn't have tried to gain on us."

Crowley heard the catch in Rose's voice when she said the word 'dead'. He took her hand. "I'm sorry."

"My own sister. Threw a bloody grenade at us! Whatever

family love I might have thought we had has clearly long since passed for her."

"Yeah. And that's not your fault, nor is there anything you can do about it."

"I can grieve." Tears stood on Rose's lashes.

Crowley pulled her into a hug. "Yes, you can do that. I'm sorry."

After a moment Rose pulled away, wiped at her eyes angrily with one grubby sleeve. "So let's get the bitch. Where do you think she went?"

They moved on, staggering toward the parking lot, ignoring the glances of the few early morning tourists.

"Denver airport," Crowley said. "At least, I reckon that's where she's probably headed."

"If she drives it, that's a good eleven hours," Rose said. "But if she catches a plane..."

They dropped into their rental car, both groaning at the relief the comfortable seats offered. Crowley tried to recall details of the local area. He pulled out his phone and hit the maps app to confirm his guesses. "The closest airport is Flagstaff." He tapped more, pulled up details of the airport. "It's small, only one airline plus private planes. Is that a likely candidate?"

"Private planes?" Rose sneered. "Exactly the kind of place where one of her rich Illuminati friends might fly in and out?"

Crowley grinned. "You're brilliant. That's a fine point. I need to call Cam."

He dialed the phone, drummed the fingers of his free hand on the wheel while it rang. Then Cameron finally picked up.

"Hey, Jake."

"I need to you to do some hacking for me immediately."

"And hello to you too, mate!"

"Sorry, man, but I'm not kidding. The situation has got really messy."

Cameron's tone became instantly serious. "Notepad at the ready. What do you need?"

"I need you to find out who has private planes at the Flagstaff-Pulliam Airport in Arizona. Then compare those names to the names of the Illuminati on the Denver airport capstone."

Cameron was silent for a moment, then he said, "What?"

"I know how it sounds. Just do it, please!" Crowley thought

for a moment as he heard keyboard taps from Cameron half a world away. He remembered the gray marble capstone at Denver airport, and the men credited with its laying. "Actually, start with the names Claude W. Gray and Benjamin H Bell."

"You got it," Cameron said. "Leave it with me and I'll get back to you ASAP."

Crowley drove, pulled out of the parking lot and headed for the highway. "Get some rest," he told Rose. "One of us might as well."

She laid her head back against the headrest and closed her eyes. Crowley tried not to think about how she must be feeling, the thought that her sister had really tried to kill them. The woman was a psychopath, no question. Wrapped up with the Illuminati and the Anubis Cult. Which he assumed were one and the same, or at least the Cult was a group within the Illuminati. And now he and Rose had finally learned what the Anubis Key was, they had immediately lost it to Lily and her lunacy. What could they be planning for it? Crowley gritted his teeth and pushed the speed up, barreling along the highway in the quickly brightening day. Whatever she was planning made no difference; their task was the same. They had to stop her.

They were almost to the airport when Crowley's phone rang in the center console. Rose jerked up in her seat and grabbed it. "Cameron," she said, and answered the phone. "Hey, Cam. Wait a sec, I'll put you on speaker. Jake's driving." She tapped the speaker, then said, "Go ahead."

"Okay, guys," Cameron said. "I'm afraid I don't have much, but it might be what you need. There is one jet at Flagstaff registered to a Graybell, Incorporated. I don't see any connection to the men you mentioned beyond the similarity in name, but it's the closest thing to a match I can find."

"That might be it," Crowley said. "You find anything else at all?"

"Well, I dug into Graybell, Incorporated and found that they're a corporation headquartered in Denver. And they have ties to a German outfit called Graue Glocke."

"Gray Bell," Crowley translated.

"Exactly."

"I know this is an odd question," Crowley said. "But any connections to the Illuminati?"

Cameron chuckled. "I'm used to odd questions from you. And yes, the Graybell corporate logo is a stylized pyramid with a smoking capstone. Could be Masonic."

At the mention of a smoking capstone Crowley and Rose exchanged a quick glance, both with eyes wide.

"You think they knew all along what the Anubis Key was?" Rose asked.

Crowley shrugged. "Who knows how much they knew, how much they told Lily, any of that. Cam, what kind of business is Graybell?"

"Let me see."

As Cameron tapped more keys, Crowley braked and turned off into the small road leading to Flagstaff airport, chain link fences, low buildings and gray concrete only a hundred meters ahead.

"Chemical," Cameron said. "They claim to be working on drought solutions... advanced methods of cloud seeding... methods for cleaning polluted water..."

"Wait!" Crowley said, remembering what Lily had let slip. "Did you say cloud seeding?" He glanced at Rose and she nodded. She remembered too.

"Is that important?" Cameron asked.

Panic swept through Crowley at the swift train of thoughts the information had set in motion. He fell automatically into the tone of command suited for the military. "Get on the horn with any authorities to whom you have connections. Let them know there's a terrorist on board that Graybell plane and it must be intercepted at the Denver Airport. I don't care what you have to do, who you have to talk to. Make them believe you."

Crowley parked the car crookedly at the side of the small road and grabbed his phone as he leaped out.

"Hang on," Cameron said. "They filed a flight plan for Los Angeles."

"That's bull," Crowley said, staring up at the sky.

"How do you know?"

"Because their plane just took off and it's definitely headed east." He watched as a sleek, white plane with Graybell emblazoned on the side climbed slowly into the clear blue sky. A smoking capstone logo was printed boldly on the vertical stabilizer.

"Bloody hell," Cameron said. "I'm on it. What are you going to do?"

Crowley grimaced, cursed. "I'm going to catch them."

CHAPTER 54

"**What do you** mean you're going to catch them?" Rose asked.

"Exactly that. Come on." Crowley moved the car to a more sensible spot on the gravel beside the short airport road, locked it up, and tucked the keys up on top of the front wheel.

"Another hire company that'll never let us rent a car again," he said with a grin. "But at least they'll get this one back."

"And now what?"

"Follow me." He stayed low and skirted the chain link fencing until he reached a double gate that was pushed closed, a heavy chain looped loosely around its uprights. Checking no one was paying attention, at least no one they could see, he tested the length of the chain. The gate shifted a good foot or so, making a gap just big enough for them to squeeze through. "Don't you love lax security?" Crowley said with a grin.

The slipped through and Crowley stayed low and near the fence as he led them along to a large tan metal hangar. He glanced around the corner and saw a small jet standing just in front of the open hangar door.

He pointed. "That's a Beechcraft Premier. I can fly it no problem."

"You fly too?" Rose asked. "You're full of surprises."

"I spent a long time in the Army, trained for the SAS. I covered a lot of bases while I was in."

"And you're really going to steal that plane?"

"Yes, but I'll return it when we're done. It's for a good cause, right?"

Movement in the hangar made them duck back into the shadows of the wall. Two businessmen in crisp suits boarded the plane, chatting casually as they went. Both carried an attaché case, but nothing else.

"That's handy," Crowley said. "It looks like they're about ready to go anyway. But where's their pilot?"

Rose tapped his shoulder and pointed as another man rounded the other side of the hangar. Sandy-haired, wearing khakis and a polo shirt, he leaned into the small plane to share a few words with the businessmen, and then secured the door behind them.

"Yep, that's pilot," Crowley said. "Quickly, get him to come over here."

"Me?" Rose said aghast. "How?"

"I don't know! Feminine wiles? Show him the goods?"

Rose arched an eyebrow. "Really? The goods?"

"Please, just do it. He'll be suspicious of a man, but a woman is always less confronting, right?"

Rose sighed, then ducked around the hangar and hurried over to the pilot. "Excuse me, I really need your help," she said. Crowley was impressed with how desperate she managed to sound.

She grabbed the startled man by the hand and pulled him toward the spot where Crowley hid. Caught off-guard, the pilot followed at first, a few stumbling steps, but then he stopped and pulled Rose to a halt.

"Miss, I don't know what you think you're doing, but you really shouldn't be in here."

"Sir, please!" Rose's voice took on a pleading tone. She sounded like a lost little girl. "You have to see this!"

"See what?"

She dragged him another few paces, within about five meters of Crowley's hiding place, before the man pulled her up short again.

"Lady, listen, I have a job to do and you shouldn't be here."

Crowley knew he needed to act. He strode out from cover and said, "Daisy, there you are! Why are you bothering that man?"

Rose looked around, agape as Crowley quickly closed the gap between them.

"Is she with you?" the pilot asked, clearly relieved that the strange woman had someone else with her.

"I'm sorry," Crowley said as he reached the pair of them. "She's a little, you know…" He circled a finger at his temple.

As the pilot began to laugh and Rose stepped aside, fury creasing her brow, Crowley's whirling finger closed into a fist and he whipped a punch across the point of the pilot's chin. The unfortunate man dropped like his strings had been cut.

"I'm a little mad, am I?" Rose demanded.

Crowley grinned. "You should have flashed him the goods." He ducked her slap and said, "Come on, help me here."

He was pleased to see Rose was smiling slightly as they

hastily pulled the pilot into a corner. She was a good sport. Crowley quickly stripped to his underwear and donned the pilot's clothes. Thankfully they were a similar size. As he dressed, Rose tied and gagged the pilot who moaned and writhed as she got the last knots in.

"Keep the gag loose," Crowley said. "We don't want to kill him, just buy some time before he raises the alarm."

"Won't the air traffic controllers know something is up?"

"Yes, but what are they going to do, shoot us down?"

"That's not funny," Rose said.

"Don't worry. They definitely don't have anti-aircraft missiles in a small airport like this. Come on."

They jogged over and boarded the plane. Rose dropped into the seat beside Crowley as he prepped for takeoff.

"What's the delay?" one of the businessmen asked. He checked his watch. "We're already late, where have you been?" He leaned forward, eyes narrowed. "Wait a minute, you're not the pilot who spoke to us a moment ago."

"My apologies," Crowley said, flashing his most winning smile. "Quick change of plans, but don't worry. You're in good hands and we're off now. We'll make up the time in the air."

He went through final prep and then taxied out towards the runway. Rose slipped the co-pilot's headset on and asked softly if he was sure he knew what he was doing.

Crowley turned his winning smile to her. "We'll soon find out."

As he taxied onto the runway a shocked and angry voice came through the headsets. "Beechcraft Premier Charlie-Foxtrot-one-niner, what are you doing?"

Crowley ignored the demand, put a finger to his lips to ensure Rose did the same.

"Beechcraft Premier Charlie-Foxtrot-one-niner, we have not yet given you clearance, return to the hangar immediately!"

Crowley wound up the Premier's engines as he lined up on the runway.

The controller's voice was a screech as another small jet came streaking toward them from the other end of the runway. "Charlie-Foxtrot-one-niner, collision alert!" But it was too late to do anything about it.

Rose let out a yelp of shock as the plane approaching them lifted its nose off the tarmac. They clearly saw the pilot's horrified face as he leaned back in his seat, hauling the small jet up. It roared over them, Crowley wincing as he was convinced he'd made the worst mistake of his life and it was all over, but the other plane's landing gear skimmed mere inches above the nose of their jet and then it was gone.

"What the hell is happening up there?" one of the businessmen yelled.

Crowley wound up the engines further and began his take-off run. "Civilian pilot," he said back over his shoulder. "Doesn't know what the hell he's doing. He's in the air now, so he won't be a problem for us anymore. Sorry about that."

He ignored the clamor from the tower and lifted the small Premier into the air. Rose seemed to relax beside him once they were up.

"What do we do when we get to Denver?" she asked.

Crowley shrugged. "Hopefully Cameron will have got the message through and the authorities will be waiting for the Graybell jet when it lands."

Rose considered that for a moment. "So what are we doing then? If Cameron can't get anyone to listen to him, we'll be arrested in Denver and Lily gets to go unscathed. If he is successful, then our part in all this is superfluous."

Crowley had hoped she wouldn't consider that, but as she had put it together, he had no intention of lying to her. "That's true," he said, opening up the engine. "But I'm planning on catching up to them before they get anywhere near Denver."

Rose twisted in the seat, face shocked. "And what exactly are you going to do when you catch up with them?"

Crowley grimaced, not taking his eyes off the vista of sky ahead of them. "Deal with the situation."

CHAPTER 55

They flew above an unrelenting landscape of flat, featureless brown. Crowley pushed the plane for all it was worth. He kept glancing at the fuel gauge, wondering if they had enough to make Denver. He didn't know what this plane's original destination was, therefore what they might have fueled up for. And he was out of practice estimating from gauges. But all he could do was keep going and hopefully reaching Denver would become moot.

Then, up ahead against the cornflower blue sky, he spotted a white dot. He pointed.

"Another plane."

"Think that's them?" Rose asked.

"We'll see, but yes, I think so. We weren't that far behind them."

He kept the small jet working at capacity and they quickly closed the gap. He stayed high and left of the other plane and soon saw the telltale symbol on the tail, the smoking pyramid. He remembered his experience in the cavern, the tiny drops of water, the writhing tentacles of black. The cultist's blackened faces as whatever that dark cloud was had asphyxiated them violently. Seeing the Anubis Key represented on the tail of the plane ahead convinced him he had to stop them, whatever the cost. He could only imagine what kind of authorities would close ranks around Lily if she made it to Denver. He had to assume that was the base of their operations, or at least a serious outpost. Lily was likely to have too many friends there.

"Could you talk to them?" Rose asked, nervousness making her voice tremble. She could obviously tell Crowley had a single-minded focus and it was scaring her. He didn't blame her. It was scaring him too. "Convince them to land?" she said.

"I can talk to them if we're on the same frequency, but would they listen?"

Rose shrugged, brow creased, lips pressed together.

They closed in and Crowley checked the number on the Graybell jet, noted the make and model. Then he keyed open a channel. "Cessna 118, come in."

No reply.

"Graybell Cessna, you are instructed to return to the Flagstaff airport immediately."

This time, the Cessna pilot replied, his voice tight with anger. "And who the hell are you?"

"Homeland security," Crowley quickly invented.

"With a British accent? Sure you are."

"You are instructed to return immediately, or else a military response will be required."

There was a long pause, and then the pilot's voice again. "Look, mate," he emphasized the word sarcastically. "I don't know who the hell you are, but I heard the same chatter from the tower that you did. I'm pretty sure you're the ass who stole a plan. Now kindly get off my channel and get a safe distance from my bird."

"Last warning," Crowley said, his voice a threatening growl.

There were several seconds of silence again, and then the Cessna changed course. Crowley quickly matched it, checking his compass. North, and then northwest.

"What the hell?" Crowley muttered.

"What are they doing?" Rose asked.

"They've changed direction, but they're not headed for Flagstaff. I don't know what they're doing."

"How long until we land in Albuquerque?" one of the passengers demanded from the back.

Crowley jumped. He had completely forgotten they were even there. "Not long at all," he said, trying to sound upbeat.

"Can you be more specific?" the man asked.

"I can, but I won't," Crowley snapped.

The passenger sputtered, quickly becoming indignant. Crowley couldn't blame the poor man, but he didn't have time to mollify him. More important things were at stake.

Rose turned in her seat. "I suggest you calm yourself, sir. Do you really want to upset the pilot?"

The businessman clamped his jaw shut and scowled. Crowley glanced back, gave both stern-faced men a quick smile, then turned his attention back to the Graybell jet.

As he pondered where they might be going, Lily's voice suddenly boomed into their ears. "Jake Crowley, or whatever your name is, you get the hell off our tail or I swear to all the gods I'll dump the capstone in Lake Mead. Try me if you don't believe me. I will trigger an apocalypse for America before I'll let you take this artifact."

Rose's mouth fell open and she scrambled for charts beside her seat.

Crowley muted the outside broadcast to address only her. "Don't bother, I know what she's talking about. That's what they've done, changed course to reach Lake Mead."

"Is it a big lake?" Rose asked.

Crowley sighed. "It's the largest reservoir in the States. Tens of millions of people get their water from it. Irrigation for farming..." He stopped talking, shook his head. "Regardless of what we know about the Key and how it reacts to water, contaminating that lake alone would be disastrous."

Tears stood in Rose's eyes again. Crowley wondered how it must feel to discover your sister was a genuine psycho. She was like some kind of comic book supervillain.

"You need to bring them down before they reach the lake," Rose said.

Crowley nodded. "At whatever cost."

Rose glanced back at the businessmen behind them, then returned her eyes to meet Crowley's. This could cost them everything, their very lives, and her look said she knew that. And she knew it had to be that way.

Crowley nodded once, then gunned the engines of the Premier and swooped down above the other plane. He tried to line his nose cone up with a wing and bumped the Cessna hard.

Lily's screaming blasted from their headsets as Crowley struggled to keep control. The Cessna dipped and twisted in the air.

"What the hell was that?" one passenger yelled.

"Sit down and buckle up," Crowley shouted back to him. "Bit of turbulence up ahead. It's gonna get rough!"

The pilot of the Cessna cursed at Crowley, then did nothing to conceal his argument with Lily, demanding she do something to get this idiot away from them.

Crowley banked, shot over the top of their cabin and bumped them again. "Return to Flagstaff!" he shouted. "I am not playing games here!"

Lily shouted instructions at her pilot and the other plane tried evasive maneuvers, changing directions quickly, rising and dropping. Crowley had lost track of where exactly they were and had no time to check his compass, to figure it out. He glanced back into the cabin and the two businessmen sat shocked into terrified silence, knuckles white on the arms of their seats.

Crowley banked around for another hit.

"We're really dogfighting with private jets?" Rose said, incredulity making her voice high. Her knuckles were white too.

"Yes, but these dogs have no teeth. I'd kill even for an old-fashioned Gatling gun right about now." He clamped his jaw in determination and decided to try something crazy. He banked around again, frantically calculating the proper angle, and lowered his landing gear. It locked down with a loud thump through the fuselage. He lined up again and shot over the other plane. The Premier shook and they all heard a loud crunch.

"What happened?" Rose yelled, almost drowned out by the hollering of the two men in the back, both now animated out of their shock by fear.

Crowley brought the Premier about and caught sight of the Cessna. He smiled. "We took out their rudder and part of their vertical stabilizer." He pointed to the tail section, where the vertical portion had torn loose. A stream of profanity filled the headsets as Lily cursed at Crowley, at Rose, at the entire world. She was eloquent.

"Are we okay?" Rose asked, ignoring her sister's ranting.

Crowley consulted the controls, shrugged. "As far as I can see."

"Our landing gear?"

"We'll find out about that when we land."

They watched as the Cessna went into a steep dive.

"Are they crashing?" Rose asked.

"Yep. Unless that pilot is incredibly skilled," Crowley said flatly.

Down below, nothing but flat desert lay in every direction. Then, as Crowley dropped altitude and banked to follow the Cessna down, in the distance, a narrow gorge, and then a highway.

"Could they land on the road?" Rose asked hopefully.

Crowley worked out the angles, then shook his head. "Not a chance. He'd have to make a forty-five-degree turn and that's not going to happen now with the damage we gave him. His best bet is to get to the ground and hope for the best. But that desert is pretty rough."

They watched as the Cessna leveled out as it approached the ground. Crowley was impressed with the pilot's skill, bringing some measure of control to the fast, forced descent. For a moment it looked like he was going to make it, but then the

Cessna shuddered and tilted.

"Damn, he's losing it," Crowley said.

The small plane hit the earth, landing on its belly, wobbled, and began to spin like a top. By some miracle, it didn't tumble and tear apart, as Crowley had expected, but continued to skid toward the gorge. The small amount of traffic on the highway had all braked to a halt as the plane slewed towards it, kicking up a whirling cloud of dust. Crowley imagined every driver leaning out the window with their cell phones set to video. This event would be all over YouTube in minutes.

The Cessna careened through the dirt, skipped and bounced as it crossed the highway tarmac, and then finally began to slow as it approached the gorge. Crowley circled, holding his breath as it finally came to a halt, teetering on the edge.

"Please," Rose whispered, then cried out as the small, wrecked plane tipped and fell in. She began to cry as smoke plumed up from below.

Crowley wanted to comfort her, but he had realized they had problems of their own. Through all the dogfighting he hadn't paid attention to the fuel gauge and now it read empty, the warning light flashing frantically from the dash.

He barked a curse and Rose looked over at him. "What now?"

"Looks like we need to make an emergency landing, too."

CHAPTER 56

Interstate 40, near Diablo Canyon.

Crowley brought the Premier around into a shallower decline and lined up on the highway. He swallowed, wondering how much damage he might have done to their undercarriage with that hit on Lily's Cessna. It would truly suck to have survived the dogfight only to die in a landing crash because their wheels were gone.

"We're really doing this?" Rose said.

"No choice." He raised his voice so the two businessmen in the back could hear him too. "Brace yourselves, this is going to be a rough landing." *Just not too rough, I hope,* he added silently to himself.

He brought them in as shallow as he could, thankfully towards a long strip of highway devoid of cars. He passed over the scar in the tarmac where Lily's plane had carved through it and touched down right on the other side. The Premier bounced and skidded a little, slewed left and right as he fought the stick to keep them true. He was thankful beyond words that the undercarriage was still there. His biggest fear had been that they would belly flop on the fuselage and skid. But while he had wheels, one of them was clearly bent or buckled. The Premier shuddered and skipped, then he gained a bit of control back as the ailerons and brakes howled. They skipped again, slewed slightly, and finally began to slow. At the last instant they lost the edge of the tarmac and rattled over rough desert. One of the businessmen screamed as something banged loudly under the fuselage, the broken wheel finally giving up, and the plane tipped and gouged its wing into the dirt. The wing broke, the plane twisted sharply to the left, and then nothing but silence and stillness.

"We're down," Crowley said, collapsing back into his seat in relief.

Rose leaned over and planted a kiss hard on his lips. "Thank you!"

They all got their belts off and got out of the plane as quickly as possible. The flat, brown landscape stretched away in all directions, the highway running a straight east-west through it like a scar. To the west, the mountains that marked Flagstaff rose from the haze. To the east, shimmering heat waves as the interstate turned into a silver mirror and disappeared over the horizon. Curious passersby slowed their cars to stare, but none of them stopped, or got out to offer help.

"Where are we exactly?" Rose asked.

Crowley pointed to a street sign. "Interstate 40. Beyond that, I'm not sure."

The two businessmen were white-faced and trembling beside them. "What the hell is going on?" one demanded.

"Engine trouble," Crowley said with a smile. "Sorry about that."

The man stared at him dumbfounded. The other one said, "But we need to get to Albuquerque."

Crowley grabbed him by the shoulders, turned him to face east, and pointed down the highway. "Albuquerque is that way. You might want to hitch a ride, though. It'd be a long walk."

He gave the man a shove, then turned and took Rose by the hand. "Come on. Let's check."

They crossed the highway and headed for the narrow canyon where the Cessna had crashed. They passed a sign that read Canyon Diablo.

"That's kinda fitting," Crowley said

They walked across rock-strewn desert, towards the spiral of smoke curling up into the clear sky. When they reached the canyon's edge, Crowley squeezed Rose's hand as they looked at the smoking wreckage far below. The plane had broken apart, the tail section just below the canyon rim, wing sections here and there. The fuselage was out of sight amidst the smoke and tumbled rock.

"I'm sorry, Rose," he said, genuinely contrite. Guilt tore at him, but he knew they had done the right thing. And Lily had tried to kill them not long before.

"I know," Rose said quietly. "Me too." Then she stiffened, leaned forward.

"What is it?"

She shook her head. "Look, there on the edge of that narrow crevasse. Am I seeing things?"

Crowley moved around to get a better view and laughed. "No. No you're not."

The familiar backpack, containing the source of all their

trouble, hung crookedly, hooked onto a small outcropping of rock. Around it were tatters of wreckage, some sections of seat and chunks of foam. But it was definitely their backpack.

"I'll be damned," Crowley said. "Wait here, that's not too far away."

He climbed down carefully, the canyon not dropping steeply until some meters past where the pack had come to rest. After a few minutes he had retrieved it and clambered back up. They both crouched to check and sure enough, the capstone was still wrapped securely inside.

"The Anubis Key," Crowley said, shaking his head.

"She's dead, isn't she?" Rose said, her voice empty of emotion.

Crowley shrugged. "I couldn't see past the edge or through the smoke." Privately he thought there was no way anyone could have survived, but he knew he didn't need to verbalize that thought for Rose. She knew it already.

She stared down into the smoke and wreckage for a moment then tipped her head back and screamed at the heavens. Her wail contained all her grief and anger, pouring out for anyone and everyone to share a moment of her pain. Crowley couldn't imagine the combined rage and frustration and sorrow that must have been coursing through her. Eventually she lowered her head, tears on her lashes that refused to fall.

"I'm sorry," he said again, putting one hand on her shoulder. It sounded like the most pointless thing in the world to say, but what else was there? She turned to him and they hugged hard for several seconds.

Then Rose sniffed and pulled away. "Come on then."

They made their way back to the highway to discover people had finally started to stop and offer assistance. The two businessmen were just climbing into a wildly painted VW microbus as they reached the tarmac again.

"You hear that?" Rose asked, tipping her head.

Crowley listened hard. "Sirens. Coming this way."

A young woman leaned out the driver's window of her Toyota and pointed at Crowley. "He's the one who landed that plane on the highway!"

Crowley turned to Rose and winked. "Let's get out of here."

CHAPTER 57

In a cheap motel in nearby Winslow, Crowley checked in under the name James Crow again. He was definitely going to have to follow up that loose end one day before long; the name, the identity, had been playing on his mind during this recent adventure and he knew it was because it was unfinished business. Maybe once this escapade was over. He frowned as he scribbled the fake signature. Was it over now? They still had to decide how best to get rid of the Key. Who could they trust?

The motel was rudimentary but clean. They found their room on the end of one row and Crowley suggested that Rose shower and rest while he went out for breakfast.

She nodded, grief and fury still haunting her eyes. "I am starving, actually."

"I can't remember the last time we ate properly."

"Or had a decent sleep."

"Maybe now we can."

Rose stared at him for a long moment, then walked over and kissed his cheek. Without another word, she went into the bathroom and closed the door. Crowley walked down the street, which was busy with early morning traffic. He found a diner, ordered breakfast rolls and coffees and carried them back. Every step of the way he found himself looking left and right, suspicious of every passing car. Any other pedestrian on the sidewalk with him looked like a potential attacker. He was glad to get back inside the motel room and lock the door behind him.

Rose emerged from the shower, wrapped in a towel. She gave Crowley a shy smile and came to sit on the bed beside him. She leaned up against him, silent in grief but clearly taking comfort from his presence. He was glad he could at least offer that.

She sniffed, catching the aroma of bacon, and he handed her food and a coffee.

"Thanks. I was afraid a girl in a flatbed Ford might have stolen you away."

He frowned, realizing she was referencing something, but lost again.

"Winslow, Arizona?" she prompted. "You did see the 'Standing on the Corner' monument? We passed right by it."

Crowley shrugged. "Right. I saw it but didn't get the reference."

She let out a soft laugh. "You're hopeless. So what's the plan?" She took a big bite of roll and made a noise of appreciation around the mouthful.

Crowley realized he was attacking his own breakfast like a starving man and slowed down, took a deep breath. "We need to figure out what to do with the capstone. The Anubis Key! I still can't believe we found it."

"And what is it?"

He shook his head. "Regardless, we can't exactly add it to our checked luggage. And that's assuming we can even fly back to England on our false IDs. I wonder what might be compromised where right now."

Rose swallowed, drank coffee. "Maybe Cameron can help?" she suggested.

"Yeah, maybe. We can get him to snoop around anyway. But that still doesn't answer the question of what we're going to do with that."

They looked at the backpack, sitting on the dresser like any other bag. Not like something that could feasibly end the world.

Rose sighed, finished her breakfast and drained the coffee. "Do we have to figure it out right this second?"

"I guess not. Why?"

She leaned over, her presence hot, the scent of cheap motel soap still on her. Crowley's pulse increased rapidly and he put his cardboard cup down on the bedside table, turned to face her. As he moved in a sharp knock at the door made them both jump.

"Dammit!" Crowley said, looking from Rose to the door and back again. "Wrong room! Go away."

A loud, firm voice from outside said, "Homeland Security!"

Crowley's heart continued to race. Rose looked at him, teeth worrying at her bottom lip. She raised her eyebrows in question. Crowley looked around the small room, no other exits barring the small bathroom window and he imagined they'd have got that covered before they knocked so boldly.

He got up, cursing quietly, and peered out the peephole. A man stood there holding up legitimate-looking credentials, but they were easy enough to fake and Crowley honestly had no idea what Homeland Security ID was supposed to look like. The man was middle-aged, average height, slightly balding. He had a friendly face with piercing blue eyes and wore a nicely tailored navy blue suit. Three other men, larger, in darker suits and sunglasses, stood behind him. They looked menacing.

"I've got people around back too, Mr. Crowley," the friendly-looking man said with a smile. "Don't bother trying to squeeze out the bathroom window."

Crowley sighed, not surprised, and looked at Rose. "They know your name," she said, as she stood and quickly pulled on jeans and a t-shirt with her back to him. "You think they're legit?"

She turned back to him, dressed. He was annoyed. Legit or not, what bloody awful timing. He shrugged. "There's not really anything we can do anyway, is there. Just stay calm and keep your wits. Let's see what happens." He opened the door.

The man outside didn't appear to be wearing a sidearm, and Crowley couldn't spot the telltale bulge of a shoulder holster. But the three men standing behind him were clearly, unapologetically armed. The man in the navy suit smiled. "I'm Agent Paul, Department of Homeland Security. May I come in?"

Crowley stood back, gestured generously for the man to enter. To his surprise, Paul left his people outside. He took a seat at a small table beside the window, perfectly at ease.

"Please, sit."

Crowley and Rose resumed their spot beside each other on the bed. Rose's hand found his and their fingers intertwined.

"You've stirred up quite a hornet's nest in a short period of time," Paul said. "Both of you."

Crowley shrugged, conceding the point. "We did what we had to do." He looked at Rose, then back to Paul. "Well, I did. She had nothing to do with anything."

Paul held up a hand, cutting him off. "Mr. Crowley... Can I call you Jake?"

Crowley scowled and Paul smiled even more broadly. "Fair enough. Mister Crowley, I have a fairly good idea of what's been going on. With both of you." He let out a small laugh, shook his head. "Honestly? I've lost track of all the calls I've gotten about you two. MI6, British Special Forces, two members of Parliament, and..." He looked meaningfully at Rose. "One very persistent director of the Natural History Museum in London."

Rose grinned, then made a contrite face, but chose to say nothing.

"No offense," Paul went on, "but I no longer find a British accent charming." He let out a long, tired sigh. "On the positive side, every person vouched for you. And, to a man or woman, they told me to say that you now owe them a favor."

Crowley grimaced. "I can imagine."

Paul's expression became serious for the first time. "But how about you tell me everything. Imagine I have no idea what's happened and you start at the beginning."

Crowley frowned. Could they trust this man?

Rose leaned close to his ear and whispered, "What if he's Illuminati?"

Crowley nodded, glad she was echoing his thinking. He doubted they would break free easily if the man was the enemy, given the number of heavily armed goons outside. Then his phone beeped. It was a message from Cameron.

Agent Paul visit yet? The text had an accompanying photo of the man sitting opposite them. He smiled.

"That Cam?" Agent Paul asked.

Crowley blew out a breath. "This stuff makes a soul paranoid as hell," he said. "Wait a minute." He dialed Cameron.

"Hey, Jakey-boy. He there?"

Crowley was pleased the message was genuinely from his old buddy. "Yeah, he just arrived. So he's legit?"

Cameron laughed. "Yeah. I thought you'd be worried. He's a good guy."

"Thanks, mate." Crowley gave Rose a reassuring nod and she relaxed.

"You got it. Come and visit me soon."

Crowley smiled, remembering his thoughts about taking a good bottle of scotch up to his old friend. "I most certainly will. Talk soon."

"Laters." Cameron hung up.

"So," Agent Paul said. "Now we're all happy that everyone is who they say they are, tell me everything." Crowley raised his eyebrows and Paul lifted his palms. "I have all day," the Special Agent said. "You have anywhere particular to be right now?"

Crowley shook his head, then stopped to think for a minute. "Okay, let's start with Rose's sister. She went missing."

It took a long time, but he managed to relay the entire story, culminating with landing the stolen plane on the highway. There really wasn't any point in leaving anything out.

Once he'd finished, Paul leaned back in his chair, palms

together, and tapped his lips with his index fingers. "Okay then," he said eventually. "And where is this capstone now? This Anubis Key?"

Crowley pointed at the backpack sitting innocuously on the pale wooden dresser.

Paul looked at it, eyes narrowed like it might attack. "Is it safe to open?"

"I suppose so. But I would strongly advise against touching it, and whatever you do, don't get it wet. Not even a single bead of sweat."

"Or feed it after midnight," Rose said.

Crowley and Paul both looked at her, equally nonplussed.

She shook her head. "Honestly, doesn't anyone watch movies anymore?"

Paul picked up the backpack, then clearly decided against opening it. He hefted it, looked questioningly at Crowley.

"It is surprisingly light," Crowley confirmed.

Paul nodded. "Well, I think I'll leave it to the scientists. So, back to all the mayhem you've stirred up. The Denver Airport is completely shut down."

"What about the underground rooms and passages?" Crowley asked.

Paul shook his head. "That's the worst part. Homeland Security has inspected the property countless times and never found anything amiss. But now, of course, it's clear that some of our own are part of the cover-up. Now we're finding all kinds of things that apparently didn't exist."

"What's down there?" Rose asked.

"Bunkers, living quarters, food, weapons, you name it. It looks like their goal was to cause an apocalypse, let the chosen few ride it out in their underground city, and then start over in a new world of their own making."

"Pretty much what we figured," Crowley said.

"The problem we now face," Paul said, "is uncovering the extent of the Illuminati's reach. You two have neutralized this particular threat early, which is great. But the downside to that is the vast majority of the Illuminati never mobilized. It'll be a challenge for the FBI to root them out. And then there's the Anubis Cult, which will be the CIA's problem."

"We ran into a small band of them in Egypt," Crowley said, remembering Professor Hamza in his Anubis outfit. "Honestly, they seemed rather foolish and inept. But then the people Lily was with are entirely more menacing."

"It's not unusual for groups like this to have small cells that are more public, but entirely uninformed. They think they're something special but actually know nothing of the actual workings of the real group members. And those real members use these fools as a smokescreen, to hide their true intent."

"Makes sense," Crowley said. "Clever."

"I guess the CIA has to figure out how much are they a part of the Illuminati? Are they a splinter group? Are there more cults like theirs, connected or otherwise?" Paul sighed and fell silent.

"What happens to us?" Rose asked.

Paul seemed to snap out of a private reverie and smiled. "You foiled a terrorist plot. You are free to leave the country, on the condition that you never talk to anyone about the Anubis Cult or the Illuminati. You'd probably be taken for fools if you did, but let's not risk it, eh? No need to cause a panic."

Crowley nodded, sure of the truth of that assessment.

"Thank you," Rose said.

"We should be thanking you. If what you've told me is true, and I don't doubt it is, then it would have been a disaster."

"How much of the story did you already know?" Crowley asked.

Paul smiled again. "Enough that I believe you've told me the truth now. One thing, though. Do you have any idea where your sister went once she turned the bag over to the man from Graybell?"

Rose frowned. "What do you mean? My sister is the one who was going to dump the stone into Lake Mead, remember. She's the terrorist."

"Oh yes, that's right." Agent Paul looked concerned. "She was definitely on the plane?"

"Definitely," Crowley said. "We talked to her in flight."

Paul pursed his lips for a moment, looked from Crowley to Rose. "We found only one body at the crash site," he said eventually. "A man." He stood, shook his head. "Don't worry. We'll find her."

Rose stared, blinked. She looked at Crowley. "So does that mean she's still alive?"

Crowley had no idea what to tell her. "I don't see how anyone could have survived that crash."

"The body could be elsewhere in the canyon," Paul said. "We haven't finished the clean up there, not by a long way. I expect we'll find her further down, thrown clear. There's a lot of wreckage further down the slope too, that's much more difficult to get to." He saw Rose's anguish and quickly added, "I'm very sorry. But we'll let you know anything we find as soon as we find it."

Rose's eyes fell and she kept her silence.

"You rental car is outside," Paul said. "Along with your belongings that we retrieved from Flagstaff airport." He handed Crowley an airline envelope. "Tickets to London. Flying out of Phoenix with a stop in New York. I didn't think it was a good idea for you to fly out of Flagstaff, so you've got a little driving to do."

"Thanks" Crowley said. "We appreciate it."

After Paul had left, Crowley turned to Rose, wondering where things stood after the unexpected interruption. She returned his gaze, her eyes haunted.

"That turned out well, all things considered," Crowley said. "No more wondering what to do with the Anubis Key. I guess we're free and clear."

Rose swallowed hard, shook her head. "I hope so."

"You hope so?"

"Jake, they didn't find Lily's body."

He sighed, looked at the ground. "You saw how wrecked the Cessna was. I saw even more wreckage below that. I'm pretty sure they just haven't found her yet."

"You think they will?"

"I can't imagine any other outcome really."

Rose swallowed and began gathering her things. "Let's get out of here, back to London."

"Right now?"

"I just want to go home."

Crowley couldn't blame her for that. "Fair enough."

Rose kissed him, and they began to pack.

EPILOGUE

In a dimly lit office, dark wood paneling on the walls, three people sat behind a ridiculously large and opulent desk. The legs were carved like writhing serpents, the gleaming surface broad and empty. Around the walls hung numerous portraits, men and women in a variety of dress styles, showing a history of several hundred years.

Two craggy-faced, gray-haired men sat on either side of a woman with severe features and gray-blonde hair pulled back tightly into a long ponytail. All three were in their seventies at least. They sat patiently, their hands resting on the smooth, clear surface. They looked stern, but patient. A clicking resounded distantly through the marbled halls leading to the large room, growing quickly louder. The tap of heels on the stone floor.

Lily Black entered, her face set. Bruising all up one cheek led to a swollen black eye. Her left arm hung in a sling, a plaster cast from the hand to the elbow. Despite the pain in her left hip and leg, she refused to limp or request a seat, no matter the agony it cost her to stand tall. Her back might never be the same again, but she would spare no expense on treatments and rehab. She stood before the three and took a deep breath to speak, but didn't get a chance.

"Not the best result," one of the stern men said.

"In fact, a complete debacle!" the woman said, her face creasing into anger. She sat forward, jabbed one elderly, gnarled finger at Lily like a weapon. "The most powerful weapon we could ever have imagined, and you lost it."

Lily forced herself to meet the old woman's eye. "Yes," she said. "I take full responsibility." Before they could punish her, she had to state her case. Distract them from the failure. "But there's something else we can follow up."

"Something else?" the other man said, the one who had not spoken before. "Something to right this awful situation?" He leaned forward, his eyes narrowed. "Something to save your life?"

Lily swallowed, gritted her teeth against the pain and stood taller. "I didn't think it would be nearly as good as the Anubis

Key, so I haven't mentioned it before now, but I think it will still serve our purposes. And I want to go after it."

"What is it?" the woman asked.

"I humbly request that you trust me here, while I do some more research." She hurried on, before the outraged woman could voice her anger. "I was right about the Anubis Key, after all. I'm good at this stuff. Let me do more research, then I can give you a full accounting. If you'll finance the work."

The woman scowled, then sat back. The three elders conferred. Finally, the old woman shrugged and sat forward once more. "Very well. Despite the result here, you have previously proven yourself most capable and determined. But know this is your last chance. Keep us informed."

Lily smiled. "Thank you. I promise you won't regret it. One other thing, though, if I might be so bold. My sister is largely harmless, and I can handle her. But while I go after this new possibility, maybe you could arrange an... accident? For Mr. Crowley?"

The woman inclined her head. "Consider it done."

End

ABOUT THE AUTHORS

David Wood is the author of the popular action-adventure series, The Dane Maddock Adventures, and many other works. Under his David Debord pen name he is the author of the Absent Gods fantasy series. When not writing, he hosts the Wood on Words podcast and co-hosts the Authorcast podcast. David and his family live in Santa Fe, New Mexico. Visit him online at davidwoodweb.com.

Alan Baxter is a British-Australian author who writes supernatural thrillers and urban horror liberally mixed up with crime and noir, rides a motorcycle and loves his dog. He also teaches Kung Fu. He lives among dairy paddocks on the beautiful south coast of NSW, Australia, with his wife, son, dog and cat. Read extracts from his novels, a novella and short stories at his website –warriorscribe.com– or find him on Twitter @AlanBaxter and Facebook, and feel free to tell him what you think. About anything..

Made in the USA
San Bernardino, CA
19 July 2017